OUTLAW HELL

Also by Jack Bodine in Large Print:

Beginner's Luck: The Pecos Kid
Reckoning: The Pecos Kid

The Pecos Kid #4

Outlaw Hell

Jack Bodine

Thorndike Press • Waterville, Maine

The Pecos Kid Book 4

Published in 2002 by arrangement with Lowenstein Associates, Inc.

Thorndike Press Large Print Western Series.

The text of this Large Print edition is unabridged. Other aspects of the book may vary from the original edition.

Set in 16 pt. Plantin.

Printed in the United States on permanent paper.

Library of Congress Cataloging-in-Publication Data

Bodine, Jack.
Outlaw hell / Jack Bodine.
p. cm. — (The Pecos Kid)
ISBN 0-7862-3829-1 (lg. print : hc : alk. paper)
1. Braddock, Duane (Fictitious character) — Fiction.
2. Large type books. I. Title.
PS3552.O366 O98 2002
813′.54—dc21 2001058530

OUTLAW HELL

CHAPTER 1

The haunch of antelope crackled and spattered over the fire, as Duane Braddock turned the spit. He kneeled in a cave near the Texas-Mexican border, gazing at endless rolling desert wastes; a bald eagle circled high in the sky.

Unrelenting silence was unhinging his mind, and every day was the same as the last. He hunted, gathered roots, hauled water, and wished he were somewhere else, like in a nice little saloon, with a relaxing glass of whisky, a piano player, and maybe, if he was lucky, some dancing girls.

But Duane Braddock couldn't simply ride away from his little niche in the mountain. He was wanted for murder in the first degree, and a posse was on his trail, not to mention Apache scouts from the Fourth Cavalry. Duane was worth more dead than alive, because he'd shot a certain overly zealous federal marshal in a town farther north. The marshal had gone loco and tried to arrest Duane for murder, a crime Duane didn't commit. Duane resisted the warrant; he didn't trust judges and juries, his father having been hanged by a trumped-up court in the Pecos country. Then the marshal made the mistake of drawing on Duane, and Duane fought back in self-defense. The marshal died of lead poisoning, and now Duane was on the dodge, living like an Apache, constantly looking over his shoulder, ready for anything.

He returned to the fire, yanked his Bowie knife out of his right boot, and examined the roasting meat. It looked about done to his practiced eyes, so he impaled it on the knife, lowered it to the rock floor of the cave, and sliced off a chunk. Sitting cross-legged, he gnawed tender sweet venison and wondered how much longer he'd have to remain in hiding.

He was nearly six feet tall, wearing black jeans and a black shirt, with a short scraggly black beard. Eighteen years old, he looked lethal as a panther, but he'd been raised in a pious and holy Benedictine monastery high in the Guadalupe Mountains, and he'd dreamed of becoming a priest someday. Duane had never realized, as he'd sung Gregorian Chant in the chapel, that he'd end up an outlaw in Mexico. How strange is a man's life, he cogitated. One day you're living at the right hand of the Father, and six months later, you're on the dodge.

Duane had been brought to the monastery at the age of one year, after his parents had died. He'd spent most of his life high in the clouds, cramming his mind with theology, philosophy, and history, with an occasional dip into the classics, and special attention to the mightiest tome of all, the Bible.

All had been going well until one day Duane lost his temper and nearly killed another acolyte, who'd made insulting remarks concerning Duane's parentage. According to monastery records, Duane's father had been an outlaw, while his mother had been employed as a prostitute. They'd never bothered to get married, and Duane was extremely sensitive about his sordid beginnings. Inarticulate with pain and rage, he'd attacked with the first thing he could lay his hands on, a cast-iron frying pan.

It frightened him to know that he could perform incredibly violent acts beyond his control. But he couldn't tolerate painful insults, and didn't like to be pushed around. A furnace of rebellion and resentment burned in his heart, and didn't require much to stoke it up. He could elucidate Saint Irenaeus's arguments against the heresies, but didn't comprehend his own personal behavior.

Since leaving the monastery, every time he'd turned around he'd fallen into a deeper pile of shit. Sometimes he believed that he carried the mark of Cain. On other occasions he thought himself capable of great achievements. He was full of energy and optimism mixed with doubts and fears. Since leaving the monastery, he'd developed a new ambition: to become a cowboy and own his own ranch someday. Now the Fourth Cavalry was after him, not to mention the posse. If only that goddamned marshal had left him alone, he thought ruefully. I try to be polite, I'm kind to old ladies, but before I know it, somebody's aiming a gun at me.

He munched pinyon nuts as he watched the molten sun sink toward red mountainous calligraphy in the distance. The glory of the universe pulsated through him, and he felt saturated with the power of the Holy Ghost. But something was missing, as if he was trying to climb onto a horse, but the saddle kept slipping.

He knew that he could live indefinitely in the desert, for once he'd spent a month with a tribe of hit-and-run Apaches. They'd taught him to track, move silently, see clearly, and hear everything, but most of all how to locate food and water on a supposedly barren land. An old *di-yin* medicine man named Cucharo had said that Duane's grandfather was a famous Apache warrior. Duane had drunk sacred *tiswin* with the Apaches, and experienced incredible visions of his grandfather that he was still trying to decipher.

Duane would've lived with Apaches forever, but couldn't abide some of their customs. For instance, if a squaw had twins, the father was obliged to kill one, because Apaches believed that twins resulted from evil sorcery. Duane knew that he could never slit his own son's throat, regardless of circumstances, and decided that the Apache way was a bit too barbaric and superstitious for what remained of his Roman Catholic tastes. So he'd left the Apaches and returned to the white man's world, where he'd shot the federal marshal.

He had stared at bare stone walls, and hadn't talked with anyone except his horse, Steve, for nearly a month. His tobacco was gone, he had nothing to read, and he was tired of cooking over an open fire. The desert was beautiful in all its multivaried splendor, but unending loneliness was rattling him.

He wished he could stop thinking about tobacco, but the desire became worse with every passing hour. Major events were occurring in the world, and he didn't know what they were. America could be in another war with Mexico, and he was on the wrong side of the Rio Grande.

Darkness fell on the desert, and he spotted a border town's faint twinkling lights to the north. Duane gazed at those beckoning beacons every night, and imagined churches, saloons full of colorful strangers, and homes where people sat with family and friends at dinner tables, while he chewed charred meat in a cave.

He knew that the posse would tire of the chase after a few weeks of nothing, and the Fourth Cavalry had more important assignments than to chase one lone outlaw forever. "Maybe it's time I returned to civilization," Duane said aloud, for he often talked to himself in the cave. "I'll use a new name, and if folks act suspicious, I'll climb onto my horse and gallop out of town pronto. They say half the people in

Texas are on the dodge, and maybe somebody in that town can tell me about my father."

Duane had heard conflicting testimony concerning his outlaw father. Some claimed Joe Braddock was an innocent small rancher who went up against the big boys. Others said he was a cold-blooded killer, rustler, and horse thief. The only man Duane met who'd actually known his father had kept mum about the details, because he didn't want Duane to ride the vengeance trail. "Best you don't know," he'd said, before dying of a gunshot wound.

His name was Clyde Butterfield, and he'd taught Duane the classic fast draw. Duane had been blessed or cursed with unusually fast reflexes, and had occasion to use his newly acquired skills several times since meeting Butterfield. Then, thanks to a whisky-soaked newspaper reporter with an overactive imagination, Duane Braddock became known as the Pecos Kid. The ex-acolyte was struggling to assimilate the dramatic changes in his life since he'd left the monastery, and often wondered who he was beneath his black wide-brimmed cowboy hat.

He gazed longingly at the town calling

across the desert, but then, suddenly, was on his feet, reaching for his Colt .44. He spun around, yanked iron, thumbed back the hammer, and aimed at his spare shirt hanging from a peg in the cracked stone wall. He didn't pull the trigger, because he didn't want to attract Apaches, the posse, the Fourth Cavalry, or anyone else looking to claim the reward on his head, but the Apaches had taught him to stay alert, with his muscles primed for action at all times.

The town on the edge of night was called Escondido, and its most prominent institution was the Last Chance Saloon. As Duane fretted in his isolated cave, customers played cards, drank, and made nefarious plans in the main room, while a man in a striped shirt played the piano off-key.

Painted women in short dresses brought the customers whisky, the blue-plate special, and romance at fifty cents a throw, the latter a specialty of the house. It was the basic border town whoop and holler, frequented by Mexican banditos, American outlaws, unemployed cowboys, vaqueros, gamblers, drunkards, whores, and heavily armed swaggering fools.

Forty-two-year-old Maggie O'Day owned

the Last Chance Saloon, and her office was at the rear of the rambling structure. It was furnished with a crude wooden desk, some chairs, a few books, and a double-barreled shotgun on the wall, opposite a painted portrait of General Robert E. Lee.

Maggie was a heavyset raw-boned woman who looked like she could lay a man out with one punch. But she wore a frilly dress, a fancy becurled hairdo, a gold necklace, and an emerald brooch, as she peered through gold-rimmed spectacles at the bottom line.

The Last Chance was raking in cabbage every night, thanks to her shrewd management. She had considerable experience in her specialized field, which she'd first learned at her mother's knee — dear old momma had been a soiled dove herself. Maggie joined the profession at the age of twelve, learned the ropes quickly, saved her money, invested wisely, married when it suited her, and now had the supreme luxury of sleeping alone every night and not worrying where her next crust of bread was coming from.

She'd never met her father, and for all she knew, he could be the poor wretch she'd seen languishing in the alley earlier that night, filthy and ragged, sucking a bottle of cheap mescal. But she had more to worry about than her unknown father. The saloon was amassing more money than she could handle easily, and she didn't trust banks, sheriffs, and certainly not the townspeople of Escondido, most of whom were outlaws.

Her wealth resided in an iron safe bolted to the wall, the window barred like a jail cell, and the door double-thick, with three of the best locks money could buy. If anybody wanted her earnings, he'd have to bring dynamite, and hopefully her bodyguards would catch them in the act. One of these days, the lid'll blow off this town, she conjectured. I hope I'm out of here by then. Her ultimate dream was move to San Francisco, buy a legitimate hotel, and be a real lady instead of queen of Escondido's whores.

A shot sounded on the street, and her hand moved involuntarily toward the Smith & Wesson lying on her desk. She always kept it handy, because anything could happen in Escondido. Then someone knocked.

Burly Bradley Metzger, her chief bodyguard, entered her office, wearing a black frock coat with a frilly white shirt and black string tie. "A gal to see you. Wants a job, I think. Should I tell her to come back tomorrow?"

"What's she look like?"

"Got a scar on her face, but not too bad. She's young."

"Send her in."

Maggie returned dreary ledgers to their drawer, as a petite woman with lustrous black hair, pale skin, and tattered clothing entered the office. Looks thirty, but probably seventeen, Maggie evaluated. "Have a seat. What's yer name?"

The girl had doe eyes and a thin horizontal scar on her right cheek. "Alice Markham. I was a-wonderin' if you needed a waitress."

"Ever been a waitress before?"

" 'Bout two years now. I'm a real hard worker, and I l'arn fast. I even knows how to read and write a bit."

Maggie selected a panatella from a mahogany humidor, lit it with a match, and blew smoke out the side of her mouth. "I can always use a hardworkin' gal, but I don't tolerate horseshit. I expect you to be on time and lookin' good every night yer scheduled to work. If you fight with the customers or the other gals, I'll throw yer ass onto the street so fast you won't know what hit you. Get my drift?"

"You won't have no trouble from me, Miss O'Day. I'm here to make money and that's all."

"Then we'll git along fine." Maggie puffed her panatella thoughtfully, for she'd been young and on the loose once too. "Let me give you a little friendly advice, 'cause you look like you might need some 'bout now. I'm probably wastin' my time, 'cause nobody ever listens to old Maggie O'Day, but you save yer money, stay away from drink, and don't give everythin' away to no smooth-talkin' cowboy — you can build up a nice little nest egg here. You got any good clothes?"

The girl averted her eyes. "They're pretty worn out, I'm afraid."

"I'll advance you some, and take it out'n yer pay. My cut is half of ev'rythin' you earn, but I provide room and board, and keep a clean place. Are you with me so far?"

The girl replied: "You won't have any trouble with me, Miss O'Day. I don't drink, don't smoke, don't gamble, and I ain't a-givin' my money to no smooth-talkin' cowboy."

" 'At's what they all say. Well, you can do as you damn well please, long as it don't interfere with my bizness. But let me tell you somethin' missy — fer yer own good. You look out fer my interests, I'll look out fer yers, and we'll git along right fine. But you ever cross me," — Maggie raised the Smith & Wesson and aimed it at Alice Markham's head — "I'll put one right between yer eyes."

CHAPTER 2

Father Diego Gonzalez was having problems with his breakfast campfire. "If only I had some paper," he muttered in mounting frustration. Back at Santa Veronica Iglesia in Durango, the nuns cooked his food and laundered his clothing, but now he was a lone traveler on the Coahuilan desert, and had to care for himself.

He'd been transferred to the new church in San Antonio, but the Franciscans weren't rich enough to provide an armed escort. It was a long arduous journey, but he felt confident that no one, not even a Protestant, would interfere with a priest doing the Lord's work.

Father Gonzalez's sweat-soaked brown robe billowed around his ample girth, and a straw sombrero was perched atop his head. He'd get weak if he didn't eat something soon, but the wood wasn't cooperating.

"Don't move," said a voice behind him.

Father Gonzalez spun around, and his eyes widened at a young cowboy in black clothes, with a red bandanna around his neck and a silver concho hatband on his black cowboy hat.

"Keep your hands in the air," the cowboy said.

"But I'm a Catholic priest!" protested Father Diego.

"We'll see about that."

The cowboy patted Father Diego down, searching for a weapon. "You don't look like you missed too many meals." He searched Father Diego's saddlebags, while aiming his gun at the rotund priest. Inside the saddlebags were a rosary, breviary, Bible, and vestments. The young man smiled sheepishly, as he holstered his gun. "Guess you really are a priest. Can I help you with that fire?"

Father Diego lowered his hands, as the strange cowboy disappeared into mesquite and juniper as silently as he'd arrived. The priest wondered how he'd gotten so close without his hearing him.

The cowboy returned after a brief interval with handfuls of foliage and wood. He arranged the material in the firepit that the priest had dug, and set it afire. Flames flickered and expanded immediately.

"There you go," the cowboy said.

"I'm very grateful," the priest said with a little bow. "I am Father Diego. May I know your name?"

"Just call me Joe. Sorry if I scared you, but there's more killers and crooks out here than you can shake a stick at. Want me to help you with that bread?"

Before the humble priest could reply, Duane was reaching for the wooden bowl. He emptied flour into it and mixed it with water. "Do you have any sourdough?"

"Not that I know of."

"Too bad, 'cause sourdough gives it that special taste." Duane kneaded and rolled biscuits, then placed them in the Dutch oven. He'd observed cooks during his brief stints as a cowboy after leaving the monastery in the clouds. "Shouldn't take long. Which way're you headed, Father?"

"San Antone. Are you a Catholic?"

"Yes sir, and I was raised in a Benedictine orphanage. I wonder if you'd hear my confession after the biscuits are done."

"We shouldn't wait to confess," replied the padre, "because we never know when our Lord will return. I'll watch them to make sure they don't burn." He raised his hand and made the sign of the cross. "In the name of the Father, the Son, and the Holy Ghost."

The young man appeared embarrassed, and the padre sought to reassure him. "There's nothing you can tell me, my boy, that I haven't heard a hundred times before. Go ahead, make a full confession, and I will absolve you in the name of Jesus."

Duane clasped his hands and bowed his head. "My last confession was approximately six months ago. Since then I'm afraid I've . . . ah . . . shot a few people."

The desert fell silent, as Father Diego stared at him. "Excuse me, but did you say you'd shot a *few* people?"

"Self-defense every time, Father. They pushed me into it."

"Self-defense *every* time? It is difficult to believe, no?"

"I don't know what it is about me that bothers folks, Father, but they're always trying to take advantage, and am I suppose to let them?"

The priest thought for a few moments, then nodded sagely, for he'd heard many strange confessions during his ecclesiastical career. "Do you have anything else to add?"

"Well," replied Duane, lowering his

voice, "I've . . . ah . . . fornicated with a few women."

"I suppose they attacked you, and tore off your clothing?"

"I know what you're thinking, Father. That I start everything in the first place. But I swear I don't. It just sort of happens."

"Holy Mother Church teaches that all events are caused. Where did the killings take place?"

"Texas," Duane replied.

"I meant what kinds of places?"

Duane frowned guiltily. "Saloons most of the time."

The priest waved his arms dramatically. "Aha, you see? What do you expect in saloons, a Holy Hour? Stay out of saloons, and sin no more. I'm sure that's where you meet the women too, no?"

"Yes," replied Duane.

"Do you have anything else to confess?"

"Well," Duane began, "I might've stolen a few horses here and there."

"You're not sure?"

"It was dark."

"Not as dark as your heart, I'm afraid. Young man, you simply cannot go on like this. Thou shalt not kill."

"What about when somebody shoots at me?"

"It is your duty to avoid sinful situations. Use your mind instead of your weapons of violence. You must view every man, no matter how low, as a brother, and every woman as the Mother of God, not a creature put on earth to satisfy your deezgusting lustful appetites. I will ask you to say one Rosary every day for *the rest of your life*. Do you have a rosary?"

"I used to have one, but I lost it."

"I'm sure that's not all you have lost." The priest rummaged in his saddlebag, and pulled out a black-beaded rosary. "It was made by Mexican nuns, and you should carry it with you always, to remind yourself of Christ's great love for you. The biscuits are almost finished, so let me absolve you."

The priest intoned ancient prayers and made the sign of the cross. "You are a very bad man," moaned Father Diego, shaking his head disapprovingly. Then he examined the biscuits and peered inside the pot of coffee. "I hope you'll stay and have breakfast with me."

"I've already had breakfast, Father. Thank you anyway." Duane reached into his pocket, pulled out a twenty-dollar double eagle, and tossed it to Father Diego. "May the peace of God be with you, sir."

"And also with you." The padre opened the pouch attached to his belt, dropped the coin inside, then lifted the Dutch oven off the coals. "Which way are you headed, stranger?"

There was no answer. Father Diego turned around, but the black-garbed cowboy had disappeared.

Alice Markham looked out the window and saw an adobe wall across the alley. Her new room reminded her of a prison cell, not that she'd ever been locked up. She had a cot, chair, mirror, and bottles of cosmetics lined on the crude wooden dresser. But at least she had a roof over her head, she thought, trying to cheer herself up.

She felt trapped. But it hadn't always been this way. She'd grown up in Ohio, daughter of a hard-scrabble farmer, who died of an illness that turned his skin yellow, leaving a wife with seven mouths to feed. Alice's mother soon married another farmer who was always mad at somebody, usually his stepchildren. Then mother became sick, they had a bad crop, and someone stole their cow. It was decided that the oldest children should leave and find work. Alice wasn't educated enough to be a schoolmarm, but did the best she could. Every month she sent money to her mother, but her life was one man after another, their faces blurred before her eyes, and she loathed herself totally.

She'd thought of destroying herself, but still hoped something good might happen someday. Alice was struggling to get ahead, but never managed to accumulate much. She'd heard business was booming in Texas, and worked her way south, with stops in Saint Louis, Dallas, and Camp Wood. Her latest move had delivered her to dirty little Escondido.

Alice hated to sleep with strangers and pretend that she enjoyed it. She desperately craved normal life, but what man would marry a former prostitute? She didn't have answers to questions that nagged her constantly, but wasn't ready to surrender her dreams either. *If Maggie O'Day can drag herself up, so can I.*

Alice looked at herself in the mirror, and noted that her profession was taking its toll in faint threadlike wrinkles about her mouth and eyes. She was a sensitive romantic soul forced to sell her most precious possession for a pittance, but she could see no avenue to improve her situation, and refused to beg. Stuck in hell, all she could do was pray for a miracle.

That night she had to work as a gaudy harlot yet again. Some customers would be old enough to be her father, others would smell of horses, and one might cut her face for the fun of it. She leaned closer to the mirror and perused the scar on her cheek. It had come from a straight razor in the hand of a trooper from the Fourth Cavalry. If she hadn't pulled back in time, he would've taken her head off.

Alice would carry the scar to her grave, and no cosmetic could cover it adequately. Sometimes she considered it grotesque, but other times saw it as a badge of honor. Alice Markham was an odd mixture of defiance, shame, and tarnished innocence. She didn't trust anybody, not even her own mother.

She sat in front of the mirror and smeared cosmetics on her cheeks and lips, as night came to Escondido. Gradually the pallid country bumpkin became a painted Jezebel with a naughty gleam in her eyes. "When you're a whore," she whispered to the face in the mirror, "every night is Halloween."

CHAPTER 3

The Pecos Kid rode down the main street of Escondido, his eyes alert for the posse members and the Fourth Cavalry. Light from saloons spilled onto the planked sidewalk, illuminating armed men swaggering along, while others sat on benches, watching the passing show. Laughter and the tinkling of a piano could be heard from within saloons, and a few whisky-soaked souls were passed out cold in alleyways.

Duane tried to appear casual, but maintained his hand near his Colt .44. He wondered if the padre had recognized him, but Texas was full of outlaws far more notorious than he. He hoped no one would pay attention to the lone stranger.

A whiff of broiling steak came to him from the Silver Spur Saloon, mingling with the fragrance of whisky, beer, and manure in the middle of the dusty street. The Pecos Kid rode all the way through town, because Clyde Butterfield, the old gunfighter, had taught him the importance of knowing the territory.

He passed a Protestant church, a hardware store closed for the night, and a barber shop with a painted pole. There was an adobe hotel, the stable, and a tobacco shop, but saloons were the primary business in Escondido. No guns aimed at him from behind windows, and he saw no one with a badge. He steered Steve through the proscenium door of the stable, climbed down from the saddle, and looked around cautiously. If anybody made a false move, it'd be draw and fire.

An old bearded man came out of the shadows. "He'p you, sir?"

"I'd like you to take care of my horse. Give him plenty of oats, and you got any apples around?"

"I can buy some in the morning, sir."

Duane flipped him a five-dollar coin. "Take good care of Steve here, and I'll take good care of you."

"I'm Amos Twilby." The old man bit the coin with his two remaining teeth, then dropped it into the front pocket of his jeans. "The best hotel is the Belmont, and the best saloon is the Last Chance. They give you a good pour, and got the best gals in town."

Duane pulled the saddlebags off Steve's back and positioned them on his own shoulder. As he neared the door, he looked both ways, hand near his Colt. It felt odd to be in civilization again, but a short beard covered his features, and he didn't think anybody would recognize the man who'd shot Marshal Dan Stowe.

Duane found the tobacco store a few doors down, but it was closed for the night. Not sure of his next move, he sat on the bench in front, leaned against the wall, and placed his right hand on the walnut grip of his Colt.

Two cowboys walked by, laughing heartily and smoking cigarettes. Duane smelled tobacco, and his lungs cried for more, but the store wouldn't open until morning. Only one other place to buy tobacco — the saloons.

But if he went to a saloon, he might be recognized by a drunkard from his past, and the overfed priest had said that saloons were the cause of all Duane's troubles. Unfortunately, killers and backstabbers loafed in saloons, and a calamity could befall an unsuspecting citizen at any moment. Yet, on the other hand, he had to admit that the most fascinating individuals could often be found in drinking establishments, plus entertainment and free food were sometimes provided.

He needed a cigarette desperately. I'll just stroll into the nearest saloon, buy some tobacco, and leave immediately. I'm not *that* morally weak. He touched the rosary beneath his shirt as he stared across the street at a sign that said Desert Palace Saloon.

A chill came over him, which he attributed to the cool night breeze.

Four cowboys rode tall in their saddles down the middle of the street, their hat brims slanted low over their eyes. They all wore guns, and Duane wondered which sheriff was chasing them. He waited till they passed, then crossed over.

A Mexican in a sombrero was sleeping on the bench in front of the Desert Palace. Woman's laughter came to him from inside, music to Duane's lonesome ears. I shouldn't go in there, but what's the point of being young if you can't do crazy things?

He opened the batwing doors and stepped out of the light, hand near his Colt, his eyes scanning cowboys, vaqueros, gamblers, waitresses, and gentlemen in fancy suits. It looked pretty much like every other saloon he'd ever seen, with a painting of naked ladies cavorting in a meadow above the bar.

No one seemed to recognize Duane, and he spotted no tin badges. He squared his shoulders and headed for the bar, the silver conchos on his hatband flashing the light of oil lamps. The bartender looked up as he approached. "What's yer poison?" He had hair to his shoulders and wore a patch over his right eye.

"Tobacco and some papers."

The bartender grinned. "You ain't drinkin' tonight, cowboy?"

Duane felt nearby eyes turn toward him, and decided to play it cool and easy. "Whisky," he said.

The bartender tossed a small white cotton bag of tobacco onto the counter, then poured a glass of whisky. Duane paid, carried his purchases to an empty table against the far wall, rolled a cigarette, and surveyed the scene around him.

Tough-looking men played cards, slogged down whisky, or conspired in every corner of the saloon. Some were scarred, others wore tattoos, and a few looked like they'd shoot you for the hell of it. They all behaved as if a posse would show up at any moment.

A middle-aged prostitute approached,

bent over, and asked, "Can I git you somethin' cowboy?"

Her breasts spilled out of her skimpy dress, and he gazed at the alabaster orbs. "Not right now."

She walked away, wiggling her behind, and Duane felt billygoat desire. If it hadn't been for women, he might still be in the scriptorium, studying Saint Augustine's *City of God*, instead of drinking whisky in a lawless Texas border town. He knew, deep in his heart, that he could've remained in the monastery if he had apologized to the old abbot and done lots of penance, but a perverse part of his mind had been curious about the outside world. He'd been especially attracted to pretty Mexican girls who'd attended Mass at the monastery on Sundays, and they'd started Duane down a path that had led ultimately to the Desert Palace Saloon.

Light flickered from brass oil lamps hanging from nails banged willy-nilly into the walls, as outlaws and banditos seemed to be roasting in the red flames of Dante's Inferno. The saloon exuded an atmosphere of meanness and viciousness that you could scrape from the walls, with everybody armed, half drunk, and ready to fight.

I've ended here because of my bad temper and pretty girls, no doubt about it, Duane was forced to conclude. Maybe I should've listened to the old abbot. Since departing the monastery, Duane had been engaged to a saloon singer named Vanessa Fontaine, and then to Phyllis Thornton, pretty daughter of a prosperous rancher. Both had left him in the lurch for reasons he didn't fully understand, Miss Fontaine running off with an officer in the Fourth Cavalry, and Miss Thornton returning home to daddy. Duane was determined never to trust another woman again, based on his limited experience.

Whores seemed the best solution to his billygoat problem, but he'd learned that a man can't buy love, and love is what makes it worthwhile. I'm going to finish my whisky, and then buy myself a steak with all the trimmings. When my belly is full, I'll check into the best hotel in town and get a good night's sleep. Duane had no money shortage, because the Apaches had given him some gold nuggets, which he'd cashed in at a bank in Morellos.

If I don't look for trouble, he thought, I'm sure it won't come looking for me.

At the bar, a horse thief named Sylvester

Krumm sat with his mug of beer and a cigarette. He puffed thoughtfully as he gazed across the room at a young man in a beard and black shirt, his silver-conchoed hat tilted forward so no one could see his features. The bartender approached with the bottle of whisky. "Hit you again?"

"Damn right," replied Krumm. "Say, d'ya know that kid over thar, the one what just bought the whisky. He's a-sittin' agin' the wall."

The bartender shrugged. "Never see'd 'im afore."

"That's the Pecos Kid!"

"Who's the Pecos Kid?"

"His name's Duane Braddock, and he's the one what shot Otis Puckett about two moons ago."

The bartender widened his eyes. "*That's* the galoot what shot Otis Puckett?"

"I see'd it happen meself. It was a leetle town north of here, name of Shelby, and I was just a-passin' through. Puckett braced 'im, and the Kid shot him straight out."

"You sure that's same Kid?"

"Sure as I am of my own name, although I've been drinkin' so much this week, I forgot what I'm a-callin' myself these days. But it was somethin' to see, lemme tell yez.

His hand moved so fast, one moment it was empty, the next moment it was firin' away."

The bartender regarded him skeptically. "The way you pour it down, friend, I bet *everything* looks like it's firin' away."

A brown cowboy hat with a beaded Navajo hatband turned on the stool next to Krumm. "Who'd you say that feller was?"

"The Pecos Kid."

"What'd he do?"

"Shot Otis Puckett."

"Horseshit. Otis Puckett lives in Laredo with his fambly. No dumb kid's ever gonna kill Otis Puckett." The man in the brown hat raised his voice. "You don't know what yer a-talkin' 'bout, asshole!"

The saloon fell silent. The bartender lowered his head behind the bar, and outlaws backed toward doors, while others dropped behind tables. Duane was already on the floor, Colt in hand, ready to fight his way out of the saloon, although he had no idea what was going on.

Both antagonists faced each other in the golden effulgence of oil lamps. The gauntlet clearly had been thrown down. The man in the brown cowboy hat was named Jones, and he peered into Krumm's eyes. “Make yer fuckin’ move,” he said, “or admit yer lied. What’s it’s a-gonna be?”

Krumm saw murder in Jones’s eyes, and something told him to give way. He made a half-smile, like the underdog offering his throat to the victor, and headed for the door.

“Hold on,” said Jones. “You ain’t ’pologized yet.”

Krumm quickened his pace, showing his tail as he fled for the street. Jones rushed after him, grabbed his shoulder, slammed him against the wall, and pressed his gun barrel against Krumm’s nose. “I ain’t a-gonna tell you again.”

Krumm’s eyes bulged out of his head, as the grim reaper danced crazily before him, dressed as a cowboy. “Sorry,” he said, trying to hold his voice steady. “Guess I made a mistake.”

Jones spun him around and kicked his ass toward the door. Krumm flew outside and landed on the sidewalk, as laughter erupted inside the saloon. Summoning his remaining shards of dignity, Krumm arose and dusted himself off. Then he headed for his horse, for outlaws would offer no mercy to one who’d revealed himself a coward.

Krumm ordinarily wasn't afraid of strangers, but there had been something bloody and insane in his adversary's eyes. I wonder how many men he'll kill before the sun comes up? he pondered, as he tightened the cinch beneath his horse's belly.

Inside the saloon, Jones placed his gun on the bar.

"On the house," said the bartender, pouring a tall one, to help settle things down.

Jones grabbed it, sipped off an inch, coughed, and said hoarsely, "That goddamned fool wouldn't know a bull's ass from a banjo. He said that kid over thar shot Otis Puckett. What a crock of shit." He pointed his gun toward Duane Braddock. "Hey kid — you ever shoot Otis Puckett from Laredo?"

"Never heard of him," replied the young man sitting against the wall.

" 'At's what I thought. Anybody ever tell you that you look like a girl?"

The young man arose from his chair, but the saloon manager advanced into the line of fire. He wore handlebar mustaches and a dirty apron. "What's the problem?"

Jones snarled. "Some folks try to make themselves big, when they ain't nawthin' but pantywaists."

The manager retorted: "You want to shoot somebody, do it outside. I'm tryin' to run a business here. Why don't you sit down and have a steak on the house?"

"I never turn down a free meal," Jones said with a shrug.

The manager placed his arm over Jones's shoulder and maneuvered him toward a vacant table. Somebody hooted as the bartender poured a free round. Cards were shuffled and dealt, whisky gulped, and outlaws accompanied soiled doves to the back rooms, as the saloon returned to its previous grungy ambiance. Duane sipped his whisky calmly, but was rankled beneath the facade. *I haven't been in town two minutes, and somebody recognized me! I'd better get the hell out of here.*

He tossed down the rest of his whisky, tucked the tobacco into his shirt pocket, and headed for the doors. He expected another insult at any moment, but emerged unscathed into the cool night air. On his way to the stable, something moved in an alley. Duane spun around and tightened his finger around the trigger of his Colt. "Who's in there?"

A drunkard burped as he staggered out, buttoning his pants. He gazed down the barrel of Duane's gun, and blinked. "Whoa," he wheezed.

"Thought you were somebody else," Duane replied.

Duane holstered his gun and resumed his journey toward the stable. I just drew on an innocent drunk, and I should've known better than to come to a border town. Duane soon arrived at the stable, where he hollered, "Twilby!"

The wizened old man emerged from the shadows. "Somebody call me?"

"Where's my horse?" Duane walked down the row of mounts, spotted a familiar black tail, and then saw Steve's head half buried in a wood bucket full of oats. So soon? Steve's eyes seemed to say. But we just got here.

Duane read disappointment on the horse's face. "I know we've just arrived," Duane tried to explain, "but somebody recognized me." Then Duane became aware that the stablemaster was behind him. "How much I owe you?"

"You jest got hyar. What the hell happened?"

"I don't think Escondido is my kind of town."

Steve whinnied with dissatisfaction and shook his head from side to side.

"He don't want to go," the stablemaster said.

"But he has to."

"What fer?"

"Somebody just threatened to kill me."

The stablemaster took a step backwards and appraised Duane in moonlight streaming through the door. "You look like a decent feller to me. How come?"

"I have no idea."

"You didn't deal off the bottom of the deck by any chance?"

"I don't gamble, and I never even saw the galoot before."

"You might never see 'im again. It's written in the good book when and whar yer a-gonna die, and there ain't a damned thing you can do about it noways. A scorpion might climb into yer bedroll tonight, or you could git hit by a bolt of lightning."

He believes in predestination, Duane realized. But I don't. Duane turned toward Steve and saw that the horse's eyes were heavy-lidded with fatigue. The animal was terrified of Apaches, for whom horsemeat was the greatest delicacy.

Duane turned toward the old stablemaster of the plains. "What're *you* on the dodge for?"

"What makes you think I'm on the dodge?"

"Everybody in this town's on the dodge. Who's the sheriff?"

"We ain't got one. Everybody minds their own bizness in Escondido, and we get along jest fine."

"Tell that to the feller who wanted to shoot me in the Desert Palace Saloon."

"You did the right thing to walk away. He might've been Jesse James, John Wesley Hardin, or El Pancho. But keep yer nose clean, you'll won't have nawthin' to worry about. Go to another saloon, that's all."

Duane recalled the thick juicy home-cooked steak that he'd intended to consume, and Steve deserved a peaceful night. I'll find trouble no matter where I go, Duane told himself, so I might as well have a good meal in Escondido. Besides, my father used to pass through border towns, and folks around here might've heard of him. "Been in this territory long, Mister?"

"All my life."

"Ever heard of the Polka Dot Gang?"

The old man cocked an eye. "Where'd you hear of the Polka Dot Gang?"

Duane's father, Joe Braddock, had been leader of the Polka Dots, but Duane couldn't admit that to a stranger. "Somebody in a saloon was talking about them once. They were supposed to be one tough bunch of hombres."

"Mebbe," replied the old man. "So many gangs have run through this town, it's hard to say. Still want yer saddle?"

"I think I'll stick around a while longer. If you remember anything about the Polka Dot Gang, I'd be mighty grateful if you'd let me know."

"When you git my age, young feller, the memory starts to go. I can't remember what I had fer breakfast."

Duane followed directions to the Last Chance Saloon, which looked like any other Escondido hellhole on the outside, except it was bigger. Men crowded the sidewalk in front, laughing, gesticulating, and passing bottles. There wasn't a woman in sight. Duane pushed through the swinging doors, stepped out of the backlight, and reconnoitered outlaws and painted waitresses wall-to-wall. No chicken bones littered the floor, and brass spittoons were highly polished. A skinny middle-aged man in a red and white striped shirt sat at the piano and plunked the keys. A sign above him said: Please Don't Shoot the Piano Player, He's Doing the Best He Can.

The only empty table was in the middle

of the floor, but Duane didn't want anybody sitting behind him. He headed for the bar, passing cardsharps, newspaper readers, and men passed out with their heads in puddles of beer. The air was full of tobacco smoke.

"Whisky," said Duane to the bartender, who had shoulders like a bull.

As the man in the apron poured, Duane turned his back to the bar. The waitresses were younger and prettier than the ones in the Desert Palace, heads of animals were mounted on the walls, and a painting of a naked lady reclining on a sofa was hung above the bar. Duane sipped whisky and waited for a table to open up on the wall.

Duane wondered if his outlaw father had ever come to Escondido in the old days. Maybe his mother had visited too, but Duane didn't even know her name. According to what he'd heard, she was like the painted harlots who served food and drinks to the men seated before him. Duane had vague memories of his mother, but they could have been just wishful thinking. She was a vast tragic emptiness in his heart.

Two men arose from a table against the side wall. Duane was off his stool instantly, carrying his glass toward the just-vacated table. An old moth-eaten Confederate flag hung on the wall above it, with a pair of crossed cavalry sabers. Duane sat and raised the whisky glass to his lips. His hand stopped in midair, as he noticed three cowboys approaching.

"This table's taken," said one of them, who had a pointed nose and foxy eyes.

"Thought it was empty," Duane replied. "Those other fellers just left."

"I said the table's taken."

Duane didn't like an unreasonable and intimidating tone. "It's taken by me," he said. "Sorry."

The three men looked at each other in disbelief. One wore a green shirt with yellow piping. "Hey kid," he said. "Get the fuck out've here before we nail you to the wall beside that flag."

Duane had to stay out of trouble in Escondido, regardless of the insult. He swallowed his pride and said, "If you want the table that bad, it's yours, my friends."

He arose and backed away, the whisky glass in his left hand so his right would be free to draw and fire. The third intruder wore a silver belt buckle with the great star of Texas emblazoned on the front. "Don't git smart with me, sonny jim, 'cause I'll shoot yer fuckin' lights out."

Duane forced himself to smile, but it came out crooked and odd. "Meant no harm, sir. Enjoy the table."

Duane continued backing to the bar, because he didn't dare turn his back to the three bully boys. They had *owlhoot* written all over them, with guns in holsters and knives sticking out of their boots. Duane returned to the bar, sat on a stool, and gazed at the swine who'd evicted him from his table.

Duane was calm outwardly, but wanted to obliterate them eternally. They respected nothing except their own selfish appetites, he thought. But it's nothing personal, they'd do the same to anybody. He tried to calm himself, because he always landed in the stew whenever he went loco. It felt as if his head were inflating with live steam. He wanted to walk to the table and give them a piece of his mind, but they'd go for their guns, so would he, and God only knew how it'd end. He touched the rosary around his neck, but devout Mexican nuns weren't sufficient to settle him down. He had the feeling that the whole world was against him, and he'd better get out of the saloon before he killed somebody, or somebody killed him.

He knocked back the rest of his whisky

and headed for the door, trying not to look at the three owlhoots. His stomach felt like a yawning chasm, and he recalled why he'd come to the Last Chance Saloon in the first place. He'd wanted a decent meal, and nearly got a bellyful of lead instead. It bothered him that three men stood in the way of his enjoying some delicious food, but again, he touched the rosary. Let God take care of them, he counseled himself.

The cool fragrant desert breeze struck his nostrils as he stepped outside. He looked up and saw stars whirling through the cosmos, worlds beyond worlds, and the mountains of the moon. I'm a tiny grain of sand in God's great creation, and maybe I shouldn't make a big dither out of everything.

He sat on the bench in front of the Last Chance Saloon, and rested his chin on his hand. It seemed a profound insight, and he wondered why he'd never thought it before. Why do I take everything so seriously? Maybe I should go back to the monastery, confess my sins to the Abbot, apologize for everything, and renew my vows to Holy Mother Church.

It seemed a fine idea, but he was starving to death on the main street of Escondido. He touched his concave stomach, and a burp erupted from his throat. Saloons were everywhere, and any one would do. He was about to rise, when someone dropped lazily onto the bench beside him. A familiar face, that of Amos Twilby the stablemaster, looked at him with one eye open and the other eye closed. "Howdy."

"What're you doing here?"

"I can't take a walk if I want to?"

"Which of these saloons serves the best steak, besides the Last Chance?"

"What's wrong with the Last Chance?"

"Just had a little disagreement with three owlhoots."

"You might try the Desert Palace, but onc't I see'd the cook spit in the soup. The cook at the Longhorn is a drunk, but sometimes he gits it right. As for the Silver Spur, it's the cheapest, but sometimes, when yer not lookin', a rat's liable to take the steak right off'n yer plate."

Duane pushed back his black cowboy hat and narrowed his eyes. "Sounds like the Last Chance is the only place to go."

"Hell, I wouldn't let anybody keep me out of the Last Chance. It's a damned fine saloon, and a few of the girls are as pretty as anything you'd see in Frisco. You can't let people push you around, boy. Yer paw wouldn't appreciate it."

"My paw?" asked Duane, as his eyes widened. He grabbed the front of the stablemaster's shirt. "Did you know my paw?"

The stablemaster appeared confused. " 'Course not. I'm jest sayin' that yer paw, whoever he was, wouldn't want a coward fer a son."

Duane let the old man go, and realized with dismay that he'd overreacted again. "I don't see the point of dying for a table in the Last Chance Saloon."

The old stablemaster leaned toward him. "You young fellers today, you got all the answers, but in my day, and it weren't *that* long ago, you push a man around, you'd better get ready to die." Twilby raised his button nose proudly into the air. "I was young onc't too, but I never let anybody keep me out of a saloon. Hell, I'll tell you what. We'll go into that saloon together, and we'll keep away from them owlhoots. But if they start up with us, I'll back you all the way. Don't worry about a thing."

The old man jumped to his feet, hauled his Colt Dragoon, and aimed it between Duane's eyes, only Duane wasn't there. Duane stood a few feet to the side, and aimed his Colt .44 at the stablemaster's right kidney. Twilby's eyes bugged out.

"How'd you do that, kid?"

"I lived with Apaches for a spell."

"Figured you had some Apache blood in you, first time I saw you. Somethin' in yer eyes, that bow-and-arrow look."

"You were pretty fast yourself, old man. You almost got me. Ever been a gunfighter, by any chance?"

The old man pshawed, as he stuffed his Dragoon into its hand-tooled holster. "Who the hell wants to be a gunfighter? They all end up in the cemetery anyways. But if'n we have trouble in that saloon, I can handle two of the galoots myself, and you can take the other one. Hell, I ain't greedy."

Duane realized that Twilby was suffering major delusions. In fact, the old man's speed was mostly gone. He'd be no good at all in a showdown.

"Ready, pardner?" said the old man with a wink, as he headed for the Last Chance Saloon.

Duane didn't want to enter, but Twilby might guess that Duane didn't trust the old man's fighting ability, a slap in the face to one with gray whiskers. A hunger cramp shot through Duane's gut, and he thought, maybe I'm being too careful. If I stay away from those owlhoots, I'm sure they'll leave me alone.

He followed Twilby into the saloon, and the old man motioned for him to come closer. "Which ones are they?"

"Against the far wall . . . with that son of a bitch in the green shirt."

"They don't look like much to me."

Duane and Twilby angled among tables as they closed the distance with the chop counter in back. The three men at the purloined table seemed not to notice them. A Negro cook in overalls stood at the stove, flipping steaks into the air. "How many?" he asked.

"Two."

The plates were filled, the tariff paid, and the new acquaintances headed for an empty table in the middle of the floor. Duane sat so that he could face the owlhoots, and glanced at them as he sliced into the slab of beef that smothered his plate. It was soft as butter and redolent with fragrant juices, accompanied by fried onions, fried potatoes, beans, and tortillas. He wolfed it down, oblivious to the world around him.

"You look like you ain't et fer a few months, kid."

Duane didn't reply, as he shoveled potatoes and onions into his mouth.

"Sure wish I could put away a meal like that," said Twilby. "But yer stomach gets old too, along with everythin' else. Hell, I know I'm not the man I used to be. But in the old days, I used to cut quite a figure, let me tell you. 'Course, Texas weren't so crowded then. Escondido was just two shacks on either side of the trail, with a well in back and a couple of shit houses. People were friendly then, and we stuck together."

"That's not the way I heard it," Duane said. "Aren't border towns places where outlaws go?"

"You've always got yer outlaw element," Twilby said, as he wrinkled his tiny nose. "Wasn't two robbers crucified alongside Jesus?"

"Who keeps law and order in this town?"

"Nobody."

"What would happen if the owlhoot in the green shirt walked up to me and said he was a-gonna blow my brains out?"

"Up to you to blow his brains out first. But most men in this town ain't a-lookin' fer trouble. They come here to git away from trouble. Know what I mean?"

"I'm surprised the Fourth Cavalry doesn't show up one morning and clean the whole place out."

"You can hear the Fourth Cavalry coming twenty miles away, and by the time they arrived all the outlaws would be gone. I know it, you know it, and the Fourth Cavalry knows it. That's why they don't come so often."

Duane examined the old stablemaster's face. It was deeply lined, with pouches of sadness beneath his eyes, his nose laced with red veins, marks of a drunkard. Twilby had a logical mind, Duane thought. Saint Thomas Aquinas himself couldn't've said it better. The stablemaster is on the dodge too, he knows the territory, and he's a good man to know. Perhaps God has sent him to me, to teach me about dangerous little border towns.

The man called Jones entered the Last Chance Saloon, and spotted his companions sitting at a table against the side wall. He puffed a cigarette as he strode toward them, his angry outlaw vision searching for possible threats. He was wanted for robbery, burglary, and murder in a variety of jurisdictions.

He approached the table. Cassidy, the bully with the silver star-of-Texas belt buckle, pulled up a chair. "Where the hell you been?" he asked. "We've been a-waitin' on you fer an hour."

Jones dropped onto the chair, rested his hand on his gun, and said, "I nearly shot some son of a bitch just now."

Their leader was Harold McPeak, thirty-five years old, former sergeant in the Confederate Army, also wanted for a variety of offenses. He wore a green shirt and had a bony face with large ears. "What happened?"

"He said somethin' he shun't."

McPeak appeared annoyed. "I thought we were supposed to stay out've trouble."

"Was I supposed to lie down and die?"

"You were supposed to be here an hour ago."

Jones looked around and grinned. "It don't look like a bad place to wait. Everybody says it's the best saloon in town. I need a waitress. Hey . . . bitch!"

She had black hair to her shoulders and bright red lips. "Yes sir?"

"Gimme a whisky."

She removed a glass from her tray and placed it before him. "Fifty cents."

He tossed the coin onto her tray with one hand and pinched her ass with the other. She forced a smile, but there was fury in her eyes. "Thank you, sir."

Jones sipped the whisky, then wiped his

mouth with the back of his hand. His clothes were ill-fitting, and he wore an egg stain on his dirty white shirt. "Where was we?"

"We was supposed to be talkin' about the next job, but yer late. If you can't be on time, you'd better start a-lookin' fer another gang."

"Okay . . . okay," Jones said. "I'm here. What's the deal?"

McPeak smiled, and said in a low tone: "Boys, we're a-gonna hit the sweetest little bank you ever saw. It's in a town called Shelterville, about five days east of here, and they got this nice old sheriff who wouldn't hurt a fly, plus lots of good church folk who'd hide at the first shot. We'll ride into town one by one in the mornin', meet at the bank around noon, and when I give the word, we'll hold 'em up, blow the safe, and head fer Mexico. We'll be out of sight before they know what hit 'em. Now, the way I see it . . ."

McPeak explained the details of the robbery, but Jones was distracted by a young man sitting in the middle of the floor, the same kid he'd seen earlier at the Desert Palace Saloon, who'd supposedly shot Otis Puckett. Jones felt annoyed by the young stranger, for reasons he didn't care to understand. Jones had a broken nose, a scar on his forehead, and puffy lips. The only girls he ever got, he had to pay for, cash on the barrel head. He'd never been in love in his life.

McPeak's voice droned onward, as Jones continued to glower at the young man. There was something about him that contrasted sharply with Jones. Jones had been raised in Baltimore and had fought other urchins for bits of garbage to eat. He'd never made a conscious decision to steal — it had always come naturally — and he recognized no law save his own best interests. He felt insulted by the young bearded man talking with the old stablemaster on the far side of the saloon.

McPeak stopped his dissertation abruptly, then turned toward Jones. "What'd I just say?"

Jones ignored his question. "See that kid in the black shirt. He's got everybody thinkin' he shot Otis Puckett."

"Hey, ain't he the same one who was a-sittin' at this table?"

"Sure was," said McPeak.

"Maybe he did shoot Otis Puckett," said the fourth man, the one with the pointed nose, Dick Mundy. "Puckett got shot a while back, I heard."

"He did?" Jones was surprised. "Are you sure?"

"I heard some cowboys a-talkin' about it. He was gunned down by a galoot called . . . lemme think . . . the Brazos Kid?"

"How about the Pecos Kid?" asked Jones.

Mundy snapped his fingers. "That's it . . . the Pecos Kid. His name's Craddock or Braddock or something like that." He turned toward the young man. "Sure don't look like much."

"Acted like a skeered rabbit," said McPeak. "Hard to believe he shot Otis Puckett. I'd say it's horseshit."

" 'At's what I think," replied Jones. "He's too purty fer his own good, and I don't like a man who trades on somebody else's reputation. I ought to go over there and kick his ass."

The more Jones stared at the so-called Pecos Kid, the angrier he became. Jones wanted to be admired, but it was always the other galoot who received the sweetest fruits, while he gnawed weeds. Stealing, killing, and fighting were his principal interests, and he had no regrets.

McPeak placed his hand on Jones's shoulder. "We don't want no trouble."

"It'll only take a minute."

"I just gave you an order."

"Shove it up yer ass."

Jones rolled to his feet, hooked his thumbs in his belt, and sauntered toward the table. He felt most alive when a good fight was in the offing.

Then Mundy arose from the table. "I don't want to miss this. To tell you the truth, I never liked that kid when I first see'd him."

"He looked a little simple to me," added the third outlaw, Cassidy. "Let's make him dance to the tune, boys."

McPeak, their leader, wore a disappointed expression on his weatherbeaten visage. He couldn't send them to the stockade, and his sergeant stripes didn't mean anything in Escondido. Guess I'll have to go along with it, he thought philosophically, as he followed them across the saloon. They can kill anybody they want, long as they help me rob that damned bank.

Duane leaned across the table and gazed into his new professor's eyes. "Suppose a lawman gets a wanted poster with your face on it. Does he look for you right away, or just nail the poster on the wall and forget it?"

Twilby sat with his legs crossed, holding a cigarette between his fingers, a twinkle in his eyes. "Depends on the lawman. Some're lazy, others like the glory, a few're in it fer the money, and some're even outlaws theirselves. If yer worried about 'em a-lookin' fer you, it depends what you did. If it's real bad, they might even send the Fourth Cavalry after you." The old stablemaster shook his head. "You don't ever want to git on the fightin' side of the Fourth Cavalry, boy. What're you wanted fer, if'n you don't mind me a-askin'."

Duane leaned closer, and uttered: "I killed a federal marshal, but it wasn't my fault."

Suddenly the table exploded in his face, and he went flying backwards. He landed on his back, went for his gun, and heard a voice say, "Don't move."

Duane's hand froze. He looked up and saw the bully in the brown cowboy hat with the three owlhoots who'd stolen his previous table. Duane blanched white, but held himself steady, tried to smile, and said, "What's wrong?"

Jones stepped forward and looked down contemptuously. "Are you the feller what says you shot Otis Puckett?"

"Who's Otis Puckett?"

"Are you gittin' smart with me, boy?"

"Not me, sir."

"I ain't no goddamned *sir.* I hear that you claim to be the Pecos Kid."

"You heard wrong."

"Are you talkin' back to me Craddock, or Braddock, or Shmaddock, or whatever yer damn name is?"

Duane realized that nothing would pacify the owlhoot. The Pecos Kid was being challenged again, and the only thing to do was make a stand. "I ain't a boy."

"Well, you sure as hell ain't a man either."

"You can say anything you want, since you've got a gun in your hand while my hand is empty. But give me a fair chance, and I'll show you who's a boy and who's a man."

Jones was surprised by the back talk. His law was the code of the gutter and he preferred to prey on the weak and defenseless. But a Baltimore guttersnipe can't back down publicly. "Are you saying that you want a little duel?" he inquired with a wry grin.

"Unless you intend to shoot me in cold blood, without a chance!"

"He's right," said the old stablemaster of the plains, who stood a few feet away. "You got to give 'im a play. Ain't fair to shoot a man in cold blood like that."

If Jones had been alone, he would've blasted the young man to smithereens, but he had to show outlaw valor before his peers. "All right," he replied. He holstered his gun, then beckoned to Duane. "I ain't killed nobody yet tonight, and it might as well be you. Let's go. On yer goddamned feet!"

Duane raised himself from the floor. He didn't have time to speculate on what Saint Ambrose would say about moral implications, as he faced Jones and unlimbered the fingers of his right hand. "Mister, I don't know you, and I don't want to kill you. As far as I know, you don't know me. Why don't you let me buy you a drink?"

Jones raised his eyebrows, because he thought Duane had shown the coward's stripe. "A few moments ago, you was a-challengin' me to a gunfight. Change yer mind so fast, Mister Pecos?"

"There's nothin' to fight over," Duane replied. "What's wrong with you?"

It sounded like a new insult to the ex-Baltimore street urchin. Jones stiffened, and poised his hand above his Remington. "I'm ready when you are."

Duane didn't want to draw first, because of possible legal ramifications. His sharp

Apache-trained eyes watched his opponent's hand closely. "Mister," he said, "I'm going to tell you something, and you'd better listen closely. It's true. I shot Otis Puckett. My name's Duane Braddock, and you don't have a prayer against me. But I don't want to kill you. Why don't we forget the whole thing?"

Jones scowled, becoming more unsure of himself, but the slime of the Baltimore gutter still flowed through his veins. "Sounds like humbug to me," he declared. "I say yer a lyin' sack of shit. What're you a-gonna do about that?"

Duane realized the time had come to stop making excuses, because nothing would stop the man. "What're *you* gonna do?"

Somebody laughed, and Jones thought a joke had been made at his expense. Warped anger billowed through his brain as he reached for his Remington. His finger touched the ivory grip at the same instant that Duane's Colt fired. A bullet pierced Jones's heart, and his lights went out instantly, but he was still on his feet, gun in hand, ready to fire. Everybody stared at him in morbid fascination as he collapsed onto the floor.

It was silent in the saloon, acrid

gunsmoke filled the air, and everyone's ears rang with the shot. Duane aimed his gun at Mundy, then at Cassidy, and finally at McPeak. "Any of you boys want a piece of me?"

The three outlaws glanced at each other, and Duane saw calculation in their eyes. They were wondering how they could take him in tandem, so he dropped his Colt into his holster, assumed his gunfighter stance, and said, "Go ahead, if you've got the sand."

They hesitated, then backed away slowly, to fight another day. All eyes turned toward the young angel of death in black jeans, black shirt, and black hat with silver concho hatband. "Must really be the Pecos Kid," somebody said.

Duane backed toward the rear door of the saloon, as everyone got out of his way. He reached behind him, turned the knob, and landed outside. Cool fragrant desert air struck him. He looked at the sky and decided that Steve was going for a ride whether he liked it or not. He was heading for the stable when the saloon door opened behind him. He spun around and aimed at the figure advancing through the night.

"It's only me," said Twilby. "Where the hell you a-goin'?"

"Some little cave in the middle of nowhere, because every time I come to a town, there's somebody who wants to fight me. I've got so much blood on my hands, I'll never get clean again. Why don't people leave me alone?"

The old stablemaster scratched his chin thoughtfully, like Saint Jerome the scholar. "I guess men git jealous of you. Yer kind've good-lookin', and some folks don't like who they are."

"Are *you* jealous of me, Twilby."

"I can live with myself, but some fellers can't. Are you really the Pecos Kid?"

"It's just a name some dirty, lying newspaper reporter gave me."

"Who taught you to shoot like that?"

"Clyde Butterfield. Ever heard of him?"

"Sure did. They say he was one of the craziest sons of bitches who ever came to Texas. How'd you know 'im?"

"He just started talkin' to me on the main street of a town called Titusville one day. Turns out he knew my father." The last sentence was out of Duane's mouth before he could stop it.

"Who's yer father?"

"Just another cowpoke. Nobody special."

Twilby took a step backwards and

cocked an eye. "He wasn't the boss of the Polka Dots, was he?"

Duane was at a loss for words, but recovered quickly. "I thought you never heard of the Polka Dots."

"When you first asked me, fer all I knew, you could've been John Law. Sure I heard of the Polka Dots, and yer Duane Braddock, eh? Well, the Polka Dots was famous up in the Pecos country. I saw yer father onc't in a little cantina down Tampico way. He was thar with some of his boys. If I'm not mistaken, that's when Clyde Butterfield was a-ridin' with 'im."

"You *saw* my father?" Duane asked. "You don't understand . . . he went away when I was one year old, and I don't know anything about him. What was he like? Did you palaver with him?"

The old stablemaster chuckled. "It's a long story, so let's sit down and have us a whisky." He placed his arm around Duane's shoulder and led him down the alley. "By the Jesus, they said yer paw had a fast hand too. A lot of people really liked 'im, but some, well . . . it's too bad what happened to the Polka Dots."

Duane couldn't resist the opportunity to learn more about his father. Like a moth drawn to flame, he followed the old stablemaster across the street to the Silver Spur Saloon. It was half the size of the Last Chance, thoroughly filthy, with a bar on the left, tables to the right, dance floor in back, no chop counter, and several elderly prostitutes. Twilby bought two glasses of whisky at the bar, then carried them to a table against the back wall. They sat and raised their glasses as word spread through Escondido that the infamous Pecos Kid was in their very midst.

Twilby leaned toward Duane and said, "I never knew yer father, or Clyde Butterfield, but everybody used to talk about 'em in the old days. Joe Braddock and Clyde Butterfield was in the Mexican War, and when it was over, they decided to go into business together with a bunch of other ex-soldiers. Texas was wide open then, and if you put yer brand on a steer, it was your'n legally. There wasn't many big ranches, and a lot of cowboys lived in the open with their chuckwagon, if they had a chuckwagon. But we had no law a-tall, and lots of feuds started over cattle. To make a long story short, some rich ranchers said yer paw and his men was rustlers, and tried to arrest 'em. A range war broke out, and the big ranchers hired fast hands from all over Texas to hunt down yer paw and his boys. They caught 'em in the Sierra Madre Mountains, and that was the end of the Polka Dots, but to this day, a lot of people in the Pecos country say the Polka Dots was innocent. 'Course, you'll find others who'd say they was killers, horse thieves, and cattle rustlers."

Duane was taken aback by this news. "I thought my father had been hung."

"Not the way I heard it. They shot him like a dog."

The image burned into Duane's mind, his father shot full of holes, writhing on the desert sands. "Do you remember the names of the rich ranchers?"

Twilby wrinkled his brow. "Don't right recall."

"If you remember my father's name, how come you don't remember the people on the other side? Are you afraid I'll go there and start trouble?"

"You show up in the Pecos country sayin' yer Joe Braddock's son, you'll git shot on sight. Get it through yer thick skull, kid: there's nawthin' you can do to bring yer paw back."

"Did you ever hear anything about Joe Braddock's woman?"

"Joe Braddock had one in every town. I meant no offense, but that's how it was."

"What towns?"

"If'n I tell you, you'll ride thar first thing in the mornin'. And you'll kill somebody, or somebody'll kill you. You can't look backwards, boy. Life is what you make it."

"But I don't remember my parents at all. It'd mean a lot if you'd just tell what you know."

Twilby pondered what Duane had said. "I don't know a helluva lot, and what you don't know won't hurt you. On the other hand, yer a grown man, and you got a right to hear the truth. Lemme think it over. I gotta go to the piss house. Be right back."

Twilby arose from the table before Duane could react. Duane watched the stablemaster go, and meditated upon the revelations just accorded him. Twilby had confirmed certain rumors and scraps that Duane had gleaned since leaving the monastery, but contradicted others. Duane was pleased that his father had gone down fighting instead of getting legally lynched on the main street of somebody's town. A man was an outlaw or hero depending on what side of the gutter you're standing on, Duane told himself.

An ancient painted harlot approached, placed hands on her bony hips, and winked lewdly. "You look lonesome, cowboy."

"Not tonight. Sorry."

"Don't you like girls?"

"Not interested right now."

She wore gypsy earrings and a rhinestone necklace, and the tops of her wrinkled smallish breasts were visible. She had three black stumps remaining in her mouth. "I'll show you a real good time."

"I'm sure you would, but I'm waiting for somebody."

The whore opened her mouth to reply, when a shot rang out behind the saloon. Duane yanked his gun and dived to the floor, and was joined by other outlaws and waitresses on the way down. The bartender peered fearfully out the back window. "Looks like somebody got shot!"

Duane aimed his gun before him, hammer back and ready to fire. Whores, outlaws, and vaqueros arose cautiously around him. The bartender opened the rear door and looked toward the privy. Then he moved cautiously toward the dark figure bleeding on the ground in front of it. "It's Amos Twilby!"

Duane pushed through the crowd, gun in hand, heart beating wildly. He erupted outside and saw the bartender kneeling over a prostrate figure on the ground.

"Shot in back of the head," the bartender said. "Wonder what kind of low-down varmint'd do a thing like that?"

Obviously he'd been bushwhacked from behind. But why? Duane kneeled beside the grisly shattered head of his newest friend, and felt nauseated, his brow furrowed with confusion. It made no sense. "What'll happen to him now?" Duane managed to ask.

"Cemetery," replied the bartender. "You a friend of his?"

"That's right. Who d'ya think did it?"

The bartender shrugged. "How the hell should I know?"

Duane tried to calm his uprooted mind and think it through. Evidently, someone had been waiting for Twilby to come out of the privy, then coldly and deliberately bushwhacked him from behind. Duane needed a drink to settle himself down.

"At least he died with his boots on," somebody said. "Somebody grab his arms, I'll take his legs, and we'll carry 'im to the undertaker."

Duane reached for Twilby's wrists, and a stranger carried Twilby's legs. The dude wore a frock coat, stovepipe hat, and salt-and-pepper beard. "Who're you?" Duane asked.

"My name's Burkett, and I've got a gunsmith shop. I wonder why somebody shot the poor son of a bitch?"

"Your guess is as good as mine," Duane replied, trying to digest the hideous deed. "You know him long?"

"A few years."

"He have any enemies?"

"Who don't have enemies? But I can't think of anybody who'd shoot 'im, except maybe one of them fellers you had a beef with earlier tonight, Mister Pecos Kid."

Suddenly the plot came together in Duane's convoluted mind. The outlaws had taken his table, then tried to kill him. Duane fought back, shot one, and the others retreated to plan their next move. They'd eliminated Twilby first, with Duane next on their list, but they wouldn't just walk up to him and start shooting. They'd catch him when he wasn't looking, as they did Twilby.

The crowd was dispersing back to the saloons. It was another random, senseless killing in a border town, with no apparent cause, no justice, and no mercy. Duane and Burkett lugged Twilby's corpse down a dark alley strewn with whisky bottles, and came to a house that carried a sign above the door: Caleb Snodgras, Undertaker.

Burkett kicked the door, and it was

opened promptly by a tall thin man with deep-set eyes, wearing a black suit, white shirt, and black string tie. "I heard the shooting and figured you'd be here directly. It's turning out to be a busy night. Right this way, please."

They followed the undertaker down the corridor to a small room with four cots. On one of them lay the naked corpse of Jones, the owlhoot shot by Duane earlier, washed clean of blood, with a red hole in the middle of his chest. A medicinal odor filled the room. The shelves were lined with vials and bottles of chemicals, while peculiar metallic implements lay on the desk. The undertaker clasped his bony hands together, his eyes glittering with barely concealed greed. "It appears that they shot him in the head. Tsk tsk. Are you friends of the deceased?"

"I am," Duane replied. "I'd like to give him a decent burial."

"Happy to hear it. You got twenty dollars?"

Duane reached into his pocket. "Where can I find a preacher?"

"The only one who went to divinity school is Reverend Herbert Berclair of Apocalypse Church. But I wouldn't disturb him at night, if I was you."

Meanwhile, Burkett backed toward the door. "Got somethin' to do," he said, as he disappeared into the night from whence he'd come.

Duane handed twenty dollars to the undertaker. "Did you know Twilby?"

"He took care of my horse, but I can't say we were pards. How long've you known him?"

"I just met him today. Is he married?"

"Hell no. Twilby generally kept to himself."

"I can't help wondering why he was so friendly with me, since I never saw him before."

"It's hard to know what's in a man's heart, cowboy. He lived in the stable with the horses."

"What happens now?"

"If we had a sheriff, he could search Twilby's room."

"Would it be against the law if I searched his room?"

"We haven't got any law in Escondido. You can do as you damn well please, provided you can back it up." The undertaker sat at his desk and took out a sheet of paper. "What's your name?"

Duane saw no point in lying, since he'd already admitted being the Pecos Kid in the Last Chance Saloon. "Duane Braddock."

The undertaker wrote *Duane Braddock* on the paper.

Duane looked over the undertaker's shoulder. "What's that for?"

"I've got to make a report for Austin."

Duane grabbed the sheet of paper and tore it into little pieces. "My name's Joe Butterfield."

"It's a misdemeanor to willfully make wrong statements."

Duane flipped a five-dollar coin onto the undertaker's desk. The undertaker pretended it wasn't there, as he wrote *Joe Butterfield* on a fresh form. "Where are you from, Mister Butterfield?"

"North of here."

"Remember the name of the county?"

"Write any one you like."

"What's your present address?"

"General Delivery."

"Which way you headed?"

"Take your pick."

"Are you kin to Joe Braddock, by any chance?"

Duane was surprised to hear his father's name again, but decided to play dumb. "Who's he?"

"A trigger-happy killer from the Pecos

country, but they finally tracked him down. You sure you aren't his kin?"

"Hell no, but somebody told me once that Joe Braddock was an honest rancher killed by hired guns."

The undertaker glanced at Duane's Colt. "I'm not a-gonna argue with you, Mister Braddock. Anythin' you say. If you ain't his kin, it's fine with me. Maybe he really was the Robin Hood of the Pecos, as some used to claim. We'll have the funeral after breakfast."

"I'll be there," Duane said.

Duane, still agitated by the bushwhack of Amos Twilby, headed back to the center of town. He was certain that the killer had been one of the three owlhoots who'd stolen his table at the Last Chance Saloon. I'll keep my eyes open for them, he swore. They won't catch me unawares as they did poor Twilby.

He walked past the general store, which was closed for the night, and noticed across the street a vacant storefront. For all I know, my father might've passed through here long ago, Duane conjectured. He felt strange amorphous emanations, as if the ghost of Joe Braddock had arrived in Escondido.

Duane vaguely remembered a tall, husky

man with a black mustache, wreathed in the fragrance of whisky and tobacco. Maybe that's why I love saloons, because they remind me of my father. Was he a good man or a low-down crook? That's what I want to find out.

And what about my mother? She'd nourished him at her breast, but was a blank in his memory, and no one had ever told him anything at all about her. Sometimes he dreamed that he was a baby sleeping in her arms, and she had blond curls adorning a worried pretty face. But what's dream and what's true? he wondered. And what does it matter who my parents were? I'm here, and that's the main thing.

That was the logical part of his mind, but a deeper layer had a voracious need. Duane felt like a straw in the whirlwind of time, desperately needing an anchor. If I knew the truth about my mother and father, then I could get on with my life. Otherwise I'll keep wondering about them forever. Maybe if I'm lucky I'll meet more people in Escondido who knew my father, or even my mother.

His mind returned to the brutal killing of Amos Twilby. Why'd he befriend me, out of all the outlaws in Escondido? He looked at me funny when I showed up at the barn, come to think of it. Maybe I look like my father. The name Butterfield sure got his attention. When Twilby sat beside me in front of the Desert Palace Saloon, what if it wasn't a coincidence? He knew more than he let on, and was testing me.

But maybe I'm driving myself plumb loco as usual. What if Twilby got shot by an old enemy, and it has nothing to do with the owlhoots who stole my table. Duane was frustrated by his inability to isolate definitive answers to pressing problems. He'd studied Logic at the monastery in the clouds, but couldn't apply it to Escondido.

What you need is a drink, a good hot bath, and a nice soft bed, he admonished himself. Twilby had recommended the Belmont Hotel, and Duane wondered which adobe structure it was. If it's the best hotel in town, it must be right on the main street, he figured. If I keep on walking straight ahead, I've got to run into it sooner or later.

CHAPTER 4

In the wee hours of the morning, after business slowed at the Last Chance Saloon, Maggie O'Day liked to climb the ladder to the roof, breathe fresh air, and look at the moon-dappled horizon. She wore a black shawl, walked with her arms folded beneath substantial breastworks, and thought about real estate.

It irked her that Escondido's economic future was limited because it was a nasty, lawless, border town, and there'd already been two shootings that very night. Gun-crazy owlhoots from all across Texas and Mexico passed through Escondido regularly, while smart investors gave it a wide berth. Maggie wished there was some law and order, at least enough to keep the fightin' and killin' under control.

She'd selected Escondido for her biggest entrepreneurial venture to date because there wasn't much competition and owlhoots tended to spend freely. She'd considered the impact of shooting and fighting before she ever put a penny into the Last Chance Saloon, and had hired a few of the most notorious local gunslingers soon after arriving. They tried to keep the peace in her establishment, but too often let drunkards shoot each other, long as they didn't kill other customers. The Last Chance Saloon turned healthy profits every night, but continual violence was shredding Maggie's nerves.

Maggie O'Day wanted to be a respectable lady walking down the fashionable boulevards of San Francisco, but it'd take twenty years to save that much money, and a gang of outlaws might steal her savings at any moment. She didn't necessarily trust her bodyguards either.

The queen of whores was lonely, though she hated to admit it. She knew other merchants in Escondido and met with them regularly. Most were her customers. Few women would talk with her, except for her employees. An irksome hunger ached within her, but she'd ignored it successfully thus far. In twenty years, I'll only be sixty-two, she tried to console herself. That's not so old, is it?

The aging process horrified her, for

she'd been delicate and pretty once. But over the years, her willpower had eroded where sweets were concerned. Sometimes she skimped on other foods so she could eat more pastries. Then, when her dresses got too tight, she'd starve herself for a few months. She'd maintain her new low weight for brief periods, then a praline would catch her eye, or a cake. Gradually, the dresses would start getting tighter again.

The street below was deserted except for a man walking in the shadows on the far sidewalk. Horses lined the rail in front of the Last Chance Saloon, and somebody was passed out on a bench on the other side of the street. Maggie found her eyes drawn to the man strolling along the sidewalk. She couldn't see his face, but his spurs jangled every time his heels came down, and a cigarette hung from a corner of his lips. Something about his gait intrigued her — she didn't know quite what it was. She watched him pass the drunkard sleeping on the bench.

Then a strange thing happened. The drunkard on the bench moved his head, then raised himself slowly. Maggie's eyes widened as she noticed the gun in his hand. It appeared that he was going to bushwhack the man who'd just walked past!

Maggie opened her mouth to scream, when suddenly, with movements so quick they appeared only as a blur, the man in jangling spurs spun around, shot the backshooter on the bench, then dropped to his stomach and fired a barrage of gunfire into the alley across the street.

Escondido thundered with shots, and a bullet ricocheted over Maggie's head. She dived toward the roof and peered fearfully over the edge at the action. "I'm hit!" shouted a voice in the alley. The man in jangling spurs, maintaining a steady rate of fire, charged the alley.

Maggie decided it was time to get the hell out of there. She descended the ladder to the corridor below, returned to her office, poured herself a stiff drink, and sat behind her desk. The shootout had begun so suddenly, she couldn't remember what she'd been thinking about before. She recalled the man in flashing spurs and wondered who he was. She opened her mouth and hollered: "Bradley!"

The door opened, and her chief bodyguard stuck his head inside. "Ma'am?"

"A few people was just shot outside. Tell the feller who won that I want to talk with 'im."

Bradley narrowed his left eye. "I ain't yer errand boy."

"Jesus Christ, everybody's so tetchy around here."

He slammed the door, and his footsteps receded down the corridor. She'd slept with Bradley a few times, out of desperation and weakness, and lately Bradley had been acting as if he owned her. She'd known it was a mistake when she first lured him to her bedroom, but he had strapping muscles and the rugged profile that she liked. He'd provided a few fleeting hours of pleasure, but now it was time to put him in his place. She would've fired him long ago if he weren't so handy with a gun.

On the planked sidewalk, Duane kneeled beside the body of the outlaw who'd been lying on the bench, pretending to be asleep. Duane recognized the pointed nose instantly. It was one of the bunch who'd tried to steal his table earlier in the Desert Palace Saloon.

He entered the alley, where another of the assailants, the one wearing the green shirt, lay dead, surrounded by curious onlookers. Duane tallied the score. He'd shot two of them just now and one earlier, but evidently the owlhoot with the silver Texas-star belt buckle had got away.

Duane lit a match, examined dirt in the alley, and touched his finger to the ground. It came up red. Apparently he'd winged his final bushwhacker. Duane followed the trail to the back of the alley and looked both ways, but couldn't see anybody. He continued into the yard where the trail of blood dried up. There were fresh hoof-marks, but Duane didn't remember hearing a horse. He had difficulty reading signs by the light of matches that kept going out. Duane heard footsteps behind him, as a crowd of saloon patrons spilled into the backyard from nearby alleys.

"It's the Pecos Kid again," one of them said.

"Anybody recognize these men?" Duane asked.

Nobody said anything. Duane knew that he'd have to look over his shoulder for the rest of his life, for one had gotten away and might show up when Duane least expected it. Why'd I leave that cave? he asked himself.

A strange apparition approached across the backyard. It was the piano player from the Last Chance Saloon, wearing his red striped shirt and red string tie, with his derby tilted over one eye. "Are you the feller what shot all them people?"

"So what if I am?" Duane replied.

"Maggie O'Day'd like to talk with you, sir."

"Who's Maggie O'Day?"

The piano player appeared surprised. "She owns the Last Chance Saloon."

"What's she want?"

"She din't tell me, but she's a good person to have on yer side. Know what I mean? Besides, if you don't talk to her, she'll probably fire me."

The piano player led him through the alley, where outlaws and banditos studied Duane's face carefully. "It's the Kid all right," one of them said.

Duane followed the piano player into the Last Chance Saloon. The girls regarded him with unabashed fascination, as he continued toward the back corridor. At its end, the pianist knocked on a door and declared: "I've found 'im."

"Send him in," said a sultry female voice.

Duane opened the door and stopped cold in his tracks. Sitting behind the desk was a stout big-busted woman with a bizarre hairdo of dyed red curls piled atop her head. "Have a seat," she said, a panatella perched daintily between her fingers. Duane dropped to the chair before her. His experience with women was limited, and Maggie O'Day exceeded his wildest expectations. She looked mean as a man, yet was pretty in an odd way, with graceful movements of her hands. "Sounds like yer a-havin' a busy night," she drawled. "What's yer name?"

Duane decided to play it to the hilt, since his identity was no longer a secret. Leaning toward her, he peered deeply into her eyes and said, "They call me the Pecos Kid."

She smiled, her eyes dancing gaily. "Howdy, Mister Pecos," she said, thrusting her bejeweled hand over the desk.

Duane had never shaken hands with a woman before, and didn't know how to proceed. Normally, a man will give a stranger a firm crunch, to let him know that no horseshit would be tolerated, but Duane couldn't do that to a woman. So he squeezed her hand gently, while she caught him in a viselike grip. Bones in his hand crackled. When she let him go, he tried to smile. "You can call me Duane Braddock."

He noticed her eyes roving over his body, stopping briefly at certain strategic places. "I was up on the roof tonight," she began, "a-gittin' a breath of fresh air, and I happened to see yer li'l gunplay in the middle of the street. I ain't never see'd nobody move so fast in my life. Yer a perfessional, I take it?"

"Not me," Duane replied. "I was a cowboy before I got in trouble with the law. Hell, I don't want to be a professional gunfighter. They all end up in the cemetery."

"Sounds like yer headed thar anyways. What was the shootin' about?"

"Bunch of owlhoots got mad at me. Don't ask me why."

"Don't take much to get some of 'em a-goin'," Maggie said. "They'd ruther shoot a man than give 'im the time of day. The trouble with this town is we ain't got no law. Say, would you be innerested in bein' our sheriff? One hundred dollars a month, with all the fines you can collect. We'll give you a jail and an office. What do you say?"

Duane calculated that the pay was more than three times what a cowboy earned, and fines could really add up. But he had plenty of money, and didn't need additional headaches. "No thanks. I was planning to move on."

"A sheriff can do pretty much what he

wants, thanks to that tin badge," Maggie said, persisting. "If a wanted poster came from Austin with yer picture on it, you could set a match to it."

"If a wanted poster came from Austin with my picture on it, I wouldn't even be here. I'm hitting the trail soon as my horse rests up. No thanks, Mrs. O'Day."

"It's *Miss* O'Day. Have you noticed anything strange about this town, Duane?"

"I never saw a nest of coyotes like this in all my days."

"You seen any children on the streets?"

"I figured there weren't any."

"They're here, but they cain't go outdoors to play. There's too much stray lead flyin' around, and we need a tough sheriff to put an end to it. There's decent folks left in Escondido, and we'd be mighty grateful if you took the job."

"This town is full of backshooters and bushwhackers. I wouldn't last a day."

"They're all scared of you now. You could do some real good here, make yer own laws if you want, and put together a nice little grubstake. How's about some whisky?"

She poured a glass and handed it to him, and he sipped sweet mellow liquid, a notch above what she served in the bar. "The more I think about it, the worse it sounds," he declared.

"Maybe yer right," she said reluctantly. "We got some real bad fellers in Escondido, no doubt about it. Yer young and I reckon you've got a lot to learn." She winked. "The girls must go plumb loco over that purty face of your'n, ay cowboy?"

Duane smiled faintly. "But they always leave after they get to know me."

"A gal looks fer a man who can take care of her, not git her strung up. You pull yer life together, you'll have all the gals you want. If it's one thing I know, it's women."

Duane examined the strange flamboyant creature before him. "You been in this business long?" he inquired.

She puffed her cigar thoughtfully. "I was born in this business."

"Did you ever hear of my father, Joe Braddock?"

She flinched barely perceptibly. "Long time ago, but I never met 'im. They say he was one wild-ass son of a bitch once he got going, and you're a chip off the old block. Lots've owlhoots pass through Escondido, and you might meet somebody who knew 'im from the old days."

"I already met one of them — Amos Twilby. Were you a friend of his?"

"He was a customer. How'd he know your father?"

"He got shot before he could tell me."

"He was a damned fine stablemaster, but I've always wondered where his stake come from. You know, if you wanted to ask about Joe Braddock, folks would feel obligated to answer a sheriff's questions. A sheriff could do pretty much as he pleased in a town like Escondido."

"You ever hear anything about Joe Braddock's woman?"

"Joe Braddock prob'ly had a lot of 'em, a goodlookin' feller like that."

"If you never met him, how do you know he was good-looking?"

"I'm just telling you what people used to say. Joe Braddock was a legend in the Pecos country, because he dared to buck the big ranchers."

"Some folks say he was an outlaw."

"Maybe he was. Hell, everybody's got an axe to grind. If the big ranchers who killed yer paw ever heard you been a-snoopin' around askin' questions, they might send vigilantes after you, too. But if you was a lawman, they wouldn't dare touch you. Think it over, cowboy. And if you want a girl for the night, just pick her out and take her upstairs, on me. It's a li'l fringe benefit of being a friend of Maggie O'Day's."

Duane sat in a dark corner of the Last Chance Saloon, sipping whisky and brooding over his first day in Escondido. After a lifetime of wondering about his father, he was finally meeting people with reliable information.

Each had confirmed the others' stories in varying degrees, but Duane was eager to know more. Maybe I can find somebody who was a friend of my father's, and there might even be an old woman who met my mother too. It's true what Maggie O'Day said: a sheriff can investigate anything he wants.

Duane's eyes roved the half-empty saloon, as he searched for the fourth owlhoot, the one with the silver star of Texas on his belt buckle. Waitresses congregated at the end of the bar, exchanging jokes with the man in the apron. The Pecos Kid had been drinking all night, and everything hit him at once. His head swam, as Twilby, his parents, and Maggie O'Day danced through the corridors of his mind. He saw himself shooting the men who'd tried to bushwhack him, and felt as if he were choking on blood. Shuddering, trying to pull himself together, he remembered that he'd been searching for the Belmont Hotel when the shooting commenced. Exhausted, he tossed down his whisky, snorted, and headed for the corridor that led back to Maggie's office.

A barrel-chested man in a narrow-brimmed derby hat blocked his way. "Whataya want?" asked Bradley Metzger.

"Maggie O'Day."

"She's busy."

"Tell her I want to talk with her."

"I just told you she's busy, kid."

Duane didn't need a fracas in the wee hours of the morning. He was about to walk away when the door to Maggie's office opened. She poked her head out and asked: "What the hell's this?"

"I wanted to talk with you," Duane replied.

"Come on in." Maggie placed her arm across Duane's narrow waist and eased him into her office, while Bradley Metzger glowered angrily on the sidelines.

"Have a seat, Sheriff," Maggie said as she closed the door.

"What's wrong with him?" Duane asked, aiming his thumb back at the corridor.

"He's a goddamned fool. What can I do fer y'all?"

"I'm on my way to the Belmont Hotel,

unless you can recommend something better."

"You spend a night at the Belmont, you'll be a-scratchin' fer the rest of yer life. There ain't a decent hotel in town, 'cause decent people gener'ly don't come here, but maybe they would if we had better accommodations. Anyways, I've got a spare room at the end of the hall, and you can use it fer a few days. Be my guest. Why the hell not? If you want a gal, just pick her out on the house. A man like you deserves the very best." She winked suggestively.

"Too tired."

She tossed a key to him. "Room twenty, last room at the end of the hall."

Duane found himself in a labyrinth lit by oil lamps hanging from pegs molded into adobe walls. An outlaw and his maid advanced from the opposite direction, cuddling like Romeo and Juliet, although it was counterfeit love. Duane frowned disapprovingly as he came to an intersection of tenebrous passageways. He looked to his left and right, and suddenly didn't know where he was. His head spun. He felt disoriented and leaned his shoulder against the wall.

A painted harlot approached through the

corridor, her frothy black hair adorned with a red rose above her left ear. "You all right, Mister Braddock?"

"Where's room twenty?"

"I can take you there." Her eyes brimmed with adulation, and she looked like a harlequin clown in the dim lamplight. "Yer a real man, Mister Braddock."

He spotted the scar beneath cosmetics on her right cheek. "Because I shot somebody?"

"Because you stood up to 'em, and din't let 'em shove you around. I wish I was fast with a gun. Nobody'd ever mess with me again."

Duane looked her over as she led him down the corridor. She was surviving as best she could, just like the Pecos Kid. "What's your name?"

"Alice Markham."

A new wave of dizziness struck him, his vision blurred, and he saw a halo glittering ethereally around her head. "Are you all right?" she asked. "Here's your room."

He fumbled for the key. She took it out of his hand and opened the door, and they entered a small adobe cubicle with a cot, dresser, and window. "Can I do anythin'?" she asked.

Her tone of voice was unmistakable, it

was on the house, and he had to admit that he wouldn't mind, but he couldn't perform ultimate love with someone he didn't even know. "Awfully tired," he said, dropping to the edge of the bed.

"Maybe some other time."

He waited a few seconds after she left, locked the door, pulled aside the burlap curtain, and peered at outbuildings, privies, and piles of trash gleaming in the light of the moon. Not a soul was in sight.

He pulled off his boots, then unfastened his gunbelt and hung it over the bedpost. He drew his gun, held it in his right hand, and lay upon the bed. His eyes closed, while his Apache hearing searched the night for dangerous sounds. He heard wind whistling over rooftops, the distant howl of a cat in heat, and a clothesline slapping a pole, as he dropped steadily into slumber.

Maggie O'Day lay with her eyes closed in her circular wooden bathtub, a glass of whisky in one hand, a panatella in the other. The hot sudsy water drew knots out of her muscles and soothed her troubled mind. Everybody knew the brassy ex-whore who drank and smoked like a man, but few ever saw the worried businesswoman who'd gambled her savings on the future of an out-of-the-way border town.

She knew that outlaws couldn't maintain the local economy forever, and Escondido needed a stable population. But no serious investor would tolerate lead flying constantly through the air. The town needed law, Maggie knew, but nobody wanted to take on murderers and desperadoes and risk a bullet through the brain for a measly hundred dollars a month.

She thought of Duane Braddock, the best prospect so far. She found him intriguing, but felt guilty for trying to convince him to become sheriff. Yet even vicious outlaws would think twice before taking on the Pecos Kid.

Maggie was half-drunk, lazy, and lonely. She rested her head against the bathtub and entertained certain thoughts about the handsome young killer. She liked his silky blue-black beard, aquiline nose, and boyish smile. Maggie yearned for her vanished youth, when she'd slept with cute cowboys like Duane Braddock, and had even fallen in love with a few. But I'm just an old bag now, she mused, and he needs a gal his own age. Maggie knew that Duane hurt inside. Her maternal feelings swelled, and she wanted to take care of him. The poor kid didn't even know who his momma was.

Duane was dreaming about Apaches in their mountain fastness when he heard a footfall outside his window. In an instant he was out of bed, gun in hand. He pressed his back against the wall at the sound of another scrape of boot sole, and his thumb cocked the hammer of his Colt as he sucked in his gut.

Then, in the still of the night, the window blew out in a sudden deafening explosion. A blizzard of buckshot smashed into the bed where he'd reclined only moments before. His ears rang, and through the roar he heard footsteps in the backyard. He stuck his head outside and saw a figure running away. He aimed his Colt and fired, but the man disappeared around the corner of a building.

The room was thick with smoke, the mattress demolished. Somebody pounded on the door. "What the hell's a-goin' on thar!"

Duane yanked open the door, and Bradley Metzger stood in the corridor, gun in hand. Feathers and bits of fabric fluttered about the room. "Almost got you," Bradley said regretfully.

Duane recalled the silver-buckled outlaw who'd escaped earlier. It must've been him, Duane thought. Then he remembered the young prostitute, Alice Markham, who'd helped him to his room. Maybe she had told him where he was.

Other bodyguards arrived, guns drawn. They didn't ask questions, because the obvious mattress lay before them, riddled with lead. Their eyes turned to Duane, who was wide awake and ready to kill. He strapped on his gunbelt, pulled on his boots, and adjusted his black hat. Silently they watched him walk out of the room and down the corridor. Prostitutes and customers inspected him from doorways as he passed. He came to the saloon, where a few drunkards still congregated, and an outlaw was passed out at the bar. Duane drew his Colt as he approached the man in the apron. "Get me Alice Markham *now*."

Without hesitation, the bartender headed for the back rooms. Duane sat at a table against the side wall, closed his eyes, and gave thanks to the Apaches who'd taught him to listen for danger. If it hadn't been for them, he'd be on his way to the undertaker's parlor. He tried to calm himself with the commandment *Thou shalt not kill,* but it didn't accomplish the result he desired. Am I supposed to stand still and let these people kill me? How can I let some son of a bitch get away with shooting my father? What about justice and free will?

Alice Markham emerged from the corridor, accompanied by a scrawny outlaw wearing a thick blond mustache. The outlaw patted her fanny, and she kissed his cheek. Then she headed for Duane.

"You wanted to see me?" she asked in a throaty sensual purr.

Evidently she figured he was next in line to her bedroom, or so it appeared. "Did you tell anybody where I was sleeping tonight?"

She stared at him for a few moments, surprised by his question. "Why should I do that?"

"Did anybody ask where I was?"

"I never said a word about you, even to the other gals." She appeared embarrassed. "I'm always a-gittin' blamed fer things I din't do."

Duane didn't know whether to believe her or not. "Sorry," he said, as he turned toward the door.

He needed fresh air and room to think. Outside, the street was deserted, while a few drunkards were passed out on benches that lined the planked sidewalk. Duane held his gun ready to fire as he scanned alleys, rooftops, gutters, and water troughs. For all he knew, the owlhoot in the silver buckle was there, drawing a bead on him. He figured that the stable was empty, except for horses, so he climbed to the hayloft, stacked some bales of hay, and reclined behind them, gun in his right hand. I'll be safe here, he hoped. Tomorrow I'll get to the bottom of this, if there is a bottom.

He closed his eyes, as his Apache ears listened for footsteps, or the click of a hammer. Floating before him in the darkness was the sallow death mask of Amos Twilby intoning solemnly over and again: "*. . . yer a grown man, and you got a right to hear the truth.*" Through the depths of a warm Texas night, Twilby's solemn chant rippled across Duane's soul.

CHAPTER 5

Duane awoke before dawn, holding his gun ready to fire. Then he looked out the window at the first red sliver of sun peeking over distant mountains. It reminded him of when he'd dwelled among the Apaches, hunted wild animals, drank *tiswin,* and had incredible visions concerning his grandfather.

Duane wished he could be back with the Apaches, living a pure life close to nature, but warriors were always returning from raids wearing Mexican and American clothing and carrying rifles, ammunition, and other booty that they'd stolen. Their entire culture was on the dodge, and it was only a matter of time before the Army hunted them down.

Duane craved a normal life with home-cooked meals and honest ranch work. He'd loved his brief stint as a cowboy, but then he'd shot Otis Puckett, and his life had turned upside down ever since. When would the madness end? he often wondered.

He found the washbasin, splashed water onto his face, and made his way toward the undertaker's house, as Twilby's chant continued to ring in his brain. *"Yer a grown man, and got the right to hear the truth."* The undertaker lived on the east side of town in an adobe house, with window frames trimmed in white. Duane knocked on the door, and the tall, severe-looking trafficker in corpses opened it. His eyes widened at the sight of the Pecos Kid.

"I'm here for the funeral," announced Duane.

Snodgras led him to a back room, where a plain wooden coffin contained the late Amos Twilby. The undertaker had bathed and shaved the corpse, dressed him in a suit, dyed his mustache, and powdered his nose. Duane was revolted by the transformation of his friend. Will I look like that when they bury me? Duane wondered.

"Have you spoken with the parson yet?" asked the undertaker.

"I'll see him at the cemetery."

"Reverend Berclair doesn't work that way. He'll have to palaver with you first, to make sure you're a good Christian. He takes his job seriously. He's not in it for the money."

Duane noticed four other corpses lying on tables nearby. One was Jones, the owlhoot in the brown hat whom Duane had shot in the Last Chance Saloon. Second was the owlhoot wearing the green shirt, and the next corpse was the one with the pointy nose, both of whom Duane had outgunned in the street the previous night. Duane turned toward the fourth corpse, and his eyes dilated at the sight of the owlhoot with the silver-star belt buckle, whom Duane had thought got away! "What happened to him?"

"Bled to death. He was found behind a stack of firewood with a bullet in his leg."

So I got him after all, thought Duane, as previous conclusions flipped in his mind. "Wait a minute," Duane said. "If a man gets shot in the leg like this, how long before he loses enough blood to conk out?"

"The bullet severed his popliteal artery. I'd say fifteen minutes to a half hour." Then the undertaker smiled proudly. "I studied to be a doctor before I became an undertaker."

Duane was struck by a disturbing new thought. If this outlaw died fifteen minutes after I shot him, then who tried to blow me to bits while I was asleep behind the Last Chance Saloon? A chill came over Duane. Is somebody who I don't even know trying to kill me?

Apocalypse Church was a white house with desert swallows flitting about the steeple and belfry. Duane had never been in a Protestant church. Most Texans were Protestants, whereas Mexicans attended the Catholic churches. He glanced behind him, to see if a bushwhacker with a shotgun was lurking in an alley.

The inside of the church was plain white, with no statues of saints, no candles burning, and no Jesus on the bare cross suspended behind the altar. A young woman prayed in the front pew, her shoulders bent in supplication before the Lord. Whoever she is, she really believes, Duane thought. He headed for the door that led to the parson's office, and the young woman's head spun around in alarm.

"Didn't mean to scare you," he said. "I was looking for the Reverend Berclair."

She was a frail-looking, pale-complexioned teenaged girl with black hair pulled to a ponytail behind her head, and she wore a gingham dress with a high collar.

"Through there," she replied, pointing toward a door.

Duane opened it. An older woman appeared in the corridor, her features austere, and she was dressed in black. "May I help you, sir?"

"I want to see Reverend Herbert Berclair about a funeral. My name's Duane Braddock."

She made an uncertain smile. "Everybody's talking about you, Mister Braddock. I'm the parson's wife, Patricia Berclair. Right this way."

As she led him to a small parlor, he noticed she was in her mid-thirties, and was tall and angular. "Make yourself comfortable. I'll get my husband."

She headed for the door, and he decided that he liked the holy lady. He sat on an upholstered chair and looked at a small bare cross affixed to the wall above the fireplace. Above the cross was a sign: He Is Risen.

Duane felt out of place in the parson's home, because Protestants generally hated Catholics, and vice versa. He'd studied the Reformation at the monastery in the clouds, and countless warring Protestant sects had confused him. Duane didn't know what was right or wrong in religion anymore, but tried to keep an open mind. He expected a pale preacher with an elongated beak to appear, but instead a big strapping fellow approximately six feet four inches tall strode into the room. He had curly dark blond hair, a deep chest, a ruddy complexion, and advanced on a shiny walnut pegleg.

"I'm Parson Berclair!" declared the booming voice. He grasped Duane's hand firmly. "Pleased to meet you."

Duane squeezed with all his might to prevent his knuckles from being crushed. "Mister Snodgras said you wanted to see me about the Twilby funeral," Duane said.

"Are you a Christian?"

"Definitely."

Parson Berclair fixed Duane in his stare. "I mean a real Christian who tries to live the gospel, not just pay lip service. If I'm going to bury your friend today, I expect a prayerful experience for all concerned, in which we relive together the passion of Christ and his resurrection into heaven."

"Wouldn't want it any other way," Duane replied.

Reverend Berclair beamed. "I've always believed that the best way to prepare for a funeral is to bare our hearts to God, ask for forgiveness, and pray for the soul of our recently departed. Most people in Escondido are outlaws, and perhaps you are too. But God loves repentant sinners most of all. Why don't you go to the chapel, and I'll call when we're ready to depart for the cemetery?"

The chapel was filled with slanting shafts of morning light that illuminated pews. Duane sat, looked at the bare cross and walls, and felt strangely bereft without the statues, symbols, and paintings of the Catholic Church. The Protestants didn't have anything except God Himself, he realized. It was an interesting concept, but he preferred Giotto and Titian to drab walls. He dropped to his knees, clasped his hands, and tried to pray.

Nothing happened, and he felt unworthy to appear before the Lord God. The plain fact was he'd broken every rule in the book since leaving the monastery in the clouds. Unable to turn the other cheek, he found himself drawn back to a more primitive biblical theme: An eye for an eye, and a tooth for a tooth. He knew it was barbaric, but also recognized that he was weak and couldn't ignore the murder of his father, the loss of his mother, and now, most recently, the killing of Amos Twilby and the subsequent attempt on his own life.

If Twilby had stayed away from me, he'd still be alive today, Duane surmised. Twilby stuck his neck out for Joe Braddock's son, and a snake in the grass shot him. Murder and robbery are taking over the world, while good people turn their cheeks. Didn't Christ throw the money changers out of the temple precincts?

On top of everything else, as if he didn't have enough worries, somebody had tried to blast him to pieces as he slept behind the Last Chance Saloon last night. Duane couldn't imagine who the bushwhacker was, and wondered when he'd strike again.

The back door of the church opened, and Duane's slender fingers darted toward his gun. He heard the laughter of five children chasing each other up and down the aisles. A stout woman accompanied them, and Duane arose from his pew as she approached.

"Sorry to bother you, sir, but this is the onliest place where the little 'uns can play during the day. You're new in town, ain't y'all?"

"Just arrived yesterday," Duane replied.

"The children cain't go outside," she explained. "There's so many guns in Escondido, you'd think there was a war on."

She smiled apologetically, then waddled to a back pew and sat where she could watch the children. Duane returned to his knees on the floor and considered what she'd said. How can children grow normally if they're pushed indoors all the time?

Their screams pierced his ears, disturbed his prayer, and provoked his hostility against the outlaws who'd taken over Escondido. They have no respect for anybody, not even women and little children. Who the hell do they think they are? It's time somebody took charge of this town.

Now hold on, he admonished himself. Don't get carried away. You're just one ex-cowboy with a price on his head. You can't save this town, and if Jesus Himself came back to earth, even He couldn't save Escondido.

Duane heard a deep voice emanate from the front of the church. "It's time."

Duane followed the Reverend Berclair to the parlor, where his wife was waiting, attired in her black dress, black lace collar, and black bonnet that contrasted sharply with her milky white complexion. They proceeded outside. The undertaker sat on the front seat of the buckboard. A planked wooden coffin lay in back. Duane knew who slept eternally inside, covered with cosmetic powder, wearing a new suit. The undertaker flicked his reins, and the horses pulled the wagon toward the cemetery.

Duane walked beside Reverend and Mrs. Berclair and the clanking buckboard. "The deceased was a close friend?" asked Reverend Berclair.

"Actually, we'd just met," Duane said. "But he was a good man, and didn't deserve to get bushwhacked."

"Remember the words of Paul the Apostle. *Even if you are angry, you must not sin. Never let the sun set on your anger, or you will give the devil a foothold.*"

"Nobody's shooting at me and getting away with it," Duane replied darkly. "That's all I know."

Reverend Berclair glanced at him. "You're on the road to hell, my boy."

"Am I supposed to look the other way and let him do it?"

"Why does somebody want to kill you?"

"I think it has something to do with my father. You ever heard of Joe Braddock?"

The preacher shook his head. "Should I?"

"He was killed in a feud with some rich ranchers near the Pecos some years back."

"I've never spent much time in the Pecos

country, I'm afraid. My wife and I arrived in Texas only recently from Alabama. We felt that God was calling us to this sinful land, isn't that so, Patricia?"

She nodded solemnly. Duane glanced at her out the corner of his eyes, and thought she might be pretty if she gained some weight. "Escondido sure is sinful," Duane said, picking up the conversation. "I never saw so many hard hombres in one spot in my life."

"It's an uphill battle, but I believe in persistence and the healing power of God. I've *seen* Him, you see."

"What'd He look like?" Duane asked.

The preacher appeared not to notice the skeptical note in Duane's question. "It happened a long time ago, during the war, at Vicksburg," he replied, and his face seemed to glow with the memory. "Cannonballs were falling, canister raked our lines, the ground was covered with dead and wounded, and behind it all, high in the sky, I saw the face of the Lord God gazing at me, an expression of indescribable compassion on his face. I literally cried for joy, but then a chunk of flying metal hit me in the leg. It was the end of the war for me, but the message was irrefutable. God directed me to take up His ministry, and simultaneously made it impossible to do otherwise. So I mustered out, went to divinity school, and here I am in Escondido."

Maggie O'Day stepped outdoors, accompanied by Bradley Metzger, and the bright morning sunlight nearly blinded her. She was a creature of the night, usually fast asleep in the early hours, but there was something she wanted to do. Duane Braddock's story had touched her, for she'd been a semi-orphan too, and had often wondered about her father. She suspected that news of Duane's mother might be available among the older women of Escondido.

"Pick me up," she ordered.

Bradley lifted her easily in his powerful arms and carried her across the street, dodging potholes, refuse, and a puddle of horse piss. They came to the far side, and Bradley lowered her to the ground. "You ain't a goin' in the Silver Spur, are you?"

She glanced at him sharply. "If I want yer opinion, I'll ask fer it. And if'n you don't like yer job, just give me a day's notice, so's I can git somebody else."

"You'll never get anybody like me," he said angrily.

"Your kind is a dime a dozen," she replied.

She held her skirts as she entered the Silver Spur Saloon, so she wouldn't attract dirt to her hem. Outlaws slept bent over tables in the filthy, ramshackle saloon, while the bleary-eyed bartender washed glasses in a tub of dirty water. "Can I help you, Miss O'Day?"

"Where's Sanchez?"

The bartender nodded toward the back corridor.

"Why don't you wash the spittoons while yer at it?" she asked. He didn't reply.

Bradley accompanied her to the corridor. Sometimes he felt like murdering her, and other times he wanted to get on his knees and beg her to marry him. She turned toward him as they approached the door. "Wait for me here."

"Be better if I went inside with you."

She looked at him askance. "Better for who? I said wait for me here."

She knocked on the door, waited a few moments, then disappeared into the office. Bradley sat on a chair near the door, placed his gun on the table, and looked around the smoky rundown saloon in the morning light streaming through smeared windows. A man in a frock coat lay unconscious on the floor, his arm hanging over a brass rail covered with rust and dried gobs of tobacco juice.

Bradley thought Maggie should stay out of filthy low-class saloons like the Silver Spur, but she never listened to him. She uses me like a horse, but she'll git her ass in Dutch someday, and turn to me for help. Maybe I will, and maybe I won't.

Sanchez was a portly olive-skinned Mexican with a short curly beard and half-closed eyes. He set out two glasses, poured whisky, then handed one glass to Maggie. "What can I do for you, Señorita?"

She turned down the corners of her mouth with distaste as she perused the room. "I've seen nicer pigpens."

"My customers like it this way," replied Sanchez. "It reminds them of home."

"Yer the dumbest businessman I ever saw, but that ain't why I'm here." She reached into her purse, pulled out her gold cigar case, selected a panatella, and lit it with a match scratched atop Sanchez's desk. "You ever hear of Joe Braddock?"

Sanchez reflected for a few moments. "What Joe Braddock?"

"He shot some folks up by the Pecos 'bout eighteen years ago. Ever heard of the

Polka Dot Gang?"

"Not that I remember, Señorita."

"Well, Joe Braddock was boss of the Polka Dot Gang, and his wife was in the business, if you know what I mean. I'm tryin' to find out who she was. Do you think you can ask yer gals if they ever heard of Joe Braddock and his women? I'd appreciate the favor."

He leaned toward her, licked his upper lip lewdly, and asked: "What'll you do fer me?"

"I'll buy yer business fer a good price after you go broke."

"Who says I'm goin' broke?"

"Them dirty cuspidors and yer cruddy floor. It might remind some men of home, but most wouldn't set foot in here."

"Maybe you and me could become partners," he said.

"Find me some news on Joe Braddock's women, then we'll talk. You know where to find me, day or night. But don't get no ideas. This is strictly bizness."

On her way back to the Last Chance Saloon, Maggie found Duane Braddock sitting on the bench in front. "Morning," he said with a smile. "I want to talk with you."

"Change yer mind about the sheriff job?"

Duane was surprised. "How'd you know?"

She turned to Bradley. "Go to the blacksmith and tell him I want a tin badge for the new sheriff."

Bradley scowled. "I told you onc't afore that I ain't yer errand boy."

She placed her fists on her hips and leaned toward him. "That's *exactly* what you are, and if you don't like it, you can pick up yer pay and leave."

She placed her arm around Duane's waist and led him through the door. They passed afternoon drunkards, the bartender stocking fresh bottles behind the bar, and a Negro sweeping the floor. Duane said: "You'd better watch out for Bradley."

"If he made a million dollars fer me, I'd kiss his ass. But until then, he'll do as I say."

They entered her office. She sat behind her desk, reached for the whisky bottle, and dangled it before his eyes. "Want some?"

"I'm not drinking anymore, but could use a little breakfast."

"Go to the kitchen and eat whatever you want. By the way, Twilby owned the stable free and clear, we got no probate in Escondido, and Twilby ain't got kin, far as we know. Since you was his best friend, the stable's your'n."

"What'll I do with a stable?"

"Make money off it. What else?"

"Is it legal for somebody my age to be a sheriff?"

"The other businessmen and I pretty much make up the laws as we go along, 'cause there ain't no lawyers here, thank God, and yer just what we've been a-hopin' fer. We'll chip in to pay yer salary. Yer hired as of right now. How's it feel to be sheriff of Escondido?"

Two prostitutes in homespun dresses and no cosmetics sat at the big kitchen table, eating breakfast in the middle of the afternoon. It was their own private residential section of the Last Chance Saloon, and Duane felt like an intruder as he chose the stool farthest from them. The girls snickered, and one said. "You ain't afraid of us, are you?"

"What makes you think I'm afraid of you?" replied Duane.

"Why're you sitting all the way down there?"

"I didn't want to interrupt your conversation."

"We was a-talkin' about you anyways. What're you a-doin' hyar?"

"I'm the new sheriff."

She fluttered her eyelashes. "You can arrest me anytime."

The girls giggled, and Duane's ears turned bright red. The face of a Negro woman appeared in the doorway. "Lookin' fer breakfast?" she asked Duane.

"Yes ma'am."

The face disappeared. Duane rolled a cigarette, as the girls whispered among themselves at the far end of the table. "I'm Shirley," one of them announced. "And this is Maxine. We was just a-sayin' 'bout how cute you were."

Duane's cheeks reddened deeply and the girls twittered at his reaction. The Negress cook appeared in the nick of time with a platter of fried eggs, sausages, beans, grits, potatoes, and biscuits slathered with butter. "If you ladies're finished, ain't you got somethin' to do?"

The girls retreated from the kitchen as Duane scooped half of a fried egg into his mouth, then reached for the toast. The Negress returned with a pot of coffee and a mug. "I guess you're the Duane Braddock that everybody's talkin' about. You sure don't look as bad as they say."

"Nothing's wrong with me that a good meal wouldn't cure." She returned to the kitchen, and Duane felt curious about her life. He didn't know much about Negroes, because there hadn't been any in the monastery in the clouds. Probably an ex-slave, he reflected, as he stuffed grits into his mouth. Texas had been a slave state, and most Negroes her age had been owned by white men in the bad old days.

A young woman with black hair in a ponytail entered the kitchen, and Duane was jolted with the awareness that she was the supplicant he'd seen earlier in church. His fork fell from his hand as he realized that she was a prostitute too! She sat opposite him, and said, "You ever find out who tried to shoot you?"

He realized with new wonder that she was also the loose-hipped enchantress who'd escorted him to his room the previous night! "No, but I remember seeing you in church this morning."

"I told you where the parson's office was."

What kind of prostitute goes to church early in the morning? Duane asked himself. The answer came with stunning forcefulness: *Mary Magdalene.* This is a God-fearing woman, Duane speculated, and if I were a good Christian I'd save her from her life of sin, but I can't even save myself.

The Negress cook brought another platter of food, as Alice Markham ate with both elbows on the table. She pretended to be tough, but Duane had seen her in church with her heart bared before the Lord. His acolyte's eyes examined the sadness in her eyes, the defiant corners of her mouth, her mock flippant manner. Underneath it, she was a pious young girl, and he felt inspired to rescue her from her squalid life. "You look so different today," he said.

"Amazin' what some paint and powder'll do."

"Do you go to church often?"

"If I didn't, I'd go loco. Do you think it's fun a-screwin' every galoot with a spare fifty cents in his pocket?"

Her blunt language gave him pause, but it was the opening he was looking for. "Do you know how to read and write and do numbers?"

"A little."

"If you learned how to read and write better, maybe you could get a job as a clerk."

"I'm too dumb to get a job as a clerk."

"You don't seem dumb to me, and I could teach you. Hell, I've spent most of my life in school. I'm willing to give it a try if you are."

She looked at him askance. "What's wrong with you, mister?"

"I thought you said you didn't like screwing galoots for fifty cents apiece."

"I've met a million cowboys who needed to save me, but all they really wanted was my li'l ass."

Again, her language stopped him cold in his tracks. "I made you an offer, and you can take it or leave it."

"It's gettin' better and better. Next thing you'll promise the moon."

He refused to be drawn more deeply into the morass where she was dragging him. I made my offer, it was honorable, and if she doesn't accept it, not my fault. He continued to wolf down breakfast, as Maggie O'Day appeared in the doorway, a tin badge in her hand. She tossed it onto the table, and said, "Here it is."

It lay before him, glowing dully in the light streaming through the windows. Cut crudely from a sheet of tin, it carried the word *Sheriff* hammered with the point of a nail. He pinned it onto his shirt and let it hang. Somehow it didn't look very impressive.

"Payday is the last of the month,"

Maggie said. "Congratulations, good luck, and if you need me fer anythin', you knows whar to find me."

She departed the kitchen, leaving Duane alone with Alice Markham and the tin badge.

"Yer the new sheriff?" she asked skeptically.

"That's right."

"You must be loco."

He couldn't disagree, and their eyes didn't meet again as they continued to breakfast on opposite sides of the table. Duane finished first, put on his black cowboy hat, and was out the door. How strange, he thought. A prayerful prostitute.

He had no idea of what a sheriff was supposed to do, and thought he should ask Maggie first. Instead, he ran into Bradley Metzger in the corridor. "I want to talk with your boss," he said.

The bodyguard wore a too-tight suit, the frock coat unbuttoned to show his low-slung holster. He looked at Duane's tin badge. "What in hell is that supposed to be?"

"Out of my way," Duane replied.

"She's busy."

The door flung open, and Maggie stood before them with sleepy eyes and a mug of coffee. "What the hell's a-goin' on here?"

Duane was first to speak. "I want to talk to you."

"Come on inter my office."

Duane made a motion toward the door, but Bradley wouldn't get out of his way. Both men glowered at each other, and Duane was getting annoyed at the bad manners of the big ugly bodyguard.

A cross expression came over Maggie's puffy features as she turned toward Bradley. "Get out of his way, you damned fool. You'd better leave the new sheriff alone, if you know what's good fer you."

"He ever starts with me," replied Bradley, "I'll shove that badge up his ass."

She pushed Bradley away from her doorway, and the bodyguard frowned at the sheriff passing him by. Maggie closed the door in his face, then sat behind a desk littered with breakfast plates. "You'd better watch out fer Bradley, 'cause he don't like you."

"I think he's in love with you."

"That's too bad, and one of these days, he keeps it up, I'll fire his ass. But I'm glad yer here, 'cause I've got good news. There's an empty store down the street next to the barber shop, and the blacksmith'll put bars on the windows later in the day. It'll be yer office. Here's the keys."

Duane caught the jangling digits out of the air. "There's something I wanted to ask you, Maggie. Did you tell anybody what room I was in last night?"

"Don't believe so," she replied. "Why'd I do that?"

"I'm trying to figure out how the man with the shotgun knew what room I was in."

"Lots've folks could've see'd you."

"Only one person saw me as far as I know, and she claims she didn't tell anybody."

"Maybe she lied, or maybe somebody else spotted you, but you didn't spot him. Or her."

"It was awful dark," Duane admitted. "Maybe it was Bradley."

She became coy. "He knows I like you."

Duane didn't know what to say.

"You blush like a girl," Maggie said with a kindly smile. "And I do like you, but I'm old enough to be yer momma, fer Chrissakes. It's just that Bradley's the jealous kind, although he has no right. But you know how it is. A man sleeps with a woman, he thinks he owns her."

Duane wasn't sure how to respond,

because no woman had ever talked to him so candidly. "I'd better set him straight."

"Be careful how you talk to him. He's dangerous."

"So am I."

Duane yanked open the door, and Bradley turned around to the barrel of a Colt aimed at his nose. Bradley's forehead wrinkled in distaste and loathing. "What's this supposed to be?" he asked.

"Did you try to shoot me last night?" Duane replied, as he searched Bradley's eyes for the lie.

"If I tried to shoot you, I wouldn't miss," hissed Bradley. "And if you didn't have that gun in yer hand, I'd kick yer ass all over this saloon."

Sometimes a man had to draw the line, Duane reflected. Bradley itched for a fight, and Duane had to admit that he did too. Tense and anxious after the events of the night, he eased back the hammer and holstered his Colt. "Let's go."

An expression of delight came over Bradley's face as he advanced down the narrow corridor, his left fist cocked for a skull-crunching blow, and his right pawing ahead, measuring the distance. Duane knew that a southpaw was defeated through maneuver, but there wasn't much room in the narrow corridor. Duane's spiritual advisor at the monastery, Brother Paolo, had fought semi-professionally prior to taking the tonsure, and taught Duane all the advanced tricks, clean and dirty, of fisticuffs.

The new sheriff of Escondido stepped forward cautiously, holding his left arm low, hoping to lure the bodyguard into overextending himself. Bradley saw the opening and shot his right fist forward, but Duane dodged out of the way, then launched a stiff right lead to Bradley's nose. Cartilage crackled beneath Duane's fist, blood spurted in all directions, and Bradley was knocked backwards by the force of the blow.

Duane went after him, to finish him off, when the proprietress stepped between them and held out her arms. "You want to fight, go outside!" she hollered angrily.

Duane headed for the back door, prepared for a backshoot from Bradley, but the bodyguard preferred to tear him apart with his bare hands. They stormed outside into the bright sunny southwest Texas afternoon. Duane removed his hat and hung it from a nail stuck into the side of a tree, then unbuttoned his shirt. Bradley blinked like an owl in the bright sunlight as he took off his frock coat. "Sonny jim," he said. "I'm a-gonna whup yer ass."

Duane decided not to remove his gun, although it was heavy and would slow him down. Men working in the vicinity drifted closer to see the action, as others called to friends far away. News spread rapidly throughout town that war was about to commence behind the Last Chance Saloon.

Duane knew that he had to trick Bradley into throwing punches, and then counter. But Bradley knew what to expect now, and was wary of another headlong rush. Both men circled each other cautiously, giving each other angles and looking for openings, as onlookers crowded around.

Thanks to Brother Paolo, Duane was a well-schooled fighter. He knew how to keep his elbows close to his body, hide his chin behind his shoulder, and snap his punches. In addition, Brother Paolo had taught him the science of lateral movement, how to guard against a thumb in the eye and head butts, and how to avoid the inevitable punch below the belt. Duane felt confident that he could outthink the bear-like bodyguard facing him with bad intentions in his eyes.

"When's the fight gonna start?" asked an

old timer in the crowd. Another replied: "Looks like one's skeered and the other wants to run away."

Bradley bent his knees and pawed with his right hand while loading up his left. Duane took a step to the side and buried his fist up to the wrist in his opponent's stomach. Bradley expelled air from all his orifices, took a step backwards, and threw his right fist forward. But Duane dodged out of the way, then smashed Bradley in the stomach with his left fist. Bradley lowered his arms, to protect a particular portion of his anatomy, and Duane threw a crunching right hook to the side of Bradley's head.

Bradley wasn't fazed by the blow, and responded with a digging left into Duane's kidney. It felt like a dagger, but Duane stood toe-to-toe with Bradley, smashed him in the mouth, whacked him on the ear, cracked him in the gut, and then danced away from Bradley's wild, flailing punches.

Bradley was furious, his lips pulped, left ear turning purple. He reached forward tentatively with his big right fist, but Duane went under it, slammed him in the gut, jabbed him in the mouth, and danced away. He believed that he had Bradley figured out, and it was only a matter of time until Bradley fell. Cocky, vain, filled with false pride, Duane darted forward for another quick combination of devastating punches.

Instead, a hamlike fist appeared in front of his eyes. A moment later something crashed into his skull, and it felt like the Last Chance Saloon had fallen upon him. Bradley had timed him coming in and hit him with everything he had.

Duane landed on his wallet. A boot came streaking toward his face, and he couldn't get out of the way. The pointed toe connected with his cheek and tore it open, and sharp pain blotted out the afternoon. Duane jumped to his feet, dodged a left hook, ducked an overhand right, and walked into a left uppercut.

It straightened him like a ponderosa pine, then sent him sprawling backwards. No ropes stopped him, and he landed flat on his back, as pigeons sang madrigals inside his skull. Bradley stood a few steps away, thumbs hooked in his suspenders. "This is some sheriff we've got here," he drawled.

The crowd laughed, and Duane felt shame roll over him like a load of cow manure. Brother Paolo had taught him never to lunge with his punches, but he'd thrown caution to the winds, and Bradley had made him pay.

"Sonny jim," said Bradley, "I think it's time fer you to climb on yer horse and ride out of town. Otherwise I'm liable to rip yer fuckin' haid off."

Duane wiped blood off his cheek, as wrath came on like a stampede of longhorns. He got to his feet, stepped toward Bradley, and flicked out a tentative jab. Bradley picked it off easily and countered with a left hook, but Duane was gone, with Bradley off balance, leaning forward, wide open. Duane slammed him on the ear, cracked him in the mouth, harpooned him in the belly, then connected with a solid uppercut to the tip of the chin. Bradley went swaying backwards, but friends in the crowd grabbed his shoulders and pushed him back toward Duane, who worked Bradley's midsection for a spell, then went upstairs and hammered his head. Methodically, Duane took Bradley apart. Bradley's knees weakened, and he wobbled around the backyard as Duane's fists pounded him relentlessly. Bradley made one last desperate attack to turn the fight around, but Duane stepped deftly to the side, loaded up his right hand, and sent it streaking toward his opponent's chin.

Bradley was lifted off his feet by the impact of the blow and landed on his back. His eyes were closed, and only his heaving chest moved.

Duane's arms were sore from punches he'd blocked, and blood oozed out of the cut on his cheek. Somebody passed him a bottle of whisky, and he rinsed out his mouth. Some of his teeth were loose, and his left eye was half-closed, but he noticed the assembled townspeople and outlaws viewing him with new interest.

"Who's next?" he asked.

Nobody said a word. An unfamiliar face handed him a bucket of water. Duane upended it over his head and washed the blood and dirt away. Then he put on his hat and slogged away from the battleground. Outlaws, vaqueros, and gamblers made way for the new sheriff, and everybody realized that a new era of law and order had dawned on a certain little Texas border town.

Duane slept the rest of the day in the loft above the stable, his Apache ears tuned for danger. He awakened at ten o'clock at night, aching all over. He climbed stiffly down the ladder and found a muscular Negro approximately Duane's age studying ledgers in a small office at a corner of the stable. "You must be Mister Braddock. I'm Sam Goines . . . yer new stable man."

Duane looked at him askance, because he appeared familiar. "Are you kin to Maggie's cook, by any chance?"

"That's my mother, Dolores Goines."

Duane realized that Maggie had sent him there, and he'd probably been a slave too. "Where can I get a bath in this town?"

"I'll fix one up for you, suh. Maggie sent over some new clothes and sandwiches."

Sam Goines pointed to a sack at the corner of the desk, but Duane's eyes were drawn to a wooden crate filled with books in the corner. "Where'd they come from?"

"I found 'em under a pile of hay."

The former acolyte was curious about the books. They were littered with dust and straw, and didn't look as if Twilby had been interested in them. Maybe a professor on the dodge went broke and gave them to Twilby in payment for stable fees, Duane speculated. Haphazardly, he picked up a black leatherbound volume from the middle of the pile and wiped the cover with his sleeve. It said, in gold letters, *The Prince* by Niccolo Machiavelli.

"If you like books," Sam Goines said, "my mother's got lots of 'em that she's been carrying around fer years."

The Negro sounded educated, with good diction. "Where'd you go to school?" Duane asked.

"The Freedman's Bureau."

Duane had heard of the Freedman's Bureau. It had been formed by the federal government to assist ex-slaves. After Sam Goines left to perform his chores, Duane opened the book. A passage was underlined in black ink: *The way men live is so far removed from the way they should, that anyone who abandons what is for what should be will end pursuing his downfall rather than his preservation.*

Duane flipped a few pages, and read: *Is it better to be loved than feared? The answer is that the most benefits would accrue to he who is both loved and feared. But since the two seldom appear together, anyone forced to choose will find greater security in being feared than being loved.*

It seemed like Machiavelli was speaking directly to him. Duane recalled reading about the old Florentine diplomat at the monastery in the clouds, and knew that Machiavelli had been an advisor to the aristocracy of Old Italy but fell out of favor and died in obscurity. Some historians considered him the epitome of wickedness, while others said the silver-tongued courtier had looked reality in the face and had merely spoken the truth. Duane searched for more advice that he could apply to his new job in Escondido.

A man striving in every way to be good will meet his ruin among the great number who are wicked. You can't deny that, Duane agreed. In fact, it's exactly what happened to me. He touched the cut on his cheek, and it was caked with a scab. His left eye was nearly closed, his ribs ached, and teeth rattled painfully as he chewed a steak and onion sandwich. If I had any sense, I'd go back to the monastery and spend the rest of my life studying, praying, and singing Gregorian Chant. But unfortunately I don't have any sense.

CHAPTER 6

Dane took a leisurely bath in the light of oil lamps. He dressed in new black jeans with a blue shirt that Maggie had bought him, then pinned the tin badge above the left pocket. It was time to go to work.

Slipping outside, he saw a big crescent moon hanging over the rooftops of Escondido. He eased down the alley beside the stable, pressed his back to the wall, held his gun in his right hand, and peered at three riders approaching in the middle of the street, smoking cigarettes and staring ahead balefully. Along the street, saddled horses stood hitched to rails, illuminated by lamplight gleaming within saloons. Duane holstered his gun and stepped onto the planked sidewalk, listening for clicks of hammers being cocked.

He headed toward the Last Chance Saloon, his right hand near the butt of his gun, his black hat slanted low over his eyes, encircled with his hand-worked silver concho hatband. He pushed open the doors, and every eye in the house turned toward him.

"Looks like the new sheriff," said a half-loaded cowboy at the end of the bar.

It was Friday night and the saloon was packed with the usual outlaw element plus cowboys and vaqueros from nearby ranches in town for a hot time. The bartender poured drinks rapidly, while waitresses carried glasses to patrons quaffing, gambling, arguing, and sleeping amid the constant tumultuous uproar. Then a man climbed onto the bar, pulled his gun, aimed it at the ceiling, and pulled the trigger. The saloon echoed with the explosion, as gunsmoke furled the air. "Let's put some goddamned life into this place!" he bellowed.

Bradley appeared in the doorway, his face looking like the Union Pacific Railroad had run over it. "Who fired that shot!" he yelled, but most patrons paid no attention to him. "Goddamned sons of bitches!"

Bradley yanked his gun and charged toward the bar as Duane entered the corridor that led to Maggie's office. Maggie looked up from her desk as he opened the door. She wore a purple satin dress. "What's the latest, Sheriff?"

"We ought to pass a law against firing guns in public places."

"Consider it passed, and it's a damned fine idea. By the way, yer office is ready. You can go there whenever you want. And if there's anythin' you require at the Last Chance Saloon, and I mean *anything*, it's on the house." She winked suggestively, then placed the end of her pen in her mouth.

Duane leaned forward earnestly. "Are you sure you never told anybody where I was sleeping last night? Think it over before you answer."

"I din't tell nobody, but somebody could've see'd you enter the room, although you might not've see'd him."

Horses at the rail gazed at Duane mournfully as he departed the Last Chance Saloon. He headed for the barber shop, as outlaws and cowboys scrutinized the first sheriff of Escondido. "Is he *really* as good as they say?" asked a bullwhacker from San Angelo.

Next to the barber shop sat a small adobe building with iron bars on the windows and a freshly painted sign over the front door that said Sheriff.

Inside, it was dark and smelled of new wood. Duane lit the lamp, illuminating a desk, chair, and cot. On the far wall hung a framed military officer with swooping brown mustaches, gold shoulderstraps, two rows of gold buttons on his gray tunic, and a gold sash at his waist. Duane had no idea who he was.

He sat at the desk and contemplated his tin badge. It was the last thing he needed. He wondered if he was as loco as everybody said.

"Halp! Sheriff!"

Panicked voices came from the street. Duane drew his Colt. The door flew open, and a toothless man in a dirty apron entered, his face blotched with emotion. "One of the whores has got kilt at the Silver Spur!" The bartender ran his forefinger across his throat.

Duane was rocked by the news. Numbly, he followed the toothless man outside, where a crowd had gathered in front of the Silver Spur. Everybody looked anxiously at the new sheriff, expecting him to take charge, so he pushed his way through and entered the door. Inside the saloon, agitated cowboys and outlaws peered down the back corridor, from which a disheveled man with a mustache appeared. He saw the tin badge and said, "My name is Sanchez, and I are so glad to see you here."

Aged prostitutes with skinny legs and potbellies watched Duane from doorways as he passed down the corridor at the side of Sanchez. They came to a small dingy room where a naked woman was lying on the floor, her head nearly cut off.

Duane was aghast. He'd never seen a woman who'd been murdered before, and what a gruesome crime it was, with blood everywhere, her head hanging at a grotesque angle. Everybody in the corridor was looking at him expectantly when he detected a faint bloody bootprint on the planked floor. "Who was she?" Duane asked.

"Hazel Sanders," replied Sanchez.

"Who did it?"

"There was so many people coming and going tonight, it is difficult to say."

Duane examined the bootprint. It had a pointed toe like the cowboy boots that he and most other men wore, including Sanchez.

"Was there an argument?"

"Nobody heard nothin'."

"Who found her?"

"We din't see her fer a while, so I knocked on her door. It was open, so I came inside and this is what I see. Sometimes there is a bad hombre who drinks too much and pulls a knife. She looks so sad, like a poor dead little bird, no?"

Duane felt dizzied by the nearly decapitated woman lying beside him, never to move again. "Does she have any enemies that you know of?"

"Who does not have an enemy, Señor? But I do not think anybody would kill her, my poor little darling."

Duane studied the whorehouse manager more carefully. "You haven't been fighting with her, have you?"

"I fight with all my girls, but it just means that we love each other."

"Did she have a man?"

"His name is Marty Schlack."

The Belmont Hotel was a jumble of adobe huts on the edge of town, and lights glowed dully from windows as Duane approached. He'd never investigated a murder before, had no idea how to proceed, and wondered how he'd gotten himself into such a grisly fix. The brutal murder of the prostitute had moved him deeply, but all he could do was follow through as sheriff of Escondido. He remembered a line from the Book of Job: *How . . . abominable and filthy is man which drinketh iniquity like water.*

The clerk wore a black vest and puffed a cigarette as he gazed curiously at the tin badge on Duane's shirt.

"Where's Marty Schlack's room?" asked Duane.

The clerk pointed down the hall. "Number eight."

Somebody coughed hoarsely in a far corner of the hotel, as Duane made his way down the dark passageway. It seemed like a place to get a knife in your back at any moment. He placed his hand on the cool grip of his Colt as he rapped on the door.

There was a groan on the far side, then a low gnarled voice said, "Who is it?"

"Sheriff Braddock."

The door opened, and a short man with long mustaches and an unshaven chin stood before Duane. "Since when'd this town have a sheriff?" Marty Schlack's breath smelled of alcohol, and a bottle stood like a lone sentinel next to the rumpled bed. He was in his mid-forties.

"I'm afraid I've got bad news for you, Mister Schlack. Hazel Sanders has been killed."

Schlack looked as if he'd been punched in the stomach. He muttered and stuttered in confusion, and Duane calculated that his response appeared genuine. "Maybe you'd better sit down."

Schlack sat at the edge of the bed and stared into space. His face was ashen and his hands trembled. "Who did it?" he asked weakly.

"That's what I'm trying to figure out. Did she have any enemies?"

"Not that I know of. Everybody liked Hazel."

"Do you think it could've been Sanchez?"

"Sanchez got along all right with her. Why would anybody kill Hazel?"

"You tell me."

"She never hurt nobody. I don't know." Marty Schlack covered his eyes with his hands, as his body was racked by a sob.

Duane didn't think he was acting, but he'd met many clever humbugs in the brief months that he'd been gone from the monastery in the clouds. "If you remember anything, let me know. My office is next to the barber shop."

Duane returned to the street, baffled and sickened by the murder. He hadn't realized, when he accepted the tin badge, that he'd have to solve a real crime. His only clues were a dead body and a faint bloody bootprint. Maybe a drunkard had done it, he reckoned. He'd try again someday, and get caught.

Duane needed a drink, and ahead was the Longhorn Saloon. He went inside. It was packed with outlaws, cowboys, and prostitutes, most talking excitedly about the recent murder. Three armed Negro cowboys imbibed quietly at the end of the bar, and a hush came over the saloon as Duane placed his boot on the bar rail. "Can I get a cup of coffee?"

"Sure thing, Sheriff."

The bartender reached for the pot on the counter behind him, as Duane glanced at the faces surrounding him. *I wonder if one of them is the murderer of Hazel Sanders.* The bartender served the mug, and Duane carried it to a table against the wall. He couldn't imagine killing a woman, and for what? He had no notion whatever why Hazel Sanders had been killed. She had no enemies, but sure as hell didn't kill herself. *There's a fiend loose in Escondido, and I, of all people, have to find him.*

Duane glanced up from his coffee. A drunken cowboy in a white hat stood before the table and examined Duane with a supercilious smirk. "Are you really the sheriff?" he asked.

Duane looked him coldly in the eye. "What can I do for you?"

"Ain't you a little young?"

"Young for what?" Duane replied.

The white cowboy hat appeared amused. "To run a town."

Duane whipped out his Colt and pointed it at the cowboy's right eye. "I've got a new jail down the street. How'd you like to be the first customer?"

The cowboy blinked, then his face went pale. "Looks like you got the drop on me."

"Looks like I did."

"Maybe some other time," the cowboy replied, backing toward the bar.

"Up to you." Duane holstered his gun as he returned to the chair. For all I know, that's the killer, he conjectured. He sipped thick black coffee and looked at the man in the apron taking a break at the end of the bar by smoking a cigarette. Duane carried the empty mug toward him for a refill.

"Did you know Hazel Sanders?" Duane asked, as the bartender poured more coffee into the mug.

"Sure, but I was a-workin' here all night. Hope you don't think I kilt her."

"Who d'ya think might've done it?"

The bartender shrugged good-naturedly. "Yer the sheriff, not me."

Nobody's going to solve this killing for me, Duane realized. I have no business wearing this tin badge, because I haven't the slightest notion of what I'm doing.

Then, out of the blue, somebody bellowed: "What the hell's a-goin' on hyar!" It was the same cowboy in the white cowboy hat, still looking for trouble. "How come thar's niggers in this saloon!" the cowboy demanded.

Duane leaned toward the bartender. "Who's he?"

The bartender narrowed his eyes as he perused the cowboy. "Just another son of a bitch with a snootful of whisky."

The cowboy hollered: "Hey bartender, git them damn niggers out'n hyar."

The bartender held up his hands and smiled. "It's a free country."

"Like hell it is."

The cowboy gulped down the dregs of his whisky, then slammed the glass onto the bar. He wiped his mouth with the back of his hand and glowered at the Negroes. They tried to ignore him as they continued their conversation.

"Why can't niggers keep to their own kind?" the cowboy asked. "I din't go through five years of war so's I have to drink with niggers!"

The Negroes mumbled nervously among themselves at the end of the bar. They were outnumbered at least ten to one in the saloon. The cowboy in the white hat opened his mouth again. "Hey, niggers! Get the hell out'n hyar!"

He prowled toward them, followed by eight rough-looking cowboy friends in various stages of inebriation. The Negroes lowered their drinks to the bar, put their backs to the wall, and looked ready to go the distance.

The cowboy in the white hat came to a stop in front of them. "I don't drink with niggers," he said. "Hit the fuckin' trail."

"Wasn't a-drinkin' with you, boss," replied one of them, trying to smile. "You was all the way down the other end of the bar."

"I said hit the fuckin' trail." The owlhoot smiled thinly and rocked back and forth on the balls of his feet.

"You want us to leave, you got to make us, boss," retorted the Negro, still struggling to smile. "There's more of you than us, but I'll tell you one thang. Some of yous're a-gonna die, if'n you start up with us."

Hatred and fear crackled like forked lightning across the saloon. Men near doors ducked outside, and the man in the apron lowered his head behind the bar. Everyone else dropped to the floor, except one man. He wore a tin badge and was dressed in black jeans, with his sliver concho hatband gleaming through tobacco mists. "Let's settle down, boys," said the new sheriff of Escondido.

The cowboy snickered. "Here's this shithead again."

One of his pards replied: "Looks like John Law." The pard sported a red feather in the hatband of his green cowboy hat. He turned toward the cowboy in the white hat. "You ever shoot a lawman, Zeke?"

"A few."

Duane's hand hovered an inch above his gun grip. "You've got two choices," he said evenly, trying to sound convincing and wondering if he was succeeding. "You can leave these cowboys alone, or you can go to jail."

"There's one you ain't mentioned yet, Mister Lawman. *You* might end up in the cemetery."

Duane slapped out his Colt before anybody could move. "You're under arrest," he said to Zeke. "Get moving."

Zeke had drunk three whiskies too many, and had a trick up his sleeve that had worked before. He dodged to the side, hit the floor, rolled over, and came up with his gun in hand. A shot rang out. A red dot appeared on Zeke's wrist, and he seemed to be paralyzed. Then Zeke began screaming hysterically. Smoke filled the air as Duane thumbed back his hammer for the next round. The man with the red feather in his hat had yanked his gun and was in the act of raising it when he noticed a Colt aimed at his gut. Red Feather smiled foolishly as he returned his gun to its holster.

Duane stood on one side, with the Negroes against the wall and the outlaws facing them. Zeke writhed and yelled in front of the bar, as blood dripped from his fingers to the floor. One of Zeke's friends, who wore a dirty yellow canvas shirt, stared angrily at Duane and said: "Mister, yer a-gonna pay for that."

"We don't tolerate gunplay in this town," Duane replied.

"You goddamned nigger lover! Yer prob'ly half a nigger yerself! You might have that tin badge on yer shirt, but there's more of us'n you, and we'll git you — you can bet on it."

Duane watched the coalition form

before him. He took a deep breath and said, "I think we'd all better settle down, gentlemen."

Red Feather spat at the floor. "Settle down, my ass. You done shot my friend, and you ain't a-gonna git away with it."

Duane thought he should open fire, but decided to talk it through. "You'd better relax, cowboy." Then he turned toward the Negroes. "Might be best if you fellers moseyed on out of here."

One of the Negroes replied: "I don't run from nobody."

"This isn't worth dying over."

"What do you know about dyin'?" demanded Red Feather. "I had two brothers who got kilt in the war becuzz of damned niggers, damned Yankees, and yellow-dog bastards like you!"

"You're starting to make me mad," Duane replied.

"Who gives a shit?" Red Feather looked around in exasperation. "Why don't somebody shoot him in the back?"

Duane glanced behind him, but nobody was hauling iron. He stepped to the wall, so it would protect his rear, then aimed his gun at Red Feather. "You're under arrest too." He motioned to the door with the barrel of his gun. "Get moving."

"You ain't takin' me nowheres, kid."

"If you don't do as I say, I'll shoot you where you stand."

Red Feather laughed, and raised both of his empty hands in the air. "Go ahead . . . shoot."

Duane couldn't shoot anybody in cold blood, and the cowboy had seen through Duane's feeble bluff. But Duane couldn't back down now. He stalked toward Red Feather, still aiming his gun at his head. Finally they were within arm's reach.

Red Feather laughed again. "You don't have the sand to shoot me, you god-damned pantywaist."

Duane whacked the outlaw across the face with the barrel of his gun, and there was a *crunch* sound. The outlaw's eyes rolled into his head, and he dropped to the floor in a clump.

"Who's next?" Duane asked.

"Me," said a voice behind Duane's back. "Don't move, because I've got you covered."

Duane froze.

"Drop your gun," said the voice behind Duane.

"Not on your life," Duane replied.

"Then yer a-gonna die."

A shot rang out, the saloon filled with

gunsmoke once more, and Duane was amazed to discover that he was still on his feet. An outlaw in a black-and-white-checkered shirt lay on the floor, his gun a few inches from his hand, blood oozing from his chest. Duane knew he hadn't shot him, so who did?

A stranger in a wide-brimmed old Confederate cavalry officer's hat stepped out of the crowd, a smoking gun in his hand. He had a light-brown mustache, and a wry grin. "Howdy, Sheriff. Nice night, isn't it?"

"I'm much obliged to you, mister."

The newcomer scrutinized the outlaws and cowboys arrayed before him. "It's pointless to die over three darkies, wouldn't you say?"

The three Negro men appeared seriously startled by the savage bloodshed. Their leader tried another smile, but it came out weird. "I don't want no whisky that bad," he said. "Maybe it's time we was a-movin' on."

They headed for the door, as outlaws and cowboys made way. Duane realized that in the heat of the action, he'd stupidly exposed his back. He glanced at the stranger who'd saved his life, and wondered why. He'd never seen him before. The Negro cowboys disappeared into the night, and tension vanished from the Longhorn Saloon. Duane smiled at the stranger. "Thanks for the help, mister. It hadn't been for you, I might be dead right now. Buy you a drink?"

"Don't mind if I do."

They headed for the bar, where the man in the apron was waiting with a bottle and two glasses. "On the house," he said.

He poured whisky, then Duane and the stranger raised their glasses. The stranger said, "Here's to faster horses, younger women, older whisky, and more money."

They touched glasses, then drowned their frazzled nerves. Duane pushed up his hat brim and rested one elbow on the bar. "What name're you going by these days?"

"I'm Derek Wright, and I believe you're Sheriff Duane Braddock, alias the Pecos Kid."

They looked into each other's eyes, like flint on steel. "Just tell me one thing, Mister Wright. Why'd you save my life?"

"Didn't like the odds."

"You could've died."

"So fucking what?"

Derek Wright had square shoulders, a square jaw, and was deeply tanned. He'd spoken with the accents of an educated man, and Duane could visualize an officer in a tailored gray uniform with gold shoulder straps. "Looking for a job?"

"What've you got in mind?"

"Deputy sheriff. Pays seventy-five dollars a month, and you'd probably be sheriff before long, because I don't intend to stay in this town forever."

"I wouldn't touch your job with a ten-foot pole," replied Wright.

Duane examined his savior more closely. I wonder who he killed, or what he stole? Wright had deep lines around his eyes and the appearance of a man accustomed to sleeping under open skies.

"What'd you do in the war?" Duane asked.

"I served under General Jackson," Wright replied laconically.

Stone knew of General Stonewall Jackson, one of the South's great heroes. "Did you ever meet him?"

"I was one of his staff officers."

"What was he like?"

"He understood how to find an opponent's weak spot, and was the toughest, hardest, coldest man I've ever known."

Duane had met many worn-out ex-soldiers since he'd left the monastery. It seemed as though Texas was full of them. Some had held high positions in the Confederate Army, and then became drifters in Texas, unable to return to normal life.

"I wish you'd take the job," Duane said. "You'd probably be better at it than I. I don't know a damned thing about the law."

Duane became aware of Wright inspecting him carefully. "I heard somebody say that you shot Otis Puckett."

"It was a lucky draw," Duane confessed.

"Where'd you get your fast hand?"

"I had a good teacher named Clyde Butterfield. Ever hear of him?"

Wright nodded solemnly. "We weren't exactly friends, but perhaps you could call us acquaintances."

"He rode in a gang called the Polka Dots, back in the old days. You ever heard of Joe Braddock?"

"I wasn't in Texas in the old days, but I've heard of Braddock. He was supposed to be a rustler."

"Some say he was an honest rancher who fought a big combine from the East."

"Some say I hold up stagecoaches, but I'm really just a simple country boy."

Wright's voice was tinged with sarcasm, and Duane couldn't figure him out. Duane took another sip of whisky, then reached for his small white bag of tobacco. "Simple country boys don't walk into the middle of gunfights," he said, fumbling with cigarette papers. He dropped them to the floor, bent to retrieve them, and perused Wright's pointed cowboy boots, approximately the same size as the prints in Hazel Sanders's room. There was a dried dark drop of something on the bottom of Wright's left pantleg, possibly blood. A chill came over Duane, as he realized that he might be kneeling before the killer of Hazel Sanders. Duane raised himself to his full height and peered into Wright's eyes. Is this the kind of man who'd slit a woman's throat?

"You all right, kid?"

"Must be the whisky."

"You got to take it slow and eat something once in a while."

Duane wanted to ask where Wright had been at the time Hazel Sanders was killed, but the ex-officer had just saved his life. Duane noticed many men in the vicinity with pointed boots around the same size as the footprint in the death chamber. It wasn't uncommon to spill whisky or gravy on your pants. I mustn't let my imagination run away with me, Duane reminded himself.

"Where are you from, kid?" asked Wright.

"I thought it wasn't polite to ask where people were from in Texas."

"But I'm from Louisiana."

Duane became suspicious of Wright's question, although Wright had saved his life. Something about the ex-officer didn't seem right. "Did you hear about the prostitute who got killed?"

Duane inspected Wright's face for guilt, but the ex-staff officer was calm. "Texas is hell on women and horses, they say."

"If you were my deputy, maybe we could clean up this town."

"If we ran every hard case out, they'd just go someplace else. What's the point?"

Maggie O'Day looked up from her desk as Duane entered her office. "This is some job you gave me," he said.

"There's somethin' I want to talk with you about," she replied mysteriously. She lowered her voice and motioned for him to come closer. "I don't know if it's a coincidence, but yesterday I took a trip over to the Silver Spur, and I asked Sanchez to talk with his gals, to find out if any of 'em knowed about Joe Braddock's women. Next thing I hear — one of 'em's dead. It makes me wonder."

Duane was astonished by the sudden

unwelcome news. "Why'd you go over there in the first place?"

"Thought I'd he'p you out." She appeared embarrassed. "Seems that a body should know who his mother was, and since you said she used to be in the business, and some of the older gals work at the Silver Spur, I figgered one of 'em might've knowed somethin'. Hope I din't get that poor woman kilt."

Duane didn't know what to make of it. "Why should anybody kill Hazel Sanders because of me?"

"Maybe she knew somethin' that the killer didn't want you to find out."

"Who the hell is Sanchez?"

"He was here afore I came, but he's the worst businessman in town. He could triple his income if he'd just clean up that shithouse he calls a saloon. You don't think he did it, do you?"

Silence came over the Silver Spur Saloon as the new sheriff appeared in the doorway. A few desultory drunkards sat at the bar, with several others passed out on tables. The bartender stood near the cashbox and read a Spanish language newspaper.

"Where's Sanchez."

"In his office, Señor, but I would not

bother him if I were you."

Duane rapped hard on the door, then turned the knob. A man sat in an opulently upholstered chair with stuffing bursting through rips. His shoulders were bunched, his eyes drooped, and a glass of mescal sat on the table next to him, illuminated by a faint flickering oil lamp.

"I've got to talk with you," Duane said.

"I am not well."

Duane straddled a chair backwards, rested his arms on top, and peered into Sanchez's eyes. "Wake up. I have to ask you a few questions."

A tear flowed from the corner of Sanchez's eye. "How could anyone kill such a gentle creature?"

"It was probably one of your customers. You got any idea who it might be?"

"So many people come and go here, they all look the same to me."

"Maggie told me that you were going to ask your gals about the wife of Joe Braddock. Did you do it?"

Sanchez leaned toward Duane and narrowed his eyes. "When I say I am going to do something, Señor, I do it. If you want to know what Hazel said, she did not say anything, but she was not happy, I noticed. But women, they are always that way, no?

If it is not their hair, then it is their clothes, and if it is not their clothes, it is something else, the poor little dears." Sanchez sniffled, and wiped his nose with his handkerchief.

"Did she have any friends?"

"Belle Watkins."

"Where can I find her?"

A thin pale face appeared in the crack of the door. "What do you want?"

"Official business."

She glanced at his tin badge, then widened the door. He entered her small, ramshackle room, exactly like the one in which the victim had been found. Belle Watkins was mid-forties, sickly and sad, thin, medium height, with gray-streaked blonde hair.

"I was wondering if you could tell me who might've killed Hazel."

"Don't know nawthin' 'bout it," she replied.

She appeared unsettled and frightened. Perhaps the killer had threatened her personally, Duane guessed. "Did Sanchez ask you about Joe Braddock's women?"

"I remember him sayin' somethin' 'bout it."

"Joe Braddock was my father, and I was

wondering if Hazel was killed to keep her quiet."

She fixed him in her bleary eyes. "I don't know nawthin' 'bout it," she replied, "but if'n I was you, I'd ride out of town and never think of yer father and mother again."

Duane was startled by her sudden change of mood. "What makes you say that?"

"A word to the wise," she replied mysteriously.

"Have *you* ever heard of Joe Braddock?"

"He had a gang and killed some people — that's all I know. Now if'n you don't mind, I'd like to get some sleep. It's been a long night."

Duane crossed the street, more confused than ever. Belle Watkins is scared, he concluded, as he entered the Last Chance Saloon. The bartender poured a cup of coffee, and Duane carried it to an occupied table against the back wall. Four outlaws saw him coming, gathered their cards and drinks, and searched for another venue.

Duane dropped onto one of the chairs. He felt sleepy and wide awake at the same time, with rattled nerves and aching eyeballs. I've got to stop drinking so much coffee, he reflected, as he drained the cup. For all I know, Hazel Sanders's killer could be in the Last Chance Saloon at this very moment. He scanned men reading newspapers, playing poker, and drinking whisky, while waitresses passed among them, selling drinks and their bodies.

His eyes fell on Alice Markham seated on the lap of a wizened old man in a frock coat and top hat, old enough to be her father and possibly even her grandfather. She kissed his white beard and wiggled joyfully, appeared to be enamored of him, but it was all in a night's work.

Duane felt demoralized by her tragic life, and wanted to help her. I could teach her to read, write, and do arithmetic so she could get a decent job. Where would I be if Clyde Butterfield and a few others hadn't helped me? I can't solve Hazel Sanders's murder, but maybe I can save that poor lost little gal.

He was walking toward her before he knew where he was going. Every eye in the saloon followed his progress with mounting interest. He was the man who'd shot Otis Puckett, and the son of an old-time outlaw hunted and killed like a rabid dog.

Duane came to a stop at the end of the table, and said softly, "Miss Alice?"

Her head spun around, but no expression showed on her painted face. The elderly gentleman glowered grouchily at Duane. "What can I do for you, Sheriff?" he asked, jealousy and hostility in his voice.

Duane ignored him. "Alice, I'd like to speak with you alone for a moment, if you don't mind."

"I'm working, Sheriff Braddock," the pretty painted mask replied testily.

"I said it'll only take a minute."

She hesitated, her forehead creased, and she pinched her lips together. "I'll be right back," she said to the old man.

"By God, you'd better," he replied.

Duane led her toward the table where he'd been sitting, and her hand felt like a wounded little bird in his. They sat opposite each other, and her big brown eyes drilled into him. "Make it fast," she said. "I've got bizness to take care of."

He leaned closer and said: "Listen to me carefully. I can teach you to be a clerk, so you don't have to do this work anymore. And maybe you can even start a business yourself someday. You can live with me above the stable, and as for the funny business, I swear on my mother and father that I'll *never* touch you in any way, so help me God."

She stared at him in disbelief. "I think yer loco like everybody says."

"You don't need to act like a harlot and sit on the laps of old men if you don't want to." He grabbed her hand. "Come on, let's go."

She held back, as her painted face floated impassively before him. "I don't trust you."

"You told me once that you didn't like your job. Well, people have to help people, like it says in the Bible."

"Let me get this straight," she said. "You've killed four men since you first came to town, and you're tellin' me about the word of God?"

"I don't claim to be an angel, but I'm trying to offer you a way out of the fix you're in."

"How do I know you won't change your mind tomorrow morning, and then I'll need to beg Maggie to take me back. At least I got my own money here. If I go with you, I'll be beholden to you."

Duane reached into his pocket, pulled out a handful of coins, and placed them before her. "It's yours," he said.

Her eyes goggled at the sight of so much *dinero.* "Where'd you get that?"

"It's a long story."

Duane heard approaching footsteps. It was the old white-haired man threading among drinkers and gamblers. A gunbelt showed beneath his opened frock coat. He appeared semi-inebriated, his stovepipe hat sat on the back of his head, and a food stain could be seen on his lapel.

"Miss Alice," he said, "I do believe we made a certain business arrangement."

Duane cleared his throat. "Miss Alice is no longer employed by this establishment."

The old man, whose name was Dillard, ignored Duane's remark. He directed his gaze at Alice and said, "If you don't come with me, I'm afraid I'll have to speak with your employer. Where I come from, a deal is a deal." He turned to Duane. "Just because you're the sheriff, you don't scare me one goddamned bit."

The old man went for his gun, but his arm muscles had seen better days, his judgment was contorted by too much whisky, and his eyesight had deteriorated considerably over the years. Duane plucked the weapon easily out of his hand. The old man blinked in surprise as he tried to recover his balance.

Duane held him steady with one hand. "From now on, it's against the law for you to carry a gun in this town. And if anybody sells you a gun, or gives you a gun, he'll have to deal with me."

"But . . . but . . . !" sputtered Dillard, as everyone in the vicinity laughed uproariously. The old man's face turned red with shame, as he headed for the door. "You haven't heard the last of Charlie Dillard!"

Duane handed the gun to Alice. "Know how to use one of these?"

"Just pull back the hammer and squeeze the trigger."

"Go to your room and pack your things. If anybody gives you any trouble, blow his head off. I'll meet you here in about a half hour."

She gazed into his eyes. "Mister, you ain't a-gonna let me down, are you?"

"If I do, you can keep the money."

She closed one eye and wrinkled her nose. "I still think you've got somethin' up your sleeve."

Maggie O'Day sat in her bath, sipping a glass of whisky, a scowl on her face. She couldn't stop thinking about young, handsome Duane Braddock in his tight black pants. "Maybe it's time I stopped drinking this stuff," she said to herself.

She placed the glass on the floor, just as someone knocked on the door. "It's the sheriff," said the gruff voice of Bradley Metzger.

"Send him in."

"But yer nekkid!"

"I'm tired of arguin' with you. Next time you start up with me, yer fired."

"You fire me, and you'll regret it," he said irately.

"Send him in, and keep yer threats to yerself."

The door slammed, and Maggie wondered what to do about Bradley. He's gettin' to be more trouble than he's worth.

Duane appeared with his hat in hand. "Sorry to bother you, ma'am, but I . . ."

She smiled alluringly, and as she reached for the bottle, her necklace of soapsuds lowered, revealing the tops of her pendulous breasts. Duane swallowed hard at the sight of those huge, tempting cushions.

"What's on yer mind?" she asked in a throaty burr.

"I'll be taking care of Alice Markham from now on," he replied. "She doesn't work here anymore."

Maggie appeared mildly disturbed, then retrieved her studied casualness. "I didn't think she's yer type."

"She's not. By the way, Sanchez said he asked the gals about my mother, but none of them knows anything. Even Hazel Sanders's best friend is acting dumb. I don't know if Hazel was killed because of me, or what."

"I've been in a lot of whorehouses," replied Maggie. "Sometimes the gals fight among themselves, sometimes a pissed-off boyfriend shoots one of 'em, and sometimes a bastard rides out of nowhere, knifes a gal, and heads fer the next town, to do it again. You look like you could use a bath." She moved over to make room. "Want me to wash yer back?"

"Maggie, if I get into that tub with you, it'll be the end of me."

He arose from the chair and expelled himself out the door, his head spinning with confusion. A woman old enough to be my mother has invited me to . . . what? Maggie's skin had been smooth and pink, and she'd looked like a plump farm girl. Don't even think about it, he admonished himself. People will laugh if I ever took up with a woman old enough to be my mother.

He came to the main room of the saloon, but Alice wasn't there yet. A painted lady approached, swinging her hips lasciviously. "Anything I can do, Sheriff?"

"What room is Alice in?"

"Why do you want Alice, when you could have me?"

He looked her over and noticed that she was tall and thin like his first great love, Miss Vanessa Fontaine. "Her room number, please?"

"Yer no fun at all, Sheriff. Room sixteen."

He made his way down the maze, passing couples on their way to trysts. He wondered what it was like to go to bed with one stranger after another for money. It must make a woman cold in her heart, he concluded, as he arrived at Alice Markham's door.

She opened it, wearing a plain cotton dress with no cosmetics, resembling the churchgoer, not the bawdy whore.

"I'll be ready in a few minutes. Have a seat."

Duane sat at the edge of the bed and wondered how many men had slept with her. He was attracted by her tragedy and suffering, and couldn't bear the thought of a churchgoing woman selling her body to the highest bidder.

"This is the craziest goddamned thing I

ever did," she declared. "I don't even know you."

He didn't respond, because he calculated that her suspicions were bottomless, and nothing he could say would change her mind. She placed her final few belongings into her carpetbag. "I'm ready," she said.

He carried the carpetbag to the door, while she took one last lingering look around her room. Then she followed him down the corridor, out of the whorehouse, and into her new life as first female student of the Pecos Kid.

Across the street, Charlie Dillard sat at the bar of the Desert Palace Saloon and morosely sipped whisky. He was a former stagecoach robber and cattle rustler who now earned his living as a gambler, traveling from town to town, playing the odds.

He never threw a coin into a pot unless he was reasonably certain he'd win. His excellent memory of what had been dealt provided him an edge over drink-addled cowboys or outlaws, and he never hesitated to use a fast shuffle if he thought no one was paying attention. He earned a good living, stayed in the best hotels, and wore fine tailored clothing in the latest styles from the East.

But now he was damned mad. Alice Markham had caught his attention, because she was younger than most whores, and he'd anticipated a night with her smooth firm body. But then Duane Braddock had stolen her away. Dillard lit a black stogie and blew smoke out the side of his mouth. Sensitive about his diminishing virility, he'd been humiliated publicly by Braddock in the Last Chance Saloon. Dillard would never be able to show his face there again, and it was the best saloon in town.

The older Dillard became, the more he lusted after young women. They made him a young buck again instead of an old fart. Their firm, upthrusting breasts and smooth thighs were all that he lived for.

There wasn't a damn thing he could do about Braddock, because nobody would sell him a gun. He slammed the heel of his fist on the bar and muttered, "That goddamned Braddock bastard! Isn't there anybody in this town who's got the balls to stand up to him?"

The bartender stirred next to the cashbox where he'd been sipping a cup of coffee. "Are you a-lookin' to hire somebody fer the job?"

"Got a feller in mind?"

"There's bound to be somebody. Want me to pass the word around?"

Dillard flipped a ten-dollar gold piece onto the bar. "I'll be at the Belmont Hotel if anybody's interested in making a fast hundred dollars."

The stable smelled of hay and horses. Sam Goines came out of his office, lantern in hand. His eyes widened at the sight of the young white woman.

"Miss Markham'll be staying here for a while," Duane explained. "She'll be my student, and I might need to borrow some of your mother's books. Are there extra blankets?"

"I'll get some, boss."

Duane lugged the carpetbag up the ladder to the loft, as Alice followed. "This is where you'll sleep," he explained. "It may not look like much, but it's better than the Last Chance Saloon."

She gazed out the window at the moon hanging like a silver slipper in the blazing starry sky. What'm I doin' here, she asked herself. Meanwhile, Duane's eyes caressed her pert profile. She's not that bad-looking, but I promised I won't lay a hand on her, and by God I won't.

Sam joined them in the loft, blankets over his shoulder. He arranged a bed for Alice behind the barricade, then returned to the lower depths of the stable. Duane blew out the lantern, sat on his bedroll, and pulled off his boots.

Ten feet away, Alice stared at Duane's outline as he reclined in the darkness. I've put my life in his hands, and don't even know him. He's killed four men, they call him the Pecos Kid, but he's a churchgoer. Her experience with men was considerable and multivaried, but she'd never met anybody like Duane Braddock.

A faint snore emitted from his nostrils, as she undressed behind a pile of hay. Then, clad only in her underwear, she crawled beneath the blankets. If he comes over here, I prob'ly won't put up much of a fight, she thought with a secret little smile. Easier to deal with one man than twenty every night, so what'm I complainin' 'bout?

There was a knock on the door at four in the morning, and Charlie Dillard opened bloodshot eyes. "Who's there?"

A deep voice came through the door: "I heer'd you want to see me."

Dillard crawled out of bed, wearing

striped cotton drawers. He cocked the hammer of his Smith & Wesson, then opened the door a crack. A dark shadow wearing a cowboy hat stood in the doorway.

"I don't believe I know you," said Dillard.

"Put that gun away."

The man spoke menacingly. He wore a gun low on his hip, tied to his leg with a leather thong, gunfighter style. He entered the room and closed the door behind him.

"I want fifty dollars in advance."

Dillard couldn't make out the gunfighter's face in the darkness. "What if I give you fifty, you ride out of town, and I never see you again?"

The shadow grumbled something unintelligible as he headed for the door. Dillard grabbed his arm. "What's yer hurry? I was only makin' a joke. Here, I'll give you the fifty dollars." The old gambler fumbled with his matches. "Let me light a lamp."

The shadow plucked the matches out of his bony fingers and tossed them across the room. "Who d'ya want killed?"

"Duane Braddock, the sheriff. They call him the Pecos Kid."

"Not fer long."

Dillard reached into his pocket and

pulled out some coins. He counted them in a ray of light peeking through the window, but the stranger was shrouded in darkness, hat low over his eyes. All Dillard could see was that he was of average height and average build.

"What's your name?"

"I ain't got one."

"There's something I should tell you. Do you know that Braddock shot Otis Puckett a couple of months ago not far from here."

The stranger harumphed. "Was only a matter of time before somebody killed that fat fuck. It don't make a hill of beans to me."

Dillard passed him the coins, and their hands touched. The stranger's hand was callused and he had a rough manner. "I'll be back fer the rest in a few days."

The stranger left the room. Dillard sat at the edge of his bed and wondered who he was.

The stranger crossed the lobby and opened the front door of the Belmont Hotel. He glanced both ways along the street that stretched before him. His hand stayed near his gun, and he smiled faintly as he played with the coins in his pocket.

The assignment had arrived in the nick

of time. He'd been tapped out when he'd heard the bartender talking about the Pecos Kid. Now he had a pocketful of good times. Funny how life yanks a man around, he thought.

His name was Jason Smeade, a killer-for-hire on a vast frontier where a man notorious in one town would be unknown in the next. Smeade found his chestnut gelding in front of the Desert Palace Saloon, climbed into the saddle, and rode sullenly out of town. He didn't trust hotel rooms where enemies might sneak up on him as he'd snuck up on Dillard.

Wherever he went, there was always someone to pay for his services. He often was amazed by the hatred in the world, but felt none of it himself, nor love either. He killed calmly, professionally, and routinely, like a butcher. He never had a second thought, and remorse was unknown to him.

His horse plodded along, and Smeade held his gun in his right hand as he peered into windows for possible rifles and pistols aimed at him. He never knew when he might see a face from his past.

He rode onto the desert, as a coyote howled in a far-off cavern. Smeade didn't believe in heaven or hell, and had nothing to live for. When it was your time to go, that was it, thought Smeade. Somebody's gonna kill Duane Braddock sooner or later, and it might as well be me.

Smeade searched the darkness for a cave or hollow where no one could sneak up on him. If it rained, he'd wrap himself in his poncho. Better to be wet than dead, he figured, as he rocked back and forth in the saddle.

Smeade had killed so many men, he'd stopped counting long ago. His picture adorned numerous walls, and he'd had a few run-ins with lawmen in the past, but a weasel could always find a crevice in which to hide. Maybe he'd go to Hermosillo after he killed the Pecos Kid, he thought, as the gelding marched steadily into the black desperate night.

Alice awoke with a start, a premonition in her heart, and at first didn't know where she was. She smelled hay, then noticed the Big Dipper gleaming through the skylight. She perched on her elbows and gazed across the loft at the form sleeping beneath blankets. He hadn't attacked her yet, and she wondered what his game was. He's prob'ly a-tryin' to catch me off guard, but I'll be ready for 'im when he comes. I'll put up a bit of a fight, and then give in. She smiled secretly again, and touched her lips to the fuzzy blanket.

"Everything all right?" asked the darkness.

She'd thought he was fast asleep, but maybe now he'd make his move. "I'm fine," she replied.

"Get some sleep. I want to start your lessons early tomorrow."

She was more surprised than disappointed when he rolled over. The hayloft became still again, except for crickets chirping love songs on the desert. He don't act like other men, she thought, but he's only a-tryin' to trick me. When I least expect it — that's when he'll grab my ass. They're all bastards no matter how pretty they are. You just can't trust 'em.

She drifted to sleep, dreaming of the farm back in Ohio. She was standing in her bedroom with her stepfather, and he removed her clothes roughly. Only four years old, she was afraid he'd spank her. But he didn't spank her. He was doing something even worse. She'd dreamed the incident often during her tumultuous life, but could never, in the morning, remember the most terrible thing that ever happened to her.

CHAPTER 7

Next morning, Duane leaned back in his office chair, puffed a cigarette, and pondered the murder of Hazel Sanders. How do real sheriffs investigate crimes? he asked himself. What would Saint Thomas Aquinas do if he were sheriff of Escondido?

The door opened, and Derek Wright, wearing his old Confederate cavalry officer's hat, strode into the office. "Howdy," he said with a charming smile. "You offered me a job last night, and I've decided to take it."

Duane's distrust was reawakened, as he recalled the dark drops on Wright's pants. The ex-officer sat on the far side of the desk and crossed his legs, and Duane glanced at his pointed cowboy boots. "If you're crazy enough to take the job, I'm crazy enough to hire you. We don't have an oath, and you can start right now. Why d'you want to be my deputy?"

"I'm flat broke on my ass. That a good enough reason?" Wright glanced around the office. "Nice spread you've got here."

Duane pointed to the Confederate general hanging on the wall. "Do you know who that is?"

"That's Albert Sidney Johnston, one of the greatest generals the Confederacy ever had."

"What was so great about him?"

Wright appeared surprised. "How come you don't know who Albert Sidney Johnston is?"

"I was raised in an orphanage far from here, and there are big gaps in my education, I'm afraid."

"Some say that Albert Sidney Johnston could've saved the Confederacy, but he got shot at Shiloh early in the war."

"If you ask me," the ex-acolyte said, pontificating, "I don't think anything could've saved the Confederacy, because slavery was morally wrong."

"Is that so? Well, there are folks in New York, Boston, and Philadelphia who work in factories and live far worse than my daddy's slaves. Do you know what a New York slum looks like? Yankees blame us for everything that's wrong in the world, but they should clean up their own backyards first. Listening to you talk, it's no wonder somebody's trying to kill you."

Let he who is without sin cast the first stone, Duane thought. "If you become my deputy, somebody might try to kill you, too. Do you need money that bad?"

"In a word, yes, and there aren't any other jobs in Escondido that I'd be interested in right now."

"Why don't you become a cowboy?" asked Duane.

"Ranch work is what darkies are for. What's my first assignment, Sheriff?"

"Who d'ya think killed Hazel Sanders?"

Wright shrugged. "How the hell should I know?"

"I'm also trying to figure out who took a potshot at me night before last."

"I don't imagine a sheriff would be the most popular person in town. Why'd *you* take the job?"

"That's what I'm trying to figure out," Duane replied.

Maggie O'Day sat behind her desk, a cameo brooch in a gold frame pinned to the mammoth right breast of her orange silk dress. "Look what the cat just drug in," she said, a panatella sticking out the corner of her mouth.

Duane sat on the chair in front of her. "I just hired a deputy named Derek Wright. Ever hear of him?"

"I can't keep track of all the saddle bums who come to town. What's he done?"

"That's what I'm trying to figure out."

"Tell the blacksmith to make another badge. His name's Rafferty, and his shop's at the other end of town." She appeared ill at ease, scratched her arm, and puffed on the panatella nervously. "I . . . want to apologize fer last night. I'd had a few drinks . . ." She let her voice trail off. She felt like a naughty little girl.

"Nothing to apologize for," Duane replied. "If things were a little different, no telling what might've happened. I wonder why the new deputy wants the job."

"How much'd you offer him?"

"Seventy-five dollars a month. Can you afford it?"

"Law and order are worth whatever we have to pay. Besides, we prob'ly won't have to ante yer salary much longer, at the rate yer a-goin'. If you keep on a-tryin' to take on whole saloons like last night, you won't last long."

The blacksmith's shop was an adobe hut at the edge of town. As Duane approached, the clanging of a hammer could be heard from within. The shop had a double-wide door, just like the stable, and above it hung a sign that said Blacksmith, P. J. Rafferty.

Next to a roaring fire, a sweating man with a hammer pounded a length of steel, sending orange sparks flying through the air. He was bald, but had long black sideburns, and sweat glistened on his shirtless, muscular torso. Duane stood to the side and rolled a cigarette as he waited for the blacksmith to take a break. The sign on the wall said:

Man to man is so unjust
You hardly know which one to trust
I've trusted so many, to my sorrow
So pay me today, and I'll trust you tomorrow

Duane noticed ropy muscles across the blacksmith's back and arms. Rafferty looked like Thor, the god of War, as he slammed the anvil. Duane wondered if Rafferty was wanted like everybody else in Escondido, including the new sheriff. Finally, the blacksmith lowered his smoking hammer. "What can I do fer you?"

Duane studied him carefully. Perhaps he

was the one who'd aimed the shotgun through the window night before last, or who'd killed Hazel Sanders. "I need another tin badge. It should say Deputy Sheriff across the front."

"Who's the lucky man?"

"Derek Wright. Know him?"

The blacksmith shook his head, then took a few steps to the side so he could get a better view of the street. He appeared thoughtful. "Are you really Joe Braddock's son?"

"As far as I know."

"You look a little like him."

Duane became electrified. "You knew my father?"

"I had a shop in the Pecos country long time ago, and yer dad come to see me once. His horse had broke a shoe." The blacksmith peered into the street, to make sure no one was within earshot.

"What're you afraid of?" Duane asked.

The blacksmith ignored his question. "I didn't know Joe Braddock had a son."

"He died when I was one year old, and I don't know much about him. What was he like?"

"Him and his boys was on the run at the time I met him, and they was plumb tuckered out."

"Who were they on the run from?"
"Sam Archer."

Duane stared at the blacksmith. For the first time, from the most unexpected place, he had gotten a name. "Who's Sam Archer?"

"Big rancher in the Pecos country. He fought fer the Republic in the old days." The blacksmith looked askance at Duane. "Yer Joe Braddock's son, and you don't know 'bout Sam Archer?"

"That's right. What did Sam Archer have against my father?"

"You really don't know?" The blacksmith appeared surprised. "Wa'al, there was a range war, and Sam Archer hired some guns. They tracked yer father and his gang all the way to Mexico. Accordin' to the way I heer'd it, they surrounded yer father's men, closed in, and shot all of 'em dead, though some say a few got away."

Duane imagined a small embattled crew of ranchers and farmers surrounded by cold-blooded professional gunfighters. "But somebody told me once that my father was hanged."

"No, he weren't hanged. I was in the Pecos country at the time, and I remember."

"Where's the Archer ranch?"

"Near Edgewood. I hope yer not plannin' to go thar."

"Why not?"

"If Old Man Archer hears that Joe Braddock's son is in the territory, he'll have you shot on sight. Mister Archer is a hard man, you hear me?"

"The Pecos country is a long way from here. Why are you afraid of him in Escondido?"

The blacksmith's eyes scrutinized the street. "Listen to me, boy. Sam Archer ain't nobody to fiddle with, and he's got spies and judges in his pocket all over Texas." The blacksmith was alert as a cat, his eyes surveying the street.

"Did you know Joe Braddock's woman?"

"Joe Braddock had a lot of 'em. I remember him and his boys in my shop like it was yesterday. A lot of folks really looked up to the Polka Dots, as we used to call 'em. When yer paw was in my shop, he was a-talkin' about how the fight with the Archers reminded him of the Mexican war."

Overcome with emotion, Duane couldn't speak. Finally, after years of wondering and searching, he'd received the true story out of nowhere. It gave him comfort to know that his father died with his gun in his hand and his boots on, fighting for his rights.

"I think you been in my shop long enough, Sheriff," the blacksmith said. "We wouldn't want folks to git thinkin' the wrong thoughts. And you'd better not tell anybody what I said about that old son of a bitch, Sam Archer. It might be bad fer my health."

Duane climbed the ladder to the hayloft, his head bursting with significant new information. Alice sat with her back to a bale of hay, and looked up from her Bible as he lay down, placed his hands behind his head, and gazed at the ceiling.

If Sam Archer has spies all over Texas, I wonder if one of them tried to shoot me behind the Last Chance Saloon, Duane mulled. Belle Watkins appeared frightened and evasive when I asked her about Hazel Sanders. What's she hiding? And who the hell is Derek Wright? How can I make Belle Watkins talk? But maybe she doesn't know anything, and Hazel's death is unconnected to me. What if I'm blowing everything out of proportion in my overactive imagination? Maybe I should leave for the Pecos country immediately and have a little chat with Old Man Archer.

He gazed at the woman studying the Bible on the far side of the hayloft. I can't abandon her after making so many promises, because she'll only become a prostitute again. No, I'll have to wait at least a month until she's better trained in the three Rs.

Duane heard footsteps in the stable below, drew his Colt, and lowered his head. "Who's there?"

"Trouble at the Silver Spur," said Derek Wright, as he climbed the ladder to the loft. His smiling face cleared the top of the hay. "A bunch of cowboys are ready to go at it." Then he turned toward Alice and removed his old Confederate cavalry officer's hat. "I don't believe I know the lady."

Duane made introductions, and Wright looked at Alice with more than passing interest. "Pleased to know you, ma'am."

"Let's take care of those cowboys," Duane said.

Duane descended the ladder, as Wright gave one last lingering appraisal of Alice. "There are about twenty cowboys on each side," the ex-officer explained. "Maybe we should lay back and let them kill each other."

The two lawmen walked down the middle of the street and came to the Silver

Spur Saloon. Duane pushed open the doors, and every head turned toward him. Self-conscious, he made his way to the bar, placed one foot on the rail, vaulted into the air, and landed atop the counter.

Everyone stared at the angel of death standing above them. "We don't tolerate fighting in this town!" he hollered. "If you've got a disagreement, take it someplace else. Otherwise you're going to jail, and if you resist, my deputy and I can't be responsible for what might happen to you!"

They gazed at him with awe, curiosity, and contempt. "Who in hell's that young feller on the bar?" somebody asked drunkenly.

"That's the Pecos Kid."

The saloon became silent, except for a cowboy with a handlebar mustache and a skeptical expression. "Nobody's puttin' me in jail," he declared.

Duane cracked out his Colt and pointed it at the cowboy's mouth. "That's where you're wrong."

Beads of sweat broke out on the cowboy's face. The draw had been so fast, he hadn't seen it coming. "Yes sir."

Duane pivoted and aimed at another cowboy. "How about you?"

"I'm not looking for trouble," he said, holding his hands in the air. "I'm in town fer a good time — that's all."

"Make sure it stays that way."

Duane jumped down from the bar and holstered his gun. Derek Wright angled his head toward a table against the wall. "Let's have a drink."

"We don't drink on duty," Duane replied.

"*We* don't? You didn't tell me that before I took the job."

"If you want to get shot, go ahead and drink. I'll see that you receive a decent burial."

The bartender poured two mugs of coffee, and Duane and Wright carried them to a table against the wall. Wright pushed up his brim with his thumb. "Where'd you meet the gal?" he asked.

"Friend of mine."

"For a long time?"

A spark shot out of Duane's eye. "Leave her alone."

"I thought you and she were just friends."

Duane was becoming increasingly dubious about Derek Wright. "Are you working for Sam Archer by any chance?" he asked out of the blue.

Wright's right cheek twitched barely perceptibly, but Duane's Apache eyes saw everything. "Settle down, kid," the ex-officer growled. "I'm not your enemy."

"You ask a lot of questions. I can't help wondering why."

"Just making small talk. What're you afraid of? The whole world isn't against you. Relax."

Duane wondered if he was suspecting Wright unfairly. The twitch in the ex-officer's cheek could've meant anything. Wright had offered to help, which was more than anyone else had done. "Sorry," said Duane. "This town's making me jumpy, I reckon."

"Maybe it's time to move south. It's real nice in Monterrey this time of year. I was heading in that direction myself. Maybe we can travel together."

"My next stop is the Pecos country."

"There's nothing up there except scorpions and rattlesnakes."

"I'm going to kill Sam Archer," Duane replied.

"Who's he?"

"He paid a bunch of gunslingers to kill my father, and I'm going to shoot his lights out."

"And you think I'm working for him?"

"Anything's possible."
"I think I've been insulted."
"Up to you."
"Sounds like you're trying to follow in your father's footsteps."
"If you're working for Old Man Archer, you can tell him this. I lived with Apaches for a spell, and know all the tricks. One night he'll wake up in his bedroom, and my gun will be pointed against his temple."
"And then what?" asked Wright.
"You figure it out."
"I didn't think you were a cold-blooded killer. Didn't you grow up in a monastery?"
"A long time ago," Duane said, "but I'm no saint these days. Old Man Archer's going to pay for what he did to my father, that's all I know. You can warn him that I'm coming, and nothing will stop me."

Cowboys and outlaws sprawled on benches in front of saloons, passing bottles and talking about what they'd do when the sun went down. Others sat alone, nursing their bottles, and a few appeared to be dozing.
One was a mean-looking outlaw in dusty trail clothes and a black leather vest. He was Jason Smeade, recently hired killer,

and he watched Duane Braddock striding along the far sidewalk. It'll be dark soon, Smeade estimated, and he ain't even bein' careful. I'll bushwhack him from an alley. The poor son of a bitch won't know what hit him.

Sam Goines pushed a wheelbarrow of manure across the stable as his boss entered through the front door. "What happened to Twilby's personal belongings?" asked Duane.

"It's in two burlap bags in the office, and his records're in the desk. I was planning to give his clothes to the church."

"Don't give away anything until I say so."

The office had a rough-hewn desk, ramshackle chair, and coatrack hanging at a crooked angle on the wall. Duane spotted two burlap bags near the desk. Upending them, he spilled old clothes, belts, and boots onto the floor, then searched through the rubble, but found nothing of interest or value.

He sat at the desk, opened the drawers, and found business records in a barely legible scrawl, a bag of dried-out tobacco, some cigarette papers, and a pair of socks rolled up. Duane suspected that Twilby was the missing piece of the puzzle, and that was why the old stablemaster had been killed. I wonder why he kept a pair of socks in his desk.

Absentmindedly, Duane picked up the rolled pair of socks. They were green, woolen, and scratchy. He unrolled them, while reflecting upon Twilby's furtive behavior. Like the blacksmith, he'd been cautious, but evidently not cautious enough. Duane's sensitive fingertips noticed a fabric stuffed into the toe of one sock. Curious, he probed inside and pulled it out. His eyes widened at a black bandanna with white polka dots unraveling in his hand!

He stared at it for several seconds, as implications sank through the tissues of his mind. Perhaps Twilby had been in the Polka Dots, and had sentimentally safeguarded his old bandanna in a designated spot. Duane visualized a younger, leaner Twilby riding with a wild outlaw gang across rolling desert wastes, and in front of them all, leading the way, was the leanest meanest Polka Dot of all: Joe Braddock himself.

Duane imagined a tall, wide-shouldered rancher slapping leather as he raced toward the Rio Grande, followed by his pards. A surge of righteous power passed from the riders into Duane, and he felt ennobled by their gallant fight. My father stood for justice against Sam Archer and the big money combine, but they killed him in the prime of his life, taking him away from his wife and baby son.

Duane pictured a small encircled band of men under heavy fire in the crags and gullies of the Sierra Madre Mountains. Bullets screamed around them, ricocheting off boulders, ripping them apart. But they fought on bravely, bleeding and hopeless. He saw his father with gaping wounds in his body, his life literally leaking away, struggling to hold the gun steady for one last shot.

Duane's eyes filled with salty tears. My father stood steady like a man, he realized, unlike those who slink away with tails between their legs. He battled for me and my mother and all the little people of the world. And the bastards gunned him down. Duane stared into space, as tears rolled down his cheeks. Mr. Archer, no matter what it takes, I'm going to hunt you down and kill you, I think.

The door opened, and Duane hastily stuffed the polka dot bandanna into his pocket. Derek Wright entered the office with a big smile and his hands in the air. "Don't shoot — it's only me. Something wrong?"

Duane hastily wiped tears from his face. "Got something in my eyes."

Duane looked away as he rolled a cigarette with the sure, practiced movements of an old cowhand. He scratched a match atop the desk, puffed gloomily, and imagined another office, with wood paneling and fashionable furniture, where rich men in fine Eastern clothing plotted the destruction of the Polka Dot Gang. I'm going to find those bastards if it's the last thing I do.

"You look like you're about ready to tear this town apart," Wright said. "What's eating you?"

"There's some things a man doesn't talk about."

"Sometimes it's best to get them off your chest. If you ever feel the need . . ."

Duane interrupted him. "What's going on in the saloons?"

"It's Saturday night, and the town's full of cowboys. I expect we'll have a few fights before long."

Duane wanted to be alone. "I'm going for a walk."

On the street, the ex-acolyte ambled

aimlessly with his thumbs hooked in his belt and his hat slanted low over his eyes. He felt a compelling need to hop on his horse, head for the Pecos, and have a talk with a certain Mr. Archer. But I mustn't ride off half-cocked, he told himself. I'll have to lay careful plans, then hit the trail.

Ahead was Apocalypse Church, lights glowing through windows, doors open late for stray worshippers. Duane ascended the stairs and saw a small sprinkling of citizens in the pews. He sat in the back row, bent his head, and yearned for revenge. He recalled Saint Thomas Aquinas's doctrine of the just war, and now appreciated what the divine doctor of the Church had been indicating.

But a man's on thin ice when he sees himself as an instrument of God's justice, he acknowledged. Maybe my father really was an outlaw and what if he got what he deserved? Duane felt uneasy in the presence of the Almighty. He'd drawn his Colt too many times.

Then he recognized Alice Markham in a front pew, her head bowed in prayer. A feeling of contentment came over him, because at least he'd performed one decent act since departing the monastery in the clouds. She's not a prostitute anymore, because of me. I can't leave her just yet, because of Old Man Archer.

Duane reached into his pocket and took out the Polka Dot bandanna. It made him feel eerie, as if his father were nearby. He recalled the night he'd killed for the first time, behind the cribs in a small town named Titusville. An angry, loudmouthed drunkard had forced him into a showdown, and Duane imagined that his father had been behind him, guiding his hand in the classic fast draw.

The bandanna grew warm in his hand. Twilby had worn it, and Joe Braddock must've seen it with his own eyes. The bandanna carried his father's fierce fighting spirit, and tingled the son's fingertips.

Oh God, please help me avenge the murder of my father.

But how, he wondered, can I ask God to help me kill somebody? Duane felt torn between his feelings and the moral law. I'll go to the Pecos country, but I don't have to kill anybody, do I? Maybe I can have Old Man Archer arrested, but he's got judges in his pocket all across Texas.

"I was just thinking about you," said the voice of Alice Markham.

It knocked him from his reverie. He arose beside her, and a powerful magnet seemed to draw him closer. She had a small upturned nose, a beguiling mouth, and those doleful eyes. "You look like the Madonna," he replied.

"You're making fun of me."

"I'll walk you back to the stable."

Cowboys and outlaws strolled the sidewalks, as Duane and Alice moved among them. Light from saloons illuminated faces in the night, a wagon rolled down the middle of the street, and saddled horses jammed at hitching rails.

"If it hadn't been for you," she mused, "I'd be a-workin' right now." She shuddered at the thought. "I don't know how I did it."

"You'll never have to do it again," he replied.

A shriek of woman's laughter could be heard from within the Last Chance Saloon. "You can't imagine what it's like to let strangers tetch you," said Alice. "I made believe I weren't thar."

The Pecos Kid and his woman were carefully observed by numerous eyes at that moment, and two belonged to Jason Smeade, sitting on a bench before the gunsmith's shop, which was closed for the night. Smeade was waiting for a time when Duane Braddock would be alone, tired, and with a few whiskies beneath his belt.

Then, when the sheriff least expected it, Smeade would plant a bullet into the back of his head.

Just a few more hours, Smeade said to himself. And I'll be on my way to Hermosillo.

At the Last Chance Saloon, two cowboys were staring at each other from opposite sides of the bar. They had never seen each other before.

One was Buck Duluth of the Bar J, and the other was Frankie Magill of the Diamond C. They'd spent the last week herding cattle, eating beans, and sleeping four hours every night if they were lucky. Angry, frustrated, lonely, and thoroughly dangerous, they sipped whisky and glowered evilly at each other as other men played cards and held conversations all around them. For some reason, despite all the other cowboys and outlaws in the saloon, they had focused seven days of repressed rancor at each other. Then, finally, Duluth got to his feet, hooked his thumbs in his belt, and hollered: "What the hell're you a-lookin' at!"

"That's what I'm a-tryin' to figger out," yelled Magill from the far side of the saloon.

They strode toward each other, as everyone in the vicinity got out of the way, and the piano player ran down the corridor for help. Duluth and Magill came to a stop a few feet apart, and the crowd coalesced around them, grinning like a pack of coyotes in anticipation of blood.

"If yer a-lookin' fer trouble," Duluth said, raising his fists, "you came to the right place."

Magill responded with a long, looping right toward Duluth's head, while Duluth shot a stiff left jab toward Magill's nose. Both fists connected simultaneously, and each was staggered by the other's blow. Dazed, they both wobbled backwards, shook the fog out of their ears, and prepared for the next charge.

"Hold it right thar," said Bradley Metzger, who pushed his way to the front of the crowd. "You want to fight — do it outside!"

Duluth replied, "I'll fight whar I goddamn please."

Bradley reached for his gun, but Duluth fast-drew his Colt and aimed it at Bradley's head. "Out of the way, you fancypants bastard, or I'll kill you."

Bradley tried to smile, but it came out sickly. "Put that gun away," he said.

"I'll put it away when I damn well please," Duluth replied.

Bradley stepped backwards, as Duluth transferred his aim to Magill. "I ought to shoot you," he said.

Suddenly, out of the night, a heavy metallic object crashed into Duluth's head. He collapsed onto the floor like deadweight, and a man in a blue shirt with a tin badge stood behind him, aiming a Colt at Magill.

"Let's settle down," said Sheriff Duane Braddock.

Magill lowered his gun. "I ain't a-lookin' fer no trubble, Mister Lawman."

Duane held the Colt on him a few moments, then holstered it. The bartender poured him a cup of coffee, and the Pecos Kid carried it to a table against the back wall. Muttering friends of the unconscious cowboy ferried him out the door, as Duane sipped coffee. The saloon was crowded with outlaws and cowboys, and everyone was looking at him. It felt as if tiny needles were sticking into his skin. A waitress sashayed toward his table and asked if he wanted anything. "A steak with all the trimmings," he told her out the corner of his mouth.

He rolled a cigarette and found himself

thinking about the monastery in the clouds. Scholarly Benedictine priests had delivered brilliant discourses about Evil, but it was an abstraction high in the clouds. Down in the real world Evil was vicious, mindless, and all-devouring. If Christ couldn't save us, how can I?

A dark shadow approached, and Duane's fingers reached toward his Colt. It was Bradley Metzger who lowered himself onto the chair opposite Duane. "I reckon I ought to thank you. It 'pears that you saved me a big fuss."

Duane looked at the black eye, split lip, and puffed cheeks before him. They'd fought down and dirty to the bitter end two days ago, and now Bradley was apologizing? "I'd do it for anybody. Don't take it personally."

"I owe you one. If I can help with anythin', let me know."

Bradley walked toward the back of the saloon, where he was swallowed by cigar smoke and piano music. If a man like that can apologize after I beat the daylights out of him, maybe there's hope for mankind, Duane thought. People aren't half bad if you give them a chance.

The waitress returned with a steak platter and set it before Duane. As he attacked it with knife and fork, stuffing gobbets of meat into his mouth, he noticed a short-haired black-and-white-spotted mongrel dog with a squashed bulldog face near his knee. It licked its chops and grinned at Duane as if to say: *How's about a piece of steak fer old time's sake, pard?* Duane sliced off the bone and tossed it to the dog, who caught it in its teeth and slunk away to the smoky depths of the saloon.

When Duane was halfway through the meal, a heavyset man with a short curly black beard and dirty silverbelly cowboy hat approached the table. He wore a gun in a holster and a knife in each boot. "Mind if I sit down, Sheriff Braddock?" he asked.

"Up to you," Duane replied.

The man dropped to the chair opposite Duane. "My name's Arnold, and I've got a business proposition fer you." He looked both ways. "I'd like to have somebody kilt. What's yer goin' price."

Duane stared at him.

Arnold winked conspiratorially. "I been in a few towns, and I've knowed sheriffs who kept little businesses on the side, if you git my meanin'."

"The only business I have is a stable. You'll have to find somebody else."

"I want the best, and that's you. They say every man has his price. What's your'n?"

"I wonder if I should arrest you."

Arnold leaned closer. "You're the law in this town, Sheriff. You can arrest whoever you want, or you can look the other way. I knows that sometime a lawman don't like to come out and admit anythin', so I'll slip you one hunnert dollars 'neath the table, and you'll get the final hunnert after you shoot one son of a bitch who deserves to die anyways."

"Mister, I'm trying to run a decent town here. Maybe it's time you moved on."

Arnold smiled knowingly. "I git it. Yer just a-jackin' up the price. How's about two-fifty? He lives in El Paso, and you can ride there and be back inside a month."

"If I ever see you in this town again, I'm going to arrest you. Now if you don't mind, I'd like to finish my supper."

"How's about three hundred?"

Duane yanked his Colt. "Get out of town."

"I can't figger you out, kid. Are you who they say?"

"I'm worse," Duane replied, aiming down the barrel of his Colt.

Arnold arose and backed away. Duane

waited until he was out the door, then resumed his meal. They believe I'm as wicked as they, he figured. Every time I turn around, it's something more scurrilous than last time. Places like Sodom and Gomorrah still exist, and I'm sheriff of one of them.

He cleaned off his plate and was sopping the gravy with a hunk of biscuit when he heard a voice on the street. "Sheriff, help!"

Duane was on his feet in an instant. He drew his gun and headed for the doors when they exploded open and a man in a frock coat appeared, his eyes darting around in panic. "Somebody's kilt the blacksmith!"

Duane couldn't move for a few moments, then he ran toward the doors, burst outside, and sped toward the blacksmith's shop. A crowd was gathered in front, their heads silhouetted by flickering flames in the forge. They appeared stunned and alarmed as he pushed through them. The stink of scorched flesh smacked him as he spotted the blacksmith lying face down in his forge, a dent in back of his head, sizzling like a barbecue.

Paralyzed, Duane stood near the forge and reflected upon his conversation with the blacksmith. Then Duane remembered

Twilby's murder and the seemingly unrelated slashing of Hazel Sanders. The sheriff's mind swam with the enormity of the crimes. He felt nauseous and reached toward a post for support. It can't be, he thought. His once-solid world cracked apart, as standards of justice that he'd lived by all his life came crashing down around his ears.

The crowd peered through the front door of the blacksmith's shop. "Looks like he's a-talkin' to himself," somebody said with a chortle.

"Strangest thang I ever see'd," another replied. "Just a-standin' thar a-watchin' Rafferty cook."

The townspeople tried to understand their young, deadly new sheriff. Some feared him, others were doubtful concerning his sanity, but most esteemed his fast hand. "I wonder if he's a-gonna stand thar all night?" somebody asked. "Poor Rafferty'll be cooked to a crisp if somethin' ain't done soon."

Their voices brought Duane to his senses. He grabbed Rafferty's boots, pulled him out of the forge, then examined the wound in back of the blacksmith's skull, as the stench of roasting meat reached his nostrils. The death blow had been caused by a blunt instrument such as a hammer. Duane found several on the workbench, then noticed one lying near the forge. He brought it close to his Apache eyes. Blood and hair were smeared on the end.

He pored over the blunt instrument, but there was nothing that could link it to the killer. Footprints of all sizes covered the floor, many with pointed cowboy boots. Duane tried to feel the killer's emanations, but instead his throat furled at the odor of sizzling flesh.

Duane wanted to talk with someone, but who? Did the blacksmith have a secret enemy? he wondered. Is it a coincidence that he told me about my father today? What about Amos Twilby and Hazel Sanders? Are these random killings connected to Joe Braddock?

Deputy Derek Wright in his old Confederate cavalry officer's hat appeared in the doorway. "What the hell happened here?" he asked.

"He was hit in the head with a hammer, then thrown into the forge."

Wright glanced around the room and appeared genuinely befuddled. "What a mess. Who d'ya think did it?"

"That's what I'm trying to figure out.

Did you know him?"

"I've seen him around. Does he have a wife?"

The undertaker appeared at the edge of the crowd, carrying his stretcher. "Will somebody give me a hand with 'im?" he asked sleepily.

"I'll he'p you, Caleb," said a citizen standing nearby.

The undertaker and his volunteer rolled the blacksmith onto the canvas. "Busiest week I ever had," said the cheerful undertaker.

"Where does his wife live?" Duane asked.

"Not married. He lived in back of this shop."

"Any friends that you know of?"

"Kept pretty much to himself. I always figured he was wanted for something, like most everybody else in town."

The undertaker and his helper carried the baked blacksmith out of his shop, as the crowd looked at Duane expectantly. "Let's search the place," Duane said to his deputy, trying to sound official. "Maybe the killer left something behind."

As Duane and Derek Wright sifted through the blacksmith's belongings, Belle

Watkins lay with a waddie from the Circle Y in her tiny room. The whisky-smelling cowboy kissed and mauled her clumsily while she added numbers in her mind. She was planning a quick move to El Paso as soon as she raised the fare. In the midst of her calculations, a commotion erupted in the hall outside her door. The waddie bounded out of bed, drew his gun from the holster on the bedpost, opened the door a crack, and peeped outside. "What the hell's a-goin' on?"

A woman's voice came to him. "Somebody just kilt the blacksmith!"

The cowboy latched the door, holstered his gun, and crawled back into bed. But the prostitute seemed to've lost her passion. The cowboy placed the palm of his hand on her shriveled breast. "What's wrong?"

"Nothin'," she replied.

He couldn't see her face in the darkness, and didn't want to anyway. She seemed scared, but he had more important things to worry about, such as getting his money's worth. "Don't give up now," he said, pleading. "I ain't a-finished yet!"

Duane and Derek Wright worked their way across Rafferty's shop, but found only implements of the blacksmith trade. They located the room in back where he'd lived, overturned the mattress, poked through the dresser, and even searched behind the portrait on the wall of General Pierre Gustave Toutant Beauregard, hero of First Manassas. They uncovered old clothes, business records, other personal effects, and a jug of whisky from which Deputy Wright took regular nips. He offered the bottle to Duane, but Duane was preoccupied as usual by the riddle of his life.

He believed the murders had something to do with his father, although he had no proof. He recalled how Rafferty had glanced suspiciously into the street before spilling the beans about the Polka Dot Gang. Had he been afraid of somebody special, or was he just being careful in general?

I mustn't make unwarranted accusations, because that's what happened to my father. I should talk with somebody who's been in town a long time and knows everybody. Maggie's my best bet, but what if she's the killer? *It could be anybody.* Duane's head spun with confusion, and he dropped to the edge of the bed.

Wright pulled up a chair and sat opposite him. "What's wrong, kid?"

"It doesn't make sense for both of us to investigate one murder. You keep an eye on the saloons, and I'll try to figure out who killed this blacksmith. Do you have a theory, by the way?"

Wright narrowed his left eye. "I think you take this job too seriously, kid. Nobody cares about the blacksmith. He was a loner like you and me."

"Where've you been since I saw you last?"

Wright grinned. "Hell, you don't think that *I* did it, do you?"

"Everybody's a suspect."

"I was making my rounds. How about *you?*"

"I was having supper at the Last Chance Saloon. Funny how you always show up late for things."

"What's that supposed to mean?"

"It wasn't you who tried to shoot me the other night, was it, Derek?"

"If I'd tried to shoot you, kid, you wouldn't be here right now."

Belle Watkins's hands shook as she stood in front of the mirror and wiped cosmetics from her tormented features. Then she changed to a plain calico dress that fell to her ankles, and she resembled somebody's mother. She reached toward the dresser, withdrew a pint bottle of whisky from the top drawer, and took a swig. Tiptoeing toward the door, she was on her way to the sheriff's office, to ask for protection.

A couple passed in the dark corridor, forcing Belle to lurk behind her door. Then she ventured out, closed the door silently behind her, and navigated dark corridors, gasping audibly, expecting somebody to grab her in the darkness at any moment. A lone prostitute approached in the dimness, and Belle watched her closely. For all I know, it could be her.

The prostitute swished by, and Belle continued her treacherous journey toward the back door. Duane Braddock'll save me, she figured. When I tell him what I know about his mother, he'll fall on his ass.

Belle arrived at the back door, turned the knob, and peered outside. The yard was silent and gloomy. A shiver passed through her as she stepped into the yard.

"Going somewhere?" asked a voice behind her.

Her eyes distended with horror. As she opened her mouth to scream, something incredibly sharp pierced her throat. The last thing she saw was a trash barrel. Then she toppled toward the ground, where she lay still in a widening pool of blood. The dark figure made sure the cut was deep enough, then padded softly into the alley, his footsteps swallowed by the laughter of men in saloons, the plunking of a piano, and mournful cries of coyotes in far-off escarpments, serenading the moon.

Maggie O'Day liked to make regular appearances in her saloon, to see if she could catch any of her bartenders stealing. She was also a local celebrity, the ex-whore who'd become madam, and it was good for business to let men see what success could do for a woman. She wore a white-and-purple-striped satin dress with a low-cut bodice. Her hair was adorned with orange ribbons, and she dripped with jewelry. Cowboys and outlaws stared at her with wonder as she passed among them, puffing her trademark panatella cigar.

"How's it goin' boys?" she asked out the corner of her mouth.

She carried about her an air of audacious abandon, as if she might slap somebody in the mouth, or throw a table out the window. She stood at the end of the bar, and the man in the apron nervously brought her a glass of whisky. All eyes in the vicinity were on her as she raised the glass to her lips. They made her feel like a duchess instead of boss of a ramshackle whorehouse.

The piano player struggled to play "The Yellow Rose of Texas," while a crowd of drunkards howled the words off-key. Maggie wished she could hire singers and dancers, but there was no room for a stage. I need a bigger saloon, but I sure as hell don't want to stay in Escondido forever.

A tin badge flashed at the door, and then the new sheriff stepped into the Last Chance Saloon. He surveyed the scene before him, hand near his gun. Half boy and half man, he made his way across the floor as weatherbeaten cowboys and dangerous outlaws stepped to the side. When the sheriff noticed the reigning queen of the Last Chance Saloon, a smile came over his youthful features, and he inclined toward her.

She raised an eyebrow and puffed her panatella. "Who d'ya think killed the blacksmith?"

"That's what I came to ask you. Can we talk alone?"

She rolled her eyes. "Anytime."

She headed toward the back office, and Duane followed at a respectful distance, his eyes drawn inexorably toward her rear axle assembly. When they arrived at her office, she sat behind the desk, and he sprawled on the chair in front of her. "What can I do fer you?" she asked.

"Just hear me out," Duane replied. "I know it might sound strange, but bear with me. Today the blacksmith told me that he'd met my father, and tonight he's dead. Yesterday you asked about my mother at the Silver Spur Saloon, and then somebody cut Hazel Sanders's throat. The previous night, Amos Twilby told me a few things about my father, somebody shot him in the head, then somebody tried to shoot me while I was in bed. I can't help thinking that all these killings are mixed up with me and my father. Do you have any idea what might be going on?"

She thought for a few moments. "Maybe it's time to find yourself another town."

"If I'm right," Duane continued, "whoever's doing the killing probably came here within the past six months, because that's when my name first appeared in newspapers farther north. You know this town better than anybody, Maggie. Can you think of anybody suspicious who arrived here since then?"

"*Everybody's* suspicious in this town includin' you, Mister Pecos Kid."

“When you first arrived, were Rafferty, Twilby, and Hazel Sanders here?”

“Rafferty and Twilby was, but Hazel Sanders came later.”

“Were Rafferty and Twilby friends?”

“I never see’d ’em drinkin’ together, but maybe they met on the sly. You can’t tell about people in a town like this. Everybody’s playin’ cat-and-mouse with everybody else.”

Duane reached into his pocket and pulled out the polka dot bandanna. “You know what this is?”

She looked at it. “ ’Course I know what it is. It’s a polka dot bandanna. So what?”

“It was Twilby’s, and I think he was in the Polka Dot Gang with my father. A man named Sam Archer from the Pecos country had my father killed, and now he doesn’t want me to find out about it. But it’s too late — I already know just about everything. What do you think of that?”

Maggie opened her mouth to reply, when someone screamed in the corridor. A heavily rouged whore opened the door. “Somebody’s been kilt behind the Silver Spur!”

Duane jostled his way outside, and men were streaming into alleys on either side of the Silver Spur. He joined the flow of writhing bodies, and a woman shrieked: "Oh my God!" Panic and dread permeated the town like poison gas as Duane made his way through the alley. He came to the backyard and found a crowd gathered near a limp figure lying on the ground. "Lemme through," he told them, shoving drunken cowboys and vicious outlaws out of his way.

He arrived at the inner circle of painted harlots kneeling around a bloodied woman sprawled on her back, eyes wide open and staring at the glittering Milky Way high in the sky. He examined her face, and was startled to see the death mask of Belle Watkins. It can't be, he said to himself.

Sanchez stood at the edge of the crowd, weeping openly. "Somebody is killing my babies," he moaned. "Who would do such a thing?"

Duane felt as if he was going to black out. He entered the back door of the Silver Spur, found the bar, and poured himself a glass of whisky. He didn't believe in drinking on duty, but downed the contents in three rapid gulps and then waited for the kick. When it came in the middle of his chest, he coughed uproariously, but it steadied him. Then he sat on a stool and glared at himself in the mirror. This was getting serious.

Then he thought of a heinous new possibility. He drew his Colt, checked the loads, and ran toward the door. Down the street he sped and entered the lobby of the Belmont Hotel. "Can I help you, Sheriff?" asked the desk clerk.

"Is Marty Schlack in?"

"How should I know?"

"I want his key."

The clerk hesitated, then tossed it to the sheriff. Duane held the Colt ready to fire as he moved swiftly down the corridor. He found Marty Schlack's door and knocked, but got no response. He turned the knob, and the door opened a crack on a dark and ominously still room. Aiming the gun straight ahead, Duane prowled forward, ready to shoot anything that moved.

His toe touched something large and soft. He lit the lamp, and the wick illuminated Marty Schlack lying face down on the planked floor, the back of his head caved in by a powerful blow.

The immensity of the deed staggered Duane. Somebody had succeeded in killing everybody connected with his parents! It was preposterous, unthinkable, beyond his wildest hallucinations, yet it was happening, and he didn't have a clue why.

He noticed a piece of paper lying on the dresser. Holding it to the light, he read the crudely printed letters: *If I was you, I'd head for California.*

"Schlack's dead," Duane told the hotel clerk.

The clerk appeared not to understand, but Duane considered him a suspect too. He knows about all guests, and if he goes to saloons, he'd pick up other information as well, Duane surmised. Maybe he's Old Man Archer's spy in Escondido.

Baffled, Duane walked down the middle of the main street. His Apache ears heard a footstep in the darkness behind him. He spun around, but nothing was there. He moved toward the alley, and someone inside broke into a run. Duane trotted after him, boot steps echoing off unpainted wooden walls. He saw the silhouette of a man at the end of the alley for an instant before the stranger disappeared around the corner.

Cautiously Duane advanced down the alley, pausing every few steps, ready to fire. He came to the end and peeked at the backyard full of outbuildings and trash. Somebody could be hiding, drawing a bead on me, Duane realized. He crouched in the shadows and waited a while, but nothing moved. Finally, convinced that the culprit had got away, he dusted himself off and continued his trek toward the undertaker's office.

In the backyard, cowering behind a pile of firewood, Jason Smeade heard Duane Braddock's footsteps recede into the night. Smeade's face was covered with perspiration, and his breath came in gasps. He'd been creeping up on Braddock, his gun cocked, ready to finish the assignment, but Braddock had ears like a fox.

Braddock had nearly caught him, Smeade realized. Smeade had been terrified that the sheriff would search the woodpile. He didn't want a shootout at close range with the Pecos Kid. This was going to be harder than he had thought. He couldn't sneak up on the Pecos Kid. He'd have to take him from a long distance with a good rifle, like his Henry.

The undertaker's face looked like the skull of a steer as he opened his front door. "What can I do for you, Sheriff? Don't tell me there's another body!"

"I'm afraid there is," Duane said. "Marty Schlack. Ever hear of him?"

"Sure. He was the fancy man of Hazel Sanders. Where's he at?"

"In his hotel room. Know where it is?"

"Over at the Belmont Hotel. How'd it happen?"

"Evidently somebody cracked him with a heavy instrument from behind, just like the blacksmith."

The undertaker nodded thoughtfully, as Duane realized that Snodgras had known where Schlack lived. Was the undertaker the source of his own increased earnings? Duane wondered. "Where've you been in the past hour, Mister Snodgras?"

"Surely you don't think *I* killed Schlack."

"How'd you know where he lived?"

"I buried a pard of his a few months ago, and now I'm burying him. How strange is life, eh? As for tonight, I was finishing the paperwork on Belle Watkins. People are getting killed in this town faster than I can arrange funerals. But don't get me wrong — I'm not complaining." He untied the white apron that protected his clothes from the occasional fleck of blood.

An undertaker would make a good spy, Duane speculated, because he's ideally positioned for gathering facts about people. Duane recalled Snodgras asking personal questions prior to the burial of Twilby. The newest suspect led Duane into the room where the dead prostitute lay naked on a cot. Duane tried to be dispassionate as he examined her, but sheer revulsion shattered his defenses. The killer had to be loco, whoever he was.

The undertaker pulled his stretcher out of the closet. "I wonder what these killings're about."

"You tell me."

The undertaker appeared taken aback. "What makes you think I know?"

"You've been in town a long time, and I'll bet you've met just about everybody here. Were Twilby, Schlack, and the blacksmith connected in any way?"

"Not that I know of."

"Did you ever see them together?"

"I don't think so." The undertaker screwed up his eyes. "Why do you ask?"

"I have an unusual theory — that all the murders have been committed by the same son of a bitch."

The undertaker appeared incredulous. "What makes you think that?"

"Have you ever heard of Sam Archer?"

"No, but I heard of a Howard Archer once."

The undertaker's response appeared

genuine, but the Pecos Kid had met many excellent liars. Duane headed back toward the center of town, the tips of his fingers in the front pockets of his jeans, trying to assess the confusion into which he'd unwittingly been plunged. The undertaker, bartenders, shopkeepers, gamblers, the blacksmith — they all hear news. A casual word here, a phrase there, and a person could put together a chronicle of events. Maybe the blacksmith got drunk in a saloon one night, mumbled something about the Pecos country, and didn't realize who was listening. What if Twilby unburdened his heart to a friend who blurted it to someone in the pay of Sam Archer.

Duane crossed the street and approached his office on the far side. The light was out behind the window, and he wondered where his deputy was. *Derek Wright asks too many questions, and I don't trust him either.*

Duane held the key in his right hand as he neared the door. Moonlight struck the glass window at eye level, reflecting rooftops behind him. He inserted the key into the lock, when suddenly, in the glass, his Apache eyes spotted the outline of a man's bare head emerging above the rooftops behind him.

Duane dived toward the sidewalk and rolled as a gun fired behind him. The door window blew out from the force of the bullet, but Duane wasn't there. He came up with his Colt, took quick aim, and fired a shot at the head dropping behind the peak of the roof. Then Duane charged across the street, hoping to catch the fugitive descending the rear roof of the building.

"What the hell's a-goin' on thar!" yelled somebody nearby.

Duane ripped into the backyard and aimed his Colt high, but no one was scrambling down the roof. Then Duane spotted a misshapen figure sprawled on the ground. He inched closer, ready to fire again, but the man wasn't going anywhere.

He lay on his back, eyes wide open and staring, with a bloody ugly hole halfway down his nose. He looked like a saddle burn, and his Henry rifle lay a few feet away. Duane dropped to one knee, looked at the face of his would-be assassin, and vaguely remembered it from the saloons. The sound of running footsteps came to his ears, as townspeople crowded through the alleys, their guns drawn, faces wrenched with fear, curiosity, and panic.

"What the hell happened this time!" somebody demanded.

"He tried to bushwhack me when I was opening my office door," replied the sheriff. "Anybody recognize him?"

A nearby cowboy shrugged. "I see'd 'im in the saloons, but I din't talk with 'im."

"I see'd 'im too," replied an outlaw with a harelip. "But he's no friend of mine, Sheriff."

"Anybody talk with him?" Duane asked.

Nobody answered, as Duane fixed his eyes on the dead man. So there at last is the son of a bitch who's been doing all the killing. At least I got him before he got me, Duane thought.

A man in a frock coat and stovepipe hat approached with a rifle in his hand. "Reckon this is your'n now."

Duane accepted the Henry, then pulled his victim's Colt .44, exactly like his, out of its oiled holster. The bushwhacker had the earmarks of a professional, and Duane wondered how much Old Man Archer had paid him.

"Here comes the deputy," somebody said.

Derek Wright emerged from the alley, gun in hand, and Duane felt guilty about suspecting him, the undertaker, bartenders, parson, etcetera, of the killings. It was somebody I didn't even know about, realized Duane. It illustrates the limitations of human reason, and maybe Saint Augustine was right whereas Saint Thomas Aquinas was wrong, Duane thought.

"What's going on?" asked Wright.

"He tried to bushwhack me," Duane replied. "Recognize him?"

Wright perched on one knee and bent over the dead man's face. "I might've seen him in the saloons. Kept to himself, as I recall."

"I remember him from the Silver Spur," said another voice. "He was a-tellin' the bartender that he sleeps on the desert 'cause he don't like hotels."

Duane and Wright searched his pockets and found approximately fifty dollars in coins, a penknife, and a tin box of matches, but no identification. "Somebody get the undertaker," Duane said.

Something didn't seem right to the sheriff, but he couldn't figure it out. If the stranger kept to himself, how come he knew so much about the population of Escondido? Duane tried to think his way through a convoluted web of revenge and madness, as townspeople scrutinized their new sheriff once more. Among them was

Charlie Dillard, the aging gambler who'd hired Jason Smeade to shoot the sheriff. Dillard was terrified that the Pecos Kid would figure out who'd financed the attempted bushwhack.

Dillard was thinking he ought to get out of town, as he slunk back into the shadows. But years of soft living made him reluctant to travel alone, particularly since Apaches considered the region their ancestral homeland. The stagecoach wouldn't come for another two weeks, provided Apaches hadn't burned it to a crisp, along with passengers and crew.

Dillard walked swiftly along the planked sidewalk, thinking maybe he should go to his hotel and lay low for a few days. But that was the first place the sheriff'd come looking for him. He was hoping nobody had seen that gunfighter leaving his room.

The street was deserted, as most of the townspeople were still behind the Silver Spur. Dillard felt dizzy, his heart thumped beneath his vest, and globules of perspiration covered his wrinkled brow. He entered the Last Chance Saloon and headed for the bar. Only a few drunks were sitting around, unable to walk to the action. The bartender was waiting, his shaven head gleaming in the light of the coal oil lamp.

"What happened?"

"Somebody tried to kill the sheriff. Give me a whisky."

"Did he bring it off?"

"Braddock shot him in the head."

The bartender appeared surprised as he reached beneath the bar. Dillard watched the bartender pour whisky into a glass. Then Dillard carried it to his lips and took a swig. It burned all the way down, calming his nerves and sizzling his brain. What am I worried about? he asked himself. Nobody saw Smeade talking to me, I don't think. I'm in the clear, maybe. He recalled his initial run-in with the sheriff, and Dillard's few remaining hairs bristled with humiliation. Maybe the sheriff'll remember me, or the bartender at the Silver Spur'll testify I was lookin' to hire somebody to shoot the son of a bitch.

Dillard's clothes felt damp, and his ears began to ping. He loved life, his pocket was full of jingles, and he didn't want to die. What should I do? he asked himself. If I get my horse out of the stable, it might draw Braddock's attention, and besides, he *owns* the damn stable.

Outlaws and cowboys were drifting back to the saloon, taking their places at the bar, sitting at tables, reaching for their cards, dice, and glasses of whisky and beer. Dillard heard them muttering about the sheriff's most recent victim. "A man's got to be crazy to take on Duane Braddock," somebody said. "He's got eyes in back of his goddamned head!"

Dillard lit a cigar and puffed nervously, then sipped whisky in his trembling hand. If he says anything, I'll deny everything. I don't think he'll shoot me in cold blood, but I don't want to crowd him. Dillard felt frightened of Duane Braddock, and then, when his trepidation reached fever pitch, its object appeared through the swinging doors. Sheriff Braddock had arrived and was headed for the bar.

He's coming for me, thought the old gambler, his heart chugging noisily in his ears. Dillard contemplated reaching for his gun, but he wouldn't have a chance against the Pecos Kid. He tried to smile but his lips trembled in terror, his throat constricted, and he was having difficulty breathing. The sheriff glanced at him, and something snapped inside Dillard's chest. The gambler was ravaged by pain that lasted a brief instant, and then the world went black.

Duane Braddock reached for his Colt as a man dropped to the floor in front of him.

It happened so suddenly and surprisingly Duane didn't know what it meant. The saloon went silent except for a few drunken conversations occurring against the far wall. Duane and everyone in the vicinity ogled the dead man. "Not another one," Duane muttered.

It occurred to him that he'd heard no shot. Duane bent over the body and recognized the warm corpse as Alice Markham's former swain. He didn't have a mark on him. Duane pressed his ear against the gambler's chest, but detected no heartbeat. Duane had never seen anyone die of natural causes before his very eyes.

"Probably a stroke," said somebody in the crowd. "Same thing happened to my grandaddy. One minute he was here — next minute he was gone."

The old gambler looked like he was sleeping on the floor next to the spittoon. "Somebody get Snodgras," said Duane. Then he sat at the bar and found himself feeling sorry for the poor undertaker who'd been running around all night, lugging corpses. At least this death has nothing to do with me, Duane thought. If things don't settle down in Escondido pretty soon, there won't be an Escondido left.

Deputy Derek Wright arrived at the saloon and spotted the body on the floor. "Now what?" he asked.

"Natural causes," Duane said. "Don't blame it on me."

"That's Charlie Dillard, the gambler," declared Wright. "Hell, I played a few hands of blackjack with him yesterday. I always thought he was a no-good son of a bitch." The deputy leaned against the bar and raised his finger in the air. "Barkeep?"

The man in the apron poured a glass of whisky in front of Derek Wright. Duane felt remorseful for suspecting the ex-soldier of trying to kill him, yet couldn't understand how the unknown bushwhacker had learned so much about the people of Escondido. What if there are *two* of them? Duane wondered, as he perused the profile of his deputy with new interest.

The deputy gulped whisky. "What's on your mind, kid?"

"I guess the bushwhacker was watching me for a long time, and I didn't even know it."

"I wonder who paid him to kill you."

"Sam Archer, I'll bet. I can't figure out how the bushwhacker learned so much about the people in this town, since nobody knew him."

"You didn't expect everybody to tell the truth, did you?"

"How about you, Derek. Do you tell the truth?"

The ex-cavalry officer winked. "Sometimes."

Duane had another mild headache, as his mind whirred with questions. Did the bushwhacker act alone? Was he linked to the other killings? "I hate this goddamned town," Duane said bitterly. "Wish I never came here. How about you, Derek? What're *you* doing in Escondido?"

"Working my way to Monterrey. You ever been to bed with a Mexican girl?"

Duane preferred not to talk intimately about women. He finished his cup of coffee, and the dour bartender refilled it promptly. The doors were flung open, and the cadaverous undertaker carried his stretcher into the Last Chance Saloon. He came to a halt in front of the corpse and asked, "What happened this time?"

"Just fell down and died," replied Duane. "Natural causes."

"There's so many dead people in my house, I'll have to put this one in the kitchen. Can somebody give me a hand?"

A few cowboys helped the undertaker roll the corpse onto the stretcher, then carried the stiffening gambler toward the door. Duane settled onto his barstool, sipped his cup of coffee, and tried to understand the mawkish incident. Is life that fragile?

Duane's sharp Apache eyes rested on the bartender hurrying back and forth behind the bar, pouring whisky and beer, collecting money, and perspiring onto his white shirt. Everyone who comes to Escondido stops at the Last Chance Saloon, reflected Duane. This bartender hears scraps of conversations, vows, deals, and even confessions from lips loosened by alcoholic beverages. "Hey, you," Duane said.

"What can I do for you, Sheriff?" the bartender replied, as a drop of perspiration fell from the tip of his nose to the bar.

"What's your name?"

"Smiley." The bartender wore a gold earring in his left lobe. His nose looked like it must have been broken in a fight long ago. Duane had never seen the man smile.

"When you get a chance, go to the undertaker's house and have a gander at the feller who tried to bushwhack me tonight. I'd be interested in what you know about him."

"Yes sir."

Smiley launched himself toward another part of the bar, as Duane glanced at Wright. "Did you ever feel that everything was upside down?"

"All the time," the ex-officer said with a grin. "That's life, isn't it?"

Duane wanted to confide in Wright, but still didn't trust him. "There's no point in two lawmen drinking in the same saloon. You cover this side of the street, and I'll take the other side. If you need me for anything, just holler."

On the sidewalk, balmy desert breezes wafted over Duane. He crossed over, entered the Silver Spur Saloon, and gazed at wall-to-wall cowboys, outlaws, and whores. Duane was ready for anything, including folks dropping dead at his feet.

A squat husky fellow with a black beard, black hat, and black leather vest walked toward him. "My name's Dowd. Can I have a word with you, Sheriff?"

"What's on your mind?"

"My pards and I'd like to talk . . . business."

Curious, Duane followed Dowd to a circular table in the middle of the floor, around which sat four mean-looking hombres. Duane took his place among them, keeping his hand near his Colt, while

Dowd dropped to a chair opposite him. Dowd looked both ways, lowered his voice, and said, "There's a stage that travels from El Paso to Santa Fe at the end of the month, and we was a-plannin' to rob it. How'd you like to git cut in?"

Duane sat solidly, letting the proposition sink in. "You're talking to the wrong sheriff."

Dowd leaned forward and whispered confidentially, "This ain't no ordinary stage, Sheriff Braddock. A bank is a-shippin' ten thousand dollars to another bank. It'll have a driver, two shotgun guards, and a few passengers. We'll take 'em by surprise on a lonely stretch of trail, but we could use another fast hand. You'll git one-quarter of the take if'n you throw in with us."

Duane wondered if he could arrest them before they committed the crime. Again, he recognized his ignorance of the law. "I'm going to pretend that this conversation never happened," he said as he arose from the table.

He backed away, hand near his Colt, and leaned his elbow on the bar.

"What's yer poison?" asked the bartender.

Duane didn't want to drink more coffee

because his brain was rattled enough already. "Nothing right now."

A tall, thin man with a long nose snickered at the end of the bar. Duane glanced at him, then examined other denizens of the saloon. God only knows how many vicious crimes have been concocted in this cesspool, the sheriff thought.

He knew that Texas was filled with criminals from all parts of America, and the worst of the worst ended up in border towns. Disgusted, Duane returned to his office, sat in his chair, and rolled a cigarette.

He was relaxing when suddenly the door was flung open. An elderly, spiderlike cowboy with a white mustache and sorrowful eyes stood before him, malevolence on his face. "Are you the Pecos Kid!" he demanded.

"So what if I am," Duane replied.

"They say yer the fastest hand in town, but I ain't afraid of you, do you hear me?" The drunkard wobbled from side to side as he tried to draw his gun, but his hand trembled and kept missing the grips. Duane arose, easily disarmed the drunkard, spun him around, pushed him into the jail cell, and turned the lock. Then he returned to his desk.

What should I do with him now? he asked himself. Who'll feed him, and when will his trial take place? Duane vaguely remembered reading about *habeas corpus* in the monastery in the clouds. A person accused of a crime has a right to a speedy trial. I'll hold him until he sobers up, since we don't have a judge.

The door opened and a short dumpy man with a big belly huffed into the office. "Sheriff, you've got to come right away! It's a knife fight back of the Longhorn Saloon!"

Duane followed the dumpy man into the street, where they crossed and ran into the alley on the far side. They came to a yard where a cheering crowd had gathered, and Duane elbowed through men laying bets and hollering encouragement to the combatants. Circling each other in the moonlit arena were a cowboy in his mid-forties with acne scars on his face, and a young drifter who resembled a raccoon. They held long knives in their right hands, and both had been cut already on the arms.

Duane drew his Colt as he strode into the middle of them. "Party's over, boys. Put the knives away and get out of town."

The acned cowboy sneered. "I'll get out of town when I'm *ready* to get out of town.

Step back, or I'll cut yer dick off."

Duane aimed his Colt between the cowboy's eyes. "I said get out of town."

The cowboy didn't flinch. "You wouldn't shoot me in cold blood."

Duane grinned and said, "You're right." Then he lowered his gun as if to holster it, but suddenly brought it up and smacked the cowboy across the face. The cowboy went stumbling backwards, as Duane snatched the knife from his hand. Then he turned toward the other cowboy. "Put that knife away."

"Make me."

Duane scowled as he stalked toward the cowboy.

"Keep yer distance, Sheriff. Otherwise I'll cut you."

Duane had been trained in close combat by the Apaches, and suddenly clamped one hand around the cowboy's wrist, while simultaneously bashing the cowboy in the head with the barrel of his Colt. The cowboy dropped in a heap and didn't move.

A familiar figure appeared at the far end of the alley. "What happened this time?" asked Deputy Wright.

"Why is it you always show up late?" Duane asked testily.

The ex-officer shrugged. "I was making my rounds when somebody called me. Listen kid, you don't like what I'm doing, go fuck yourself. I don't need money this bad." The ex-officer tore the badge off his shirt, tossed it to Duane, and walked away.

The tin badge bounced off Duane's chest and fell to the ground. As he bent over to pick it up, Duane realized that he'd insulted Wright. A sheriff should be more diplomatic in his dealings with others. He dragged the unconscious knife-fighters into his office, opened the jail, and threw them in with the earlier drunkard. Then he sat behind the desk and wondered if he should fill out a report — but for whom? And what in the name of all that's holy am I doing with this tin badge?

He craved normality, but only received weird situations. He wondered what it was like to go home to a good hot meal every night. At least in the monastery I had books and nobody tried to kill me. When Mexican girls came to Mass, I should've looked the other way.

His face downcast, he sauntered toward the stable. Behind him, in the saloon district, he could hear laughter, pianos, shouts, and garbled conversation. If these people want to kill each other, it's no skin off my ass.

A lone light glowed within the stable, and Sam Goines shoveled horse manure in the middle of the floor. "Somebody who wants to talk with you in the office," he said.

"Who?"

"You'll find out when you get there."

The sheriff couldn't imagine what was going on. No lamp shone in the office, and its occupant couldn't be seen through the window. Duane opened the door. "Who's here?"

"Have a seat," said a woman in the darkness. "Don't strike a match."

Duane recognized the voice: Dolores Goines, Sam Goines's mother and Maggie's cook. Duane groped for a chair in the darkness. He made out her slim, erect figure sitting in the corner, hands folded in her lap.

"First of all," she said, "you've got to promise that I never told you these things, and we never even talked here."

"Anything you say," Duane replied, "What's on your mind?"

"About eighteen years ago, I worked in a certain saloon in the Pecos country," she began.

It fell silent in the office, as Duane caught his breath.

She continued. "One night some riders showed up, lathered and tuckered out. They had a woman with 'em, about the same age you are now, too sick to travel. The boss knew the woman and took her in, then the riders left, and sometime later a posse caught up with 'em down Mexico way. Now don't interrupt. The woman who was left with us, she was pregnant, and there was a man who hated her and tried to dirty her name by sayin' she was a whore. But she wasn't a whore, she was the daughter of one of the other men who rode with the Polka Dots."

Dolores Goines paused, for Duane was completely devastated. He struggled to find his voice. "What was my mother's name?" he managed to ask.

"Kathleen O'Shea. It wasn't long after that when she gave birth to a beautiful baby boy. But she was sickly, and then we heard that her man had been killed down in Mexico. Miss Kathleen didn't get well, and just kind of wasted away. Near the end, she made us promise we'd take her little boy to a Catholic orphanage far away, because she was afraid the rich old man would kill him, just as he'll kill me if he finds out what I told you."

Duane felt like a block of stone. Again, when he'd least expected it, he'd discovered the truth that he'd yearned for all his life. "I swear to you that I'll never mention this conversation in my life," he told her breathlessly. "Please . . . what was my mother like?"

"Whenever I think of Miss Kathleen, she was always reading the Bible. She was younger than your father — twenty years at least — and don't you believe them that say the Polka Dots was outlaws. They was fighting for their rights, and they sure gave Old Man Archer a run for his money."

"Did you ever actually talk with my mother?" asked Duane.

"She was always saying about Jesus and prayer. Her hair was like gold, and she was almost as tall as you. She hoped you'd be a priest when you growed up, but you're too much like your daddy, I can see that."

Duane didn't know which question to ask first. "Did you know that Twilby was in the Polka Dot Gang?"

"It's news to me."

"If he was, do you think Old Man Archer might've had him killed?"

She leaned forward, and her eyes glittered catlike in the darkness. "I wouldn't put anything past Sam Archer," she said. "He's the cruelest, meanest man I ever heard of, because he always has to win. I never talked about the Polka Dots since I left the Pecos country, not even to Miss O'Day, 'cause you don't know who's listening. I wouldn't want nobody to think I was having a talk with Joe Braddock's son right now, so I'd better get back to the Last Chance. Now listen to me, boy. You shouldn't never head for the Pecos. But you're a hothead like your father, and I'm just wasting my breath. Your mother was a fine religious woman, and you should be proud of her. That's all. I've got to get back. Good night."

Her skirts rustled past him. She opened the door and was swallowed by the night.

Duane lay in the loft and thought of what Dolores Goines had told him. Now at last he knew his mother's name: Kathleen O'Shea. He let the syllables roll through his mind and imagined a strong, hardworking farm girl who fell in love with an ex-soldier and rancher old enough to be her father and then went on the dodge with him. What a couple they must have been, he pondered. According to records in the monastery office, they never bothered to get married.

Now Duane felt more attached to the world, thanks to a Negro woman he barely knew. But he'd always expected the truth would be like Dolores Goines had said. His parents had been good, honest country folk who'd fought greedy, powerful men and got slaughtered. They never had a chance and probably knew it, but didn't let it stop them. Or maybe they thought right would prevail in the end and God would save them.

Why is it that the worst people get the richest rewards, while good folks work hard to barely survive? he wondered. I know the promises of Christ in the next world, but what about now? How can I let Sam Archer get away with killing my parents?

Duane couldn't take a vacation to Mexico while Sam Archer was walking around, thumbing his nose at everything Duane's father and mother had stood for. It's never too late to settle a score, Duane reasoned.

He whispered solemnly into the night: "Mister Archer, I'm going to find you someday — you can bet your bottom dollar on it. Where you're concerned, there's no mountain too high to climb, no desert too far to cross, no burden too great to bear. Maybe I'll arrest you, and maybe I'll have the sand to shoot you in cold blood, which is what you deserve, you son of a bitch. You might be sleeping real peaceful now, but you damned sure won't be sleeping peaceful long."

On the other side of the stable, her head propped on a pillow, Alice Markham watched Duane tossing, turning, and mumbling to himself. She thought he must be loco, the way he carried on every night. Sometimes he frightened her. What'll I do if he shoots himself?

But she didn't think he'd shoot himself. He wasn't *that* loco, although nobody in his right mind would become sheriff of Escondido. But in other ways, he was the smartest and best-educated man she'd ever met.

Somehow she couldn't stop thinking about him. He looks like a child and a man thrown together, but some of the parts don't fit. Duane didn't have a fat gut like most of the men she'd gone to bed with, and whenever he looked at her, his eyes pierced her brain.

She wondered if she was falling in love with him, or maybe he was just odd and interesting, like a desert bird that didn't know where to land. She'd met innumerable men in her career and hated most of them, although she'd never, under any circumstances, admit it. But she couldn't hate Duane Braddock. I wonder what he'd do if I crawled over there and got under the covers with him.

She felt naughty, rambunctious, and bizarre. Tough on the outside, she needed love but mixed it with other concoctions. He might jump out of his skin, but he's probably as lonely as me. We could have fun together, and it won't hurt nothin'. Neither of us is a virgin anymore. She enjoyed new sensations and didn't worry about possible consequences. The worst he can do is send me away, but she'd seen the naughty gleam in his eye as he'd looked her up and down that morning. I believe he likes me.

She pushed the covers off. She wore only a thin cotton gown as she crossed the space that separated them, and the cool night air made her shiver. He lay on his side, knees drawn up beneath his Apache blanket, looking peaceful as a baby, when suddenly he sprang like a rattlesnake. She jumped backwards as he aimed his Colt at the center of her chest. "What's wrong?"

he asked sleepily, his arm rock steady.

She was so surprised she couldn't speak. Her lips moved but no sound came out.

He smiled. "Guess you're walking in your sleep."

She dropped to her knees beside him. "I was feelin' lonely," she said in a small voice. Slowly, languidly she draped herself over him and touched her lips to his cheek. "Don't you like me just a little bitty-bit, Duane Braddock?"

"You know I do, but I've got an awful lot on my mind."

She touched her tongue to his throat. "Care to talk about it?"

"I don't think this is a good idea," he said in a strained voice.

"You don't have to marry me or anything. I don't care." She darted forward like a minx and touched the tip of her tongue to his lips.

Surprised, Duane felt her breasts against his naked chest. He wanted to deliver a sermon on the temptations of the flesh, but somehow words wouldn't come. She unbuttoned his jeans, and he forgot speculations, deliberations, and vows. He hugged her tightly, kissed her ear, and before he could stop himself, he whispered, "Vanessa."

She stiffened atop him. "Who?"

"It's nothing," he stuttered. "Come here."

She slapped his hands away. "Who's Vanessa?"

"Old friend of mine."

Alice Markham felt cheap, used, and maligned. He doesn't like me, she figured. He needs to pretend I'm someone else.

"What's wrong?" he asked. The fluctuating moods of women never failed to astonish him.

She put her gown back on. "I forgot myself for a moment."

"She was somebody I knew a long time ago," he said, trying to explain. "I don't know what made me say her name. I'm sorry."

"You said it because you're still in love with her, whether you admit it or not." She walked back to her blankets, covered herself, and sobbed.

Duane couldn't imagine where Vanessa Fontaine's name had come from. He'd been trying hard to forget her and figured he'd succeeded, but evidently she still occupied a bedroom in his mind. Tall, willowy, aristocratic, vain, she'd accepted his proposal of marriage, but then ran off with a fancypants lieutenant in the Fourth Cavalry. When last seen, Vanessa Fontaine was heading toward Denver in a stagecoach, out of his life forever. He remembered her long, sinuous legs that she liked to wrap about him, and it bothered him to know that she held such power over him, although she wasn't even there.

He held the Colt in his right hand and reclined on the blankets once more. It's been a helluva day, he told himself, as he closed his eyes.

CHAPTER 8

A bag of mail arrived by stagecoach at Fort Richardson, Texas, two weeks later, and the good news spread quickly across the remote windswept outpost. Troopers in stables, orderly rooms, and on the parade ground eagerly anticipated missives from home at the end of the day.

Fort Richardson was Fourth Cavalry headquarters, sixty miles south of the Red River, smack in the middle of Apaches, Comanches, Osage, and Kiowa. Like any military unit, the Fighting Fourth carried on its roster clerks who sorted the mail. They were Private Mike Staglioni of Naples and Private Bill O'Shaughnessy of County Cork. Their office was behind the command post headquarters, and their strategic assignment was to attack the newly arrived letters, packages, catalogues, and appeals. Their commanding officer, Colonel Ranald Slidell MacKenzie, sat in his office down the hall, anxious for his mail like any trooper in the ranks.

The clerks searched the pile quickly, tossing the colonel's letters to the side. Then, after double-checking each piece, the clerk with the most time in grade, Private O'Shaughnessy, held the specially designated packet in his left hand, marched forthrightly to the colonel's office, and knocked on the door.

"Come in," said a firm parade-ground voice.

"Your mail, sir." O'Shaughnessy dropped it onto the desk, took a step backwards, saluted smartly, and said, "Anything else, sir?"

MacKenzie didn't look up from the pile in front of him. "That's all, Private O'Shaughnessy."

O'Shaughnessy backed toward the door, examining the famous Civil War hero at close range. Colonel MacKenzie had fought at Second Bull Run, Fredericksburg, Chancellorsville, and Gettysburg, among other major battles, and had left behind three fingers in the soil of Virginia. At the age of thirty-seven, he was the second youngest colonel in the U.S. Army, and War Department insiders said he'd be a general before long.

MacKenzie heard his underling close the door, as he perused newly arrived communications from the outside world. A West Pointer born in New York City, he'd been given the Fourth Cavalry only last December. Prior to that, he'd been commanding officer of the Negro Forty-first Infantry at Fort MacKevitt.

MacKenzie wore a walrus mustache and a blue Army shirt with matching pants adorned by yellow stripes down each side, tucked into highly polished black cavalry boots. His hair was short, dark brown, parted on the side, and neatly combed. Sifting through the stack for important messages, he found one that had been sent from the Department of War. He tore open the envelope and read an inquiry from General Sherman himself. "What are you doing about Apache depredations in your Department?"

Colonel MacKenzie knew that congressmen and senators were breathing down Sherman's back, demanding quick solutions to complex problems, but Colonel MacKenzie preferred the art and science of gentle persuasion. He'd seen too many bloody battlefields to be impetuous with other men's lives.

The morning passed slowly as he worked

through requisitions for supplies, reports of troop dispositions, accounts of skirmishes with Indians, complaints about a variety of complex issues, recommendations for action, promotion lists, etc. The higher you go in the Army, the more you push paper, he thought with chagrin. Unshakable in battle, indomitable under pressure, Colonel MacKenzie hated the administrative side of his job.

Three-quarters down the pile, he came to a plain envelope with his name and address, but no return address or government marking. He smelled it, but it carried no perfume except possibly the faint trace of whisky.

He tore open the envelope and held the carefully printed message in front of him:

Dear Colonel MacKenzie:

All hell has broke loose down here in Escondido. Seven men shot last week, two wimmin cut to pieces, and no sign of let-up. Sheriff Duane Braddock is wanted for murders all across Texas. Dont you think its time to send the Fourth Cavalry, or are you gonter wait till we is all dead? I aint signin this cus I'm fraid somebody'll shoot me.

a citizen of Escondido, Texas

Colonel MacKenzie leaned back in his chair and lit the Kentucky burly in his corncob pipe. *Duane Braddock.* He'd read about a Braddock in other recent official reports from southwest Texas. Duane Braddock had had a few run-ins with the Fourth Cavalry already. Another kill-crazy cowboy with a fast hand and slow mind, Colonel MacKenzie concluded.

The Fourth Cavalry assisted local law enforcement whenever possible, but by the time the detachment would reach Escondido, the outlaws would be long gone. They'd set up business elsewhere, the Fighting Fourth would take the field again, and the outlaws would relocate once more. It was an ongoing chess game, but served a collateral purpose. The troopers showed the Fourth Cavalry flag around Texas, and citizens didn't feel completely defenseless.

Colonel MacKenzie needed more men and better equipment, but most Americans rejected higher taxes for military appropriations. The best soldiers had returned to civilian life after the war, their places filled by misfits, morons, criminals, and the dregs of Europe. Colonel MacKenzie had troopers in his command who couldn't speak a word of English, and some of his officers were worse than the men. Fortunately, a small core of old soldiers like himself were able to hold the Fourth Cavalry together.

Colonel MacKenzie stood behind his desk and studied the map nailed to the wall. Through the open window, he heard hoarse shouts of drill sergeants on the parade ground, while a mounted patrol passed his window, clattering hooves and equipment. Colonel MacKenzie located Escondido on the map and saw that Fort Davis was the closest U.S. Army installation.

He sat at his desk and wrote the order:

TO: COMMANDING OFFICER
FORT DAVIS, TEXAS

Reports have been received by this headquarters of increased outlaw activity in Escondido. Dispatch a detachment there immediately, if you haven't already. Arrest Sheriff Duane Braddock and hold him for questioning. I await your report on this matter.

Ranald S. MacKenzie
Colonel, 4th U.S. Cavalry
In Command

Unaware of his expanding notoriety,

Duane Braddock dined on steak and eggs that morning at a corner table of the Last Chance Saloon. He'd just finished a two-hour arithmetic lesson with Alice, and his head spun with desire. But fortunately or unfortunately, he'd made the stupid mistake of mentioning Vanessa Fontaine's name in vain, and Alice had been resentful ever since. Maybe it's all for the best, he tried to convince himself. I couldn't bring Alice Markham to the Pecos country, because her life wouldn't be worth a dollar.

Duane finished breakfast and sipped a cup of coffee. It was another peaceful day in Escondido, and no one had been shot since that bloody Saturday night more than two weeks ago. Children could play out-of-doors, and ladies promenaded on the sidewalks during the day, an unheard-of event in the era before Duane had been sheriff. No additional attempts had been made on his life, and he was starting to feel safe again.

He was biding his time before he could depart for the Pecos country. He still didn't know what he'd do when he met Old Man Archer, but a debt had to be paid and the scales balanced out. I'll worry about it when I find him, he promised himself. Duane expected to finish Alice's education in a few more weeks, then he'd hit the trail.

After breakfast, he headed for the stable, where Sam Goines had already saddled Steve. Alice sat in the office and practiced her penmanship, the tip of her tongue protruding between her lips. She didn't look at Duane as he climbed onto Steve's back and rode out the door.

Duane rocked back and forth in the saddle as Steve clomped down the main street of Escondido. A group of children watched him in wonderment from the planked sidewalk, and he touched his finger to the brim of his black cowboy hat as he passed by.

As he rode onto the desert, the town fell behind him, the sun floated midway toward the horizon, and a flock of black-and-white-striped birds flew overhead. He passed Ocotillo, Spiney Star, and Nipple cactus plants, as he browsed carefully for signs of Apaches. He'd lived among them, but they numbered many bands, some at war with each other, and they wouldn't stop to ask for credentials.

It felt good to be away from the noise and filth of Escondido. The sun shone brightly, and purple mountains in the distance seemed to pulsate with light. Duane sucked the clean desert air deep into his lungs. "I'm at my best when I'm alone," he said to himself. The vast endless expanse made him realize how small and insignificant he was. This desert was here before I was born, and will be here long after I'm gone.

Sitting in the saddle, the sun beating down on him, he felt a kind of religious ecstasy. Something told him to get down on his knees and give thanks for his many blessings. "I haven't prayed for a long time, and it's about time."

He pulled back Steve's reins and started to climb out of the saddle. Suddenly he heard the *crack* of a bullet over his head. Dirt kicked into the air a few feet away, echoing thunder came to his ears, and he was already on the ground. Another shot sent a spray of rock particles into the air, as hot lead ricocheted screamingly. Duane drew his Colt, crouched behind a boulder, and cursed himself for not yanking his Henry rifle out of its scabbard. Meanwhile, his faithful mount was running away with a forty-dollar saddle on his back.

Duane discerned the direction of his assailant from how the bullet had struck the ground. It was a lone rifleman high on the ridges, probably angry at himself for missing the shots. Duane gave silent thanks to the holy impulse that caused him to climb down from the saddle. If he'd remained on course, the bullet might've struck the back of his head.

He kept low and made plans. I'll wait until dark and then head back to town. He hoped he'd meet Steve later, because it was a long way to Escondido. His assailant hadn't been an Apache, because an Apache would creep close and take no chances on missing. He was waiting for me to go for my ride, Duane speculated. Sam Archer has sent another killer to town, or maybe this bushwhacker has been here all along, biding his time. He knows I'll be on the lookout for him when I get back, and maybe he'll give himself away by a careless word or act.

Duane smoked cigarettes and waited patiently for night to fall. The more he thought about it, the more he was forced to conclude that the stranger who'd previously tried to bushwhack him hadn't acted alone. Every citizen, outlaw, and bandito in Escondido became a possible suspect once more, including Derek Wright.

At dusk, Steve poked his head through the foliage on the other side of the arroyo.

He looked both ways, then crossed over and approached shyly. Duane patted his great neck and talked to him softly as darkness fell on the desert. Then Duane climbed into the saddle and pulled the reins toward the town glowing in the distance like an open pore of purgatory.

Duane climbed down from the saddle, loosened the cinch buckle, and threw the reins over the rail. Then he hitched up his gunbelt and climbed the stairs of Apocalypse Church.

Inside were the usual members praying for forgiveness and mercy, but Alice wasn't among them. She's probably studying, and maybe I should ease up on her, Duane thought. But the sooner she learns the material, the sooner I can go after Old Man Archer. Duane sidestepped into a pew, dropped to his knees, clasped his hands together, and prayed: *Dear Lord, thank you for saving my worthless life today.*

Then his mind went blank. He didn't have the old religious fire anymore, and couldn't help wondering if religion was flummery like everything else. Injustice, deceit, and misery reigned everywhere, while preachers passed the collection plate. Duane wondered what he believed, and whether it made sense to believe anything.

"Sheriff?" asked a female voice.

It was Mrs. Berclair, the preacher's wife, smiling at Duane from the end of the pew. "My husband saw you praying here, and we were wondering if you might have a cup of tea with us. I baked some cookies today."

Duane didn't care for tea, but home-baked cookies were his specialty, and he thought it might be good to palaver with a man of the cloth. "I'll have to take care of my horse first, but I'll be right back."

"My husband is watering your horse even as we speak. This way, please." She led him through a corridor to a kitchen with a stove, straight-backed wooden chairs, and a table covered with a red-and-white-checkered cloth.

"The reverend will be here shortly," she said. "Have a seat."

Duane examined the woman's stark cheekbones, bony jaw, and thick spectacles covering hazel eyes. She wasn't beautiful but conveyed a certain warmth that he found appealing.

"You were out riding today," she said. "Aren't you afraid of Apaches?"

"I'm more afraid of the white man, to tell you the truth."

"You sure don't act it."

Duane had no idea what to say, for his death toll weighed heavily upon his heart. "It was a beautiful day," he declared, in an effort to be conversational and light, the opposite of how he felt. "Not hot like August."

The back door opened, and Reverend Berclair appeared, brimming with radiant good health, limping on his pegleg. "Howdy, Sheriff Braddock. Glad you could stop by. I just wanted to say how grateful we are for your good work here in Escondido. Things sure have settled down since you showed up." He sat opposite Duane and reached for a cookie. "You were raised a Catholic — isn't that right? Well, I've got nothing against Catholics, but a man can't let somebody in Rome do his thinking."

Mrs. Berclair poured cups of tea, as Duane stared at the preacher with new interest. "How'd you know I was a Catholic?"

The parson appeared surprised by the question. "I guess I heard somebody say so."

"Can you remember who?"

"Lots of people come through this church, Sheriff. It's hard to keep track of them all. What difference does it make in God's grand scheme?"

Duane wondered if the preacher had taken a potshot at him earlier in the day. "Did you go for a ride on the desert earlier?" he asked casually.

"What for?" asked the preacher.

Patricia Berclair smiled at Duane. "My husband is afraid of the desert, and hasn't left town since we arrived two years ago."

The preacher cleared his throat. "We've got plenty to do right here. More sinners than I ever imagined in such a small town. Why'd you ask if I went for a ride?"

"Saw some tracks of a shod horse on the desert today," replied Duane. "Just curious who was out there."

Patricia Berclair leaned forward and smiled. "They might've belonged to Mister Snodgras. I saw him riding in from the desert this afternoon. He's been taking a lot of time off lately, thanks to you." The parson's wife winked. "Maybe you should've asked him for a percentage of the profits."

Duane tied Steve to the hitching rail in front of the undertaker's house. He'd always thought there was something questionable about the man who profited from death. He knocked on the door, and presently it was opened by the undertaker. "Somebody get killed again?" he asked calmly.

Duane probed for signs of guilt. "I was riding on the desert today, and thought I saw you there. Mind if I come in?"

Duane brushed past him and entered the parlor. A wrinkled newspaper lay near the sofa; evidently the undertaker had been reading.

"If you saw me on the desert, why didn't you holler to me?" the undertaker asked.

"Too long a distance."

"Then how do you know it was me."

"I've got a spyglass."

"Good thing to have," Snodgras replied. "I've got one too. Like to look at birds. Their bones are hollow, did you know that?"

"What kind of rifle do you carry?"

The undertaker smiled embarrassedly. "I don't shoot the birds. I just look at them."

"May I see your rifle?"

A scowl came over the undertaker's solemn visage. "What do you want my rifle for?"

"Official investigation."

"I don't like the idea of somebody barging into my home."

Duane spotted the rifle mounted on hooks above the fireplace. He took it down, and it was a .40 caliber Volcanic in superb condition, recently oiled. No odor of gunpowder could be detected down the barrel.

"What're you sniffing for, Sheriff?"

"Remember when Amos Twilby was bushwhacked and you asked where I came from? Where are *you* from, Mister Undertaker Man?"

"I don't like your manner, Sheriff."

"Ever been in the Pecos country?"

"Why are you asking me all these questions?"

"How'd you like to go to jail today?"

"What's the charge?"

"Attempted murder."

"Of who?"

"Me."

The undertaker stared at him for a few moments, then smiled faintly. "You know what folks say about you? They say you're plumb loco, and maybe they're right."

"The jail's empty," Duane said, "but maybe I can find a backstabber to lock up with you, and I'll forget to confiscate the knife in his boot."

"I think you're getting too big for your britches, young man."

Duane whacked out his Colt and aimed at the undertaker's long chin. "Where are you from?"

"Des Moines," the undertaker replied instantaneously.

"Were you ever in the Pecos country?"

"Passed through on the way here."

"Ever hear of Sam Archer?"

The undertaker grimaced disdainfully. "Never, but let me point something out to you, Sheriff. We didn't hire you to intimidate honest citizens."

Duane slowly holstered his gun, then tilted his head to the side and said soberly: "I'm keeping my eyes on you, Mister Undertaker Man. Watch your step."

Patricia Berclair paced her bedroom, hands clasped behind her back, brow furrowed with thought. Am I going insane? she asked herself. Somehow, she couldn't stop thinking about Duane Braddock in his tight black jeans and brown cowboy boots, carrying a big gun on his hip. It had begun when she'd first met him, as if someone had thrown a bucket of warm water onto her.

She felt itchy and wanted to run a hundred miles. Her brain seemed to be bouncing off the walls. Above the bed was nailed a bare cross, and she dropped to her knees. "Oh my God, save me," she said.

She closed her eyes and thought of Jesus on the cross, but his features were Duane Braddock's. What does he have that excites me so? As a rule, she didn't think about men in a romantic way. Then Duane Braddock strolled into her life, with his strange crooked smile, wide shoulders, and the look of a cougar in his eyes.

She should've been doing housework or helping her husband in the office, but was instead imagining herself and Duane Braddock stark naked in bed. The devil was tempting her mightily, and she dug her fingernails into her arms to subdue the desire raging in her loins. Trembling, her knees weak, she collapsed onto the bed.

Duane Braddock needs someone to take care of him, she thought. Someone older, more mature, capable of deep understanding — me, for instance. But I'm married already, and besides, he's just a boy. Maybe I've been in this sinful little town too long and need a change. Perhaps I can encourage Herbert to take me to Austin, Houston, or anywhere but here. I need someone to talk with, like my mother or Sally, her younger sister, who was also married to a preacher.

Patricia felt alone, forgotten, and like she was losing her bearings. She'd married Herbert to help him with his work, because she'd believed he was a great man. It wasn't a gross, disgusting physical marriage like most, but a union of mind and spirit based on shared convictions.

Captain Herbert Berclair had seen God on the battlefield of Vicksburg, and lost his lust in the brilliant illumination that claimed his left leg. He and his wife slept in separate bedrooms and never had seen each other naked. Patricia Berclair was a married woman of a certain age, but was still a virgin.

It hadn't been a problem before Duane Braddock showed up. Somehow she'd been able to subdue her deepest longings, but now was writhing on the bed, scratching her arms, and kicking her legs in the air. I've got to stop thinking about him, she admonished herself. But I can't!

She wished she had a whip so she could dominate herself. Maybe a belt would do. She took a thick black leather one from the closet and laid it on the bed. Then she removed her dress and stood in her bloomers in front of the mirror.

She saw no great beauty, her knees were knobby, legs skinny, breasts nearly nonexistent. She'd always thought her mouth too wide, her nose too small, and she bore a faint resemblance to a frog. Holding the whip in her right hand, she smacked it hard across her back, the sharp sensation making her cry softly. Bowing her head, she flagellated herself repeatedly as she sobbed and shuddered in the darkness.

Light glowed through the window of the stable office, illuminating a wraithlike figure hovering over a book. Duane opened the door, as his student glanced up crossly. "I'm studying," said Alice Markham.

"Don't you think it's time you went to bed?"

"The sooner I git edjicated, the sooner I can git away from *you.* I don't want to be somebody's ball and chain."

"You've been in an awfully bad mood lately. It might not hurt to smile once in a while."

Her lips pinched and she looked like she was going to say something awful, but instead she wrinkled her brow and returned to the book. He departed the office, troubled by yet another female. He didn't love Alice, had no intention of marrying her, yet desired her warm body. Now he understood why church fathers railed against physical passion. It made no sense, provided no peace, and led to disastrous consequences for men and women alike. Unfortunately, Duane couldn't defeat his heart's longings with mere logic. *It is better to marry than burn,* said the great Saint Paul, Apostle to the Gentiles.

Duane made his way to the saloon district, scanning constantly for bushwackers and backshooters. He felt himself getting another headache from so much cogitation. Maybe I should have a drink of whisky and relax.

He angled into the Desert Palace Saloon, paid for a whisky, and carried it to a table against the back wall. There weren't many patrons, and he wondered if a bushwhacker was aiming a gun at him in the darkness. His skin felt covered with needles, and he broke out in a cold sweat. Somebody in this town is trying to kill me, and I wonder who he is.

Maybe it was a coincidence that the undertaker was on the desert at the same time as I, but maybe not. It could be this, or it could be that. The headache increased in intensity. Duane sipped whisky and tried to stop worrying, but his mind continued like an infernal devil machine.

A group of men broke into song on the far side of the room. There were eight of them out of tune and sitting at a round table. They appeared melancholy, with far-off expressions in their eyes, as they mouthed the words:

The years creep slowly by, Lorena;
The snow is on the grass again;
The sun's low down the sky, Lorena;
The frost gleams where the flowers have been

Men throughout the saloon joined the mournful old Civil War ditty. Duane had heard it sung in saloons before, for it was one of the most popular tunes of that great national catastrophe. Battle-weary troopers had crooned it around campfires, to remind them of loved ones far away, and couldn't seem to stop now that the fighting was over.

A hundred months have passed, Lorena,
Since last I held that hand in mine,
And felt the pulse beat fast, Lorena
Though mine beat faster than thine

Rustlers, bandits, gunfighters, and cowboys looked prayerful as they intoned the simple rhythm. In Duane's imagination, their cowboy hats and rough canvas shirts were replaced by wide-brimmed campaign hats and gray uniforms with brass buttons. Lamplight flickered on their bronzed features, and Duane saw the pure poetry of their souls. They'd marched to war for dear old Dixie, shared danger and hardship for five long years, ran low on supplies and ammunition, suffered, bled, and finally were conquered, losing everything in the last cataclysmic struggle.

Duane couldn't help being moved by the emotions flooding through the ramshackle saloon. He knew that most Confederate soldiers hadn't been slavers, but they didn't want folks in Boston and Philadelphia telling them how to live. They had fought for Jeff Davis and Bobby Lee, went down to bitter defeat, and then drifted West, where the weight of Reconstruction didn't crush them so heavily into the ground.

Now they were gathered in the Desert Palace Saloon, reliving the great days of their lives. Duane's curious eyes fell on his former deputy singing among them, his old Confederate cavalry officer's hat on the back of his head. They accepted Derek Wright as a comrade in arms, while the Pecos Kid lurked on the far side of the room, always the observer, never part of the group.

A hundred months — 'twas flowery May,
When up the hilly slope we climbed,
To watch the dying of the day
And hear the distant church bells chime

When the song came to an end, the saloon was still, and Smiley the bartender didn't dare pour a drink. All eyes were fixed on a time long ago when brave young men rode off to war, cheered by their women. Now they had a handful of nothing to show for their struggles, and disappointment was engraved into their faces. Somebody burped, and a bullwhacker rapped his knuckles on the bar, signaling that his glass was empty. Men dealt cards, or picked up their newspapers, but a few just stared into space, because they couldn't let go.

Somebody laughed at the end of the bar, as the saloon returned to its normal noisy ambiance. A few men got up from the table where Derek Wright sat, and Duane contemplated having a talk with his former deputy. Then he heard footsteps coming from the opposite direction. He turned toward a big burly man wearing a black leather vest, brown goatee, and brown cowboy hat.

"Mind if I join you fer a minute, Sheriff?"

"Just keep your hands where I can see them."

The burly man sat beside Duane, turned down the corners of his mouth, and said, "I'm a-goin' to shoot somebody tonight, and I'd like you to look the other way. Would you take twenty dollars?"

Duane gaped at him.

"How's about twenty-five?"

"Mister," Duane said, "you'd better hop onto your horse and ride out of town, otherwise I'll arrest you."

"I din't mean to insult you, but twenty-five dollars is all I can afford."

"If you're not gone within the next half hour, you'll be a guest in our jail. Hope you don't mind sleeping on the floor."

The would-be killer peered into Duane's eyes. "If yer not in it fer the money, what the hell're you a-wearin' that tin badge fer?"

"I ask myself the same question," Duane replied. "Were you in the war?"

The man appeared surprised. "Fifteenth Georgia Infantry. Why d'ya ask?"

"You were a good soldier once, and now you're an outlaw. I don't get it."

"I'm like the piano player, and I'm a-doin' the best I can."

The stranger arose from the table and headed toward the back door. The war must've warped their minds, Duane hypothesized. They saw too much blood and guts, they lost faith in God, and now they're reckless fools. His eyes fell on Derek Wright sitting at the big round table. How do I know he wasn't on the desert this afternoon? I wish there was one person in the world whom I could trust.

He wanted to palaver with Derek Wright, but couldn't let himself go. Here in the secular world, it's everybody pitted against everybody else, Duane realized. At the monastery, the priests and brothers tried to be decent men, unlike folks in Escondido who plot wickedness constantly.

Derek Wright stared at his glass of whisky, lost in his Civil War dreams. Duane felt ashamed for being cruel to him, but a resourceful fellow like Wright could always get along. Maybe I should go over there and ask where he was this morning.

Derek Wright looked up from his whisky. "What's on your mind, kid?"

Duane sat opposite him and asked: "Were you on the desert today?"

Derek Wright blinked in surprise. "How'd you know?"

"I was there too. You didn't mistake me for an antelope or a mule deer, and take a potshot at me, did you?"

"The antelope I shot is being served at the Silver Spur Saloon. It must've been an Apache who tried to shoot you."

"An Apache wouldn't miss." Duane looked into Derek's steely eyes. "I've been wanting to have a conversation with you for a long time, Derek. When we first met, you asked a lot of questions in a town where folks generally keep to themselves. Then you kept showing up at the wrong time, and today you were on the desert where somebody tried to bushwhack me. I know that you were an officer in the war, and you're an honorable man underneath it all, but how do I know you're not working for Sam Archer?"

Wright sucked a tooth for a moment, then replied: "I'm not asking you to trust me, and don't expect me to trust you. You know what they say about you, Mister Pecos? Only a matter of time before some *real* gunfighter shows up and shoots you."

The ex-cavalry officer tossed Duane a skeptical glance, then downed the rest of his whisky, wiped his mouth with the back of his hand, adjusted his old Confederate cavalry officer's hat on his head, and reeled away.

You can't tell people how you really feel, Duane concluded. Because they're all so tetchy. He noticed a leprechaun with a long reddish brown beard and cowboy hat, sitting on the far side of the table. "Howdy, Sheriff," the leprechaun said jovially.

"Were you in the war with Derek Wright?" Duane asked.

"Oh hell no," replied the leprechaun. "I was a cook in the Fifteenth Louisiana Infantry, but Derek Wright was an officer in the Stonewall Brigade. He's seen a lot of war."

"Is he a friend of yours?"

"Let's jest say we know each other. What're you askin' so many questions about Derek Wright for?"

"Do you trust him?"

The leprechaun didn't hesitate. "Anyday."

"Why?"

"I dunno." The leprechaun appeared flustered. "I never heard anybody say somethin' bad about him, and besides, he was in the old Stonewall Brigade." The leprechaun winked. "If you want to know more about Derek Wright, maybe you'd better ask him yerself."

The leprechaun eased off his chair, along with the others who'd been sitting at the table, and Duane found himself alone, wondering about friendship, trust, and bushwhackers. Derek Wright has a good reputation, but that doesn't mean he's not working for Old Man Archer. And for all I know, that leprechaun tried to kill me today.

Duane glanced behind him, but no one was crouching with a gun in his hand. The sheriff adjusted his black hat low over his eyes, then strolled out the door. His eyes skirted rooftops, searching for a head and a rifle. He peered into alleys for the glint of moonlight on gunmetal. Whoever he is, he'll be extra careful next time.

Duane walked into the Last Chance Saloon, and his eyes fell on Derek Wright standing at the bar, one foot on the rail, drinking alone. Duane elbowed beside him. "Sorry if I insulted you," he said. "Guess I don't know how to act around people."

Wright shrugged. "You don't know any better, but don't keep asking me to prove something to you. The only person I have to prove anything to is myself."

"I could still use a good deputy," Duane

said. "If you want your old badge back, it's yours."

"Worst job I ever had. Like asking somebody to shoot you."

"Why'd you take it in the first place?"

"There you go with your questions."

"You said it's a terrible job, but you didn't say no when I offered it to you."

"I don't have to justify myself to you."

"People have been trying to bushwhack me since I hit town, and I want to figure out who. What's wrong with that?"

"Why are you still here? Go to Monterrey, Los Angeles, or anywhere you want, long as it's far away. Don't fight the world, kid. You don't have a chance."

"There's more to this than a quick ride over the border, Derek."

"You won't be around for Christmas, but I guess you'd rather get shot, because that's what'll happen if you go to the Pecos country." Wright pulled his gun, drew back the hammer, and handed the grip to Duane. "Go ahead, take it. You might as well blow your brains out right now. Why waste time? Think of the wear and tear you'll save on your poor horse. Who cares about Christmas?"

Duane thought of candles, gaily colored wreaths, and special pastries for orphan boys at the monastery in the clouds. Maybe Derek is right, he considered. Why should I risk my life, and who cares?

In the smoky depths at the far end of the saloon, he imagined the Polka Dot Gang under attack from Sam Archer's hired guns. The bullets literally tore Joe Braddock apart, yet he fought on. There are things more important than Christmas, Duane decided, and I'm tired of arguing about it.

Duane downed the dregs of his glass, flipped a coin to the bartender, and headed for the door. He didn't even look back at Wright. He had nothing to say to the man.

Cool desert air soothed him as he walked down the main street of Escondido. I can't let my mother's and father's deaths go unpunished, that's all I know, and if Saint Thomas Aquinas doesn't like it, he can write another *Summa Theologiae.*

Duane found himself standing in front of the stable. Maybe I should just go to bed and sleep it off. The stable was pitch black, with rows of horses sleeping in the darkness. Duane heard furtive sounds in the loft, as his eyes adjusted quickly to the darkness. Horses shuffled in their stalls, and wind rattled shingles on the roof. Duane climbed the ladder slowly and held his gun ready to fire. Alice lay still in her bedroll against the wall, and a terrible foreboding came over Duane that made him rush to her side. She rolled over and looked at him in alarm, holding the blankets to her neck.

"Sorry," he said. "Go back to sleep."

"What's wrong with you?" she asked sleepily.

He heard something behind him and spun around, but there were only bales of hay. He advanced toward them, aiming his gun straight ahead.

"Is anything wrong?" Alice asked.

"There's somebody back here."

Duane spotted movement in a pile of hay heaped in the corner. "Come out with your hands up, or I'll start shooting."

The top of the pile elevated, and the naked body of Sam Goines stood like an ebony phoenix before Duane. Sam tried to smile bravely, but there was nothing he could say. Duane was flabbergasted, jealous, and possibly angry, but he wasn't sure. "Put on your clothes and go downstairs," he said in a shaky voice.

"Don't blame it on her, boss. It's all my fault. Go ahead and shoot me if you want, but leave her alone."

Duane motioned with the gun. "Get going."

Sam Goines's clothes were at his feet. He put them on quickly and backed toward the ladder. "I hope you're not going to tell my mother."

"I said get going."

Sam descended to the stable, and Duane turned toward the blanket. Alice was hiding her head in shame, and Duane didn't know what to make of it. He'd never suspected that white women slept with Negro men, and wasn't sure how he was supposed to feel. Since leaving the monastery, he'd noticed that Negroes and whites generally kept apart, but evidently everything changed when the lights went out. *Let he who is without sin cast the first stone.* He climbed behind the bales of hay, sat on his blankets, and pulled off his boots.

A small girl's voice came to him from the far side of the loft. "Are you gonna throw me out?"

"Of course not. Go to sleep."

"But . . ."

"You don't owe me explanations, and I'm not interested anyway."

Duane stretched out on his blankets, held his gun in his right hand. The loft fell silent, and he stared at the peaked roof for a long time.

Patricia Berclair sat beside her bedroom window and gazed sleepily at the moonlit backyard. Her back and shoulders hurt from the belt, and she couldn't fall asleep. She didn't know what to think of herself. I've fallen in love with a man young enough to be my son and then I whipped myself like a religious maniac. What's wrong with me? But I must never, under any circumstances, make improper advances to Duane Braddock, she told herself. I *will* control my low appetites. I can do it, but still . . .

She felt a twinge of doubt. It's natural to have certain needs, but you don't have to act on them. She pictured herself squirming in bed with Duane Braddock, and wasn't so sure. I couldn't betray Herbert, or could I?

Her reverie was interrupted by movement on the far side of the yard. She became alarmed — they were in Apache country — but a cat stepped into the moonlight and Patricia relaxed. I thought I saw a man carrying something out there, but maybe it's time I went to bed.

She crawled beneath the blankets and

closed her eyes. I'm not in love with Duane Braddock, am I?

Duane opened his Apache eyes when his Apache ears heard somebody approaching stealthily in the backyard. The Pecos Kid threw off the covers, moved silently toward the window, and smelled coal oil. He poked his head outside, and saw someone was lighting a match to the barn!

"Fire!" Duane shouted.

A shadowy figure fled as curtains of flame rose up the wall. Duane fired a wild shot, then the arsonist ducked around the corner of a building. The barn was constructed of dry old wood and was filled with hay. Flames raced along timbers, and Duane could hear crackling and sputtering all about him, as horses whinnied hysterically below.

Alice leapt out of bed, shrieking at the top of her lungs. Duane caught a glimpse of his nightgowned student fleeing toward the ladder. They descended rapidly, and were joined by Sam Goines on the main floor. Curls of smoke entered through cracks in the planks, as Duane and Sam struggled to free the neighing, stomping horses in the flickering firelight. Sam Goines grabbed the ledgers as Duane picked up the box of books, wishing he'd had the presence of mind to take his rifle, but it was too late now.

Flames cast bizarre shadows on the walls as horses stomped toward the door. Duane and Sam Goines followed them into the street, where townspeople were gathering in their nightclothes. Orange ribbons streaked up the walls of the rickety old stable, while bucket brigades formed to meet the dire threat to Escondido. Duane ran down the alley to the rear of the stable, where a barrel burned near the spot where the intruder had been. If I didn't hear him, he would've roasted three people, Duane figured. Who is this son of a bitch who's trying to cook me alive? He dropped to his hands and knees and searched for fresh tracks, but discerned a variety of confusing fragments. At the front of the stable, buckets of water splashed flames as clouds of fresh steam billowed into the air. Duane thought of his saddle, blankets, real estate, and other belongings going up in smoke.

There was a *thwack* and a roar, and the stable roof caved in, showering red sparks into the air. Duane passed buckets of water along as he scrutinized the faces around him. Townspeople, outlaws, women, and cowboys worked frantically, while a bunch of drunkards watched stupidly from the sidelines. Other citizens threw water onto buildings nearby, to prevent the fire from spreading.

This bushwhacker will burn down Escondido to get rid of me, Duane realized. The only way to catch a rat is to set a trap for him, but I'll have to be the bait, and what if he catches me instead?

The charred black skeleton of the stable stood stark and stinky in the wan dawn light. Duane and the exhausted townspeople stood before it, their clothes, hands, and faces stained with soot and perspiration. "The Lord giveth and the Lord taketh away," said Pastor Berclair. "Praise be the Lord." He turned toward Duane. "We have a guest room in the rectory, Sheriff. You're welcome to it."

"But I'm not alone. I have my . . ." — Duane didn't know what to call Alice Markham — ". . . my student," he finally expostulated.

The preacher couldn't suppress a frown, and his wife appeared scandalized. Maggie O'Day resolved the dilemma by stepping forward, a wry smile on her face. "We maintain a room for the sheriff and his student at the Last Chance Saloon."

Everything Duane owned was gone, including Steve, who'd run off without a saddle and didn't appear ready to return. He's probably galloping with a big mustang herd, Duane thought. I guess he didn't like me as much as I thought. Duane followed Maggie back to the Last Chance Saloon, as townspeople gawked at him, his silver conchoed black hat hanging down his back, suspended from his neck by a black leather strap. Maggie hollered, "Drinks on the house!"

The saloon filled with weary cowboys, outlaws, and townspeople, as Smiley the bartender lined up glasses and filled them with whisky. Duane grabbed one and carried it back toward Maggie's office, which was empty. He sat on the chair in front of her desk and tried to figure out who'd set fire to his property. It was a puzzle more compelling than anything Abelard had ever written.

Maggie breezed into the office, sat in her chair, and reached for a panatella. "You and Alice can have room twenty till you git the stable rebuilt."

"But I can't afford to build another stable."

"I'll advance you the money. What kind of town would this be without a stable?"

He gazed into her eyes. "The fire wasn't an accident, Maggie. I saw somebody with a match and took a shot at him, but he got away. I wonder who he is. You got any idea?"

She thought for a few moments and said: "No idea a'tall. But if somebody was a-tryin' to burn me down, and I couldn't figger out who he was, I'd move out of town and forget the whole mess. There's only so much you can do."

Duane knew she spoke the truth, but once again logic lost out to his rising temper. The thought that someone would go so far as to *burn* him had made a powerful impression. "I'm not running away," he said stubbornly, "and I almost caught the son of a bitch tonight. Sooner or later he'll make a mistake, and then I'll nail his ass to the wall."

Duane knocked on the door, and Alice Markham's face peered through the opening. She smiled uncertainly. "What's wrong this time?"

"I'm going to sleep on the desert," he replied, "but I expect to be back in the morning for your usual lessons."

She placed her hand on his. "I have to ask you a favor. I hope you're not gonna tell anybody about . . . well . . . a certain someone and me. If word gets around, they just might lynch us both. You know, sometimes you're a little simple, and you talk too much."

"Your secret is safe with me," he replied.

He walked out the back door of the Last Chance saloon, and the first rays of sunlight struck him like an arrow between the eyes. He lowered the brim of his hat and headed for the open desert, glancing back numerous times. He passed beyond the town boundaries and soon found himself on hard-packed dirt and grama grass.

He moved in a semicircle, then doubled back and erased his steps. Then he headed off on hilly terrain to the east of Escondido. The more he thought about the identity of his killer, the deeper the quandary became. Upon finding a stream, he took off his clothes and bathed. Then he washed the clothes and put them back on. He found a rock nearby and lay atop it like a big black lizard, letting warm morning rays dry him off.

I wonder where my nemesis is, and if he's thinking of me. He's getting discouraged, but won't give up easily. I wonder if he'll kill me before I figure out who the son of a bitch is.

* * *

Duane slept most of the day, then returned to Escondido in the late afternoon. Across from the church, he saw the sign that said General Store.

Duane had passed the establishment many times late at night when it was closed. He noticed that dolls and dresses were displayed in the window during the day, alongside cans of beans and cheeses suspended from the ceiling.

A stout Mexican wearing curly black muttonchop whiskers stood behind the counter, and Duane recognized him from the saloons. The Mexican noticed Duane's tin badge, smiled, and held out his hand. "I am happy to know you, Señor Sheriff. What I can do for you today?"

Duane shook the shopkeeper's beefy hand. "I guess you heard about the stable burning down, and . . ."

The shopkeeper interrupted him. "You must need new clothes, yes? I have just the thing."

The shopkeeper turned, but Duane grabbed his arm. "I'm here about another matter. Have you sold anybody a barrel of coal oil lately?"

"I sell coal oil all the time, Señor. This

town would be dark at night without my coal oil."

Duane examined the shopkeeper carefully. "Have you ever been to the Pecos country?"

"What for?"

"Who's your best customer for coal oil?"

"The Last Chance Saloon."

Duane left the store and headed for the Last Chance Saloon, but on his way saw a sign suspended over the sidewalk that said:

GUNSMITH
JAMES BURKETT
WE CARRY ALL MAKES.

Duane remembered that he needed to buy ammunition. Inside the shop, two hard-looking hombres gazed at a rifle lying on the counter. "Seventy dollars," said the proprietor, "and it'll earn that much in buffalo hides the first week."

The hombres turned around, saw the tin badge, and looked at each other significantly. "We'll come back later."

They lowered their sombreros, stalked out the door, and Duane inclined toward the gunsmith. "Guess I just scared away a couple of customers."

"They'll be back," replied Burkett.

"What can I do for you?"

It occurred to Duane that this was the same man who'd helped carry Twilby's corpse on the night the former Polka Dot got shot. "I'd like a box of cartridges for my Colt."

The gunsmith placed the merchandise on the counter and quoted the price. Duane paid, opened the box, and stuffed cartridges into the black leather pouch on his gunbelt.

"Anything else?" Burkett asked.

"Where were you at two o'clock this morning?"

Burkett appeared surprised by the sudden question. "In bed. Where else? Why do you ask?"

"Somebody set fire to my stable last night, and I'm trying to figure out who it was. No offense intended."

"If you don't believe me, ask my wife. Why would I set fire to your stable?"

"Don't take it personally. I'm asking everybody the same questions. I'd wager that just about everybody who comes to Escondido stops at your shop sooner or later to buy ammunition. Who, in your opinion, is the strangest man in Escondido?"

Burkett meditated a few moments, then pointed his finger at Duane. "You."

* * *

Duane found the richest woman in town seated behind her desk, adding a column of numbers. She looked up as he dropped into the chair before her.

"You look like you slept in your clothes," she said.

"Where do you keep your coal oil?"

"In the storeroom."

"Do you make notations of what comes in and goes out?"

She picked up a ledger. "What the hell d'ya think I do behind this desk all day?"

"I'm trying to find out where the coal oil came from that burned down my stable. Maybe somebody stole some from you."

"I'm the only one with a key to the storeroom, and nobody's broke down the door as far as I know. If you want to look, foller me."

She led him down the hall and unlocked a thick wooden door. Inside were canned goods, bags of beans, barrels of whisky, and a side of beef hanging from the rafters. In a far corner sat five barrels of coal oil. Maggie compared them to the ledger. "Nothing's gone from what I can see."

"How does coal oil come to this town?"

"A bullwhacker brings it once a month with his shipment of supplies to the general store, and the rest of us buy what we need. If yer a-gonna account fer every barrel of oil in Escondido, you've got quite a job. It might be easier to just git out of town."

The Silver Spur Saloon had a few customers that mid-afternoon, and a big black dog gnawed a bone in the corner. The bartender looked at Duane sleepily as Duane knocked on the office door, pushed it open, and found Sanchez sitting behind his desk, reading a Spanish newspaper and drinking whisky out of a coffee cup.

"Sorry your stable was burned down last night," Sanchez said sadly. "What a terrible thing to hoppen, no?"

"Would've been worse if I didn't wake up in time, and by the way, where were you about two in the morning?"

"It is my regret to tell you that I slept alone. Perhaps I am not the great lover that you think."

"Where do you keep your coal oil."

"In back of the saloon."

"Take me there, please."

"Why?"

Duane pointed to his tin badge.

Sanchez groaned as he took a ring of keys from a drawer in his desk. "We have hire you to protect us, but who will protect us from *you?*" He led Duane down the dark passageway that smelled like stale perfume, ancient smoke, and dirty clothing. In the backyard, Sanchez inserted a key into the lock of the storage room. It contained three barrels of oil standing side by side like sentinels. "When's the last time you looked in here, Sanchez?"

"Who the hell knows?"

"Would you know if one of your kegs was missing?"

"I have better things to do than count kegs of oil," Sanchez replied haughtily.

"Like what?"

"You have made me very tired, Señor. I am going to sleep."

"Wait a minute. Isn't this the spot where Belle Watkins was killed?"

Sanchez appeared hurt. "How can you mention such a thing? You know it pains me to think of my poor dead girls."

"Who has keys to the back door?"

"Me."

"What about your bartender?"

"When he has need, I give them to him. The rest of the time they are on my belt."

The more questions Duane asked, the more imponderable the riddle became. I can talk to every person in town, and still be right back where I started. But the damned killer has to make an error sooner or later, and I'll be ready when he does.

Later in the afternoon, after checking oil in a variety of business establishments and homes, Duane found himself standing in front of Apocalypse Church. He found the rectory and knocked on the door. It was opened by the preacher's wife, whose eyes widened at the sight of him.

"Didn't mean to disturb you, ma'am, but I was wondering where you keep your oil."

"In the shed back there." She pointed, and her finger quivered slightly.

"Could I have a look?"

"I'll get the key."

She plucked the ring off a peg near the door, then swung it back and forth in her hand awkwardly as she led Duane across the backyard. Duane thought there was something peculiar about her, or maybe she was slightly daffy, like some of the brothers and priests back at the monastery in the clouds.

She unlocked the door and beckoned for him to enter. Crates and boxes were stacked to the rafters, but in one corner sat a keg of oil. "There it is," she said, a quaver in her voice as the wind slammed shut the door behind them. They were alone in the small enclosed space.

"Did you have two barrels yesterday?" he asked.

"What a strange question," she replied.

"The person who started the fire last night used a keg of oil, and I'm trying to figure out where he got it."

"Not here," she replied. Then a curious expression came over her face. "I just remembered something. I don't know if it's significant, but I saw somebody last night just before the fire. He was headed in the direction of the stable, carrying a big object in his arms, come to think of it."

It was Duane's first lead all day, and he paused to savor its possibilities. "Where were you when you saw him?"

"In my bedroom facing the backyard. I couldn't sleep, and happened to be looking out the window. I thought my eyes were playing tricks, and maybe they were. It's hard to know at night."

Duane imagined the darkened backyard. A moving shadow could be a cloud passing the moon, or a man with a keg of oil in his arms. Again, the more information he gathered, the more intractable the solution became. He became aware of heavy breathing nearby. "Are you all right, Mrs. Berclair?"

"Not feeling well," replied she.

She raised her hand to her head, her eyes went white, and she fainted dead away at his feet. Duane stared at her for a few moments, then dropped to his knees and pressed his ear against her breast. She moaned softly.

"I think you need fresh air," he said.

He thrust his arms underneath her, lifted her, and was about to head for the door, when it was flung open violently. Parson Berclair stood in front of them, eyes bulging out of his head. "What're you doing with my wife!" he demanded.

"She fainted. Don't ask me why."

Duane carried her limp body across the yard into the rectory, as the parson fumed behind him. Duane laid her down on the sofa. Her husband tried to spill a few drops of brandy down her throat, but instead it dribbled over her chin. "She's coming around," said the parson.

She fluttered her lashes and sighed, and her eyes opened. "I'm all right now."

"She's been feeling poorly lately," Parson Berclair explained. "Women problems, I suppose. By the way, what were you doing in the shed with my wife?"

"I was trying to find out if any oil was stolen, because the fire at the stable was set with oil. Where were you last night at two o'clock in the morning, Reverend?"

"In bed of course."

Duane turned toward the parson's wife. "Is that so, ma'am?"

Her faced turned red, and her eyes darted about excitedly. "My husband and I sleep in separate bedrooms," she said.

Duane gazed at her in surprise, as the truth of their marriage sank in. Then he turned toward the preacher. "You can't prove your whereabouts at two o'clock this morning, in other words."

"Why should I have to?"

"You don't, but I'm trying to solve a certain problem, and I'd appreciate your help. Perhaps it's best if I left you alone for a while and came back later."

Duane careened toward the door and was outside before they could say anything. It was the strangest thing he'd ever heard: married people in different beds. What's the point of getting married? he wondered. I guess their souls are on a higher plane than mine.

He continued asking questions door to door for the rest of the afternoon, and made a mental note of every keg of oil in town. He learned the demoralizing truth that most men in Escondido were bachelors who slept alone and couldn't prove their whereabouts in the wee hours of the morning.

At dusk, he arrived at the undertaker's house. Although he had no proof, something in his gut told him that this was his man, especially since the undertaker's house was in the part of town where Patricia Berclair had seen the figure passing in the night.

Snodgras opened his front door and was attired in his customary black suit. "I figured you'd get here sooner or later, Sheriff. You want to see my oil keg? Right this way."

He opened a door to the storeroom in back of his house. A keg sat against the far wall, along with bottles and jars of chemicals. Duane lifted the keg and estimated that it was half full.

"If you listen close," the undertaker said tauntingly, "maybe the keg'll tell you who set fire to your stable last night."

"Where were you at two o'clock this morning?"

"Home asleep."

"Alone?"

"You're getting to be a pain in the ass

around here, boy. This was a decent town before you showed up. We had our occasional murder, but we didn't have a sheriff asking personal questions. Maybe we should abolish the office altogether. I liked it better the old way."

"I'm still the legally constituted sheriff," Duane said, "and let me tell you something. Last night, before the fire was set, a reliable witness saw somebody on the way to my stable from this part of town. He was carrying a keg of oil, and I'm not saying it was you, but you'd better hope he's not you."

Snodgras preferred to treat the threat lightly. He scratched his bald head, and said with a grin, "If you shoot me, since I'm the only undertaker in town, I wonder who'll bury me?"

"Me," replied the Pecos Kid.

Duane sat in the Last Chance Saloon, slicing a thick steak charred on the outside but red in the middle. I have no proof that the undertaker's done anything illegal. And maybe I'm prejudiced because of his grisly profession. What if I'm threatening an innocent man?

A Mexican bandito stomped down the aisle, wearing a huge white sombrero, drooping mustaches, and tight black pants with wide flaring cuffs and silver conchos sewn down the seams. He stopped in front of Duane and said, "Mind if I sit down, Señor Sheriff?"

Duane nodded. The bandito sat, looked around casually, then leaned toward Duane and said, "My horse is outside, Señor Sheriff. He is saddled and I am ready to leave Escondido. I was praying to Santa Maria for good luck on my journey, when she asked me to tell you something that happen to me last night."

The bandito glanced about again, to make sure no one was drawing a bead on him. "I was on my way to the Belmont Hotel when a man — I could not see his face — offered me two hundred dollars to kill the sheriff, you. I told him no, he ask why not, and I say because the sheriff is too fast for me."

The bandito shook his hand as if it was wet. "You are the fastest I have ever seen, Señor, and I am not so slow myself. Perhaps you have heard of me — they call me El Pancho. Let me give you a leetle advice from one who wishes you no harm. Get out of town. Why? Look here." El Pancho opened his shirt and showed a purple scar at the top of his left pectoral muscle. He grasped Duane's hand, brought it to him, and pressed it against the scar. "Can you feel it?"

Beneath the callused surface, Duane's fingertips discerned a jagged lump of lead.

"Sometime, when it rains, it hurts like hell," said El Pancho. "The doctors tell me it is poisoning my blood, but they do not cut it out because it is near an artery. It could have been avoided if I was not drunk as a pig in a certain cantina in San Pedro." El Pancho smiled. "Maybe Santa Maria is talking to me, or maybe I am just one crazy hombre, no?" El Pancho buttoned his shirt, then winked. "Watch your back, amigo. And keep your head down."

El Pancho stalked toward the door, his Mexican spurs clanging, his big sombrero pulled over his ears, a legendary Mexican gunfighter on his way toward his next opportunity.

Patricia Berclair kneeled in the front pew of the church, praying for divine assistance. Her experience in the shed with Duane Braddock had unnerved her mind. They'd been alone, he'd touched her arm, and she'd been on the verge of ripping his clothes off! Only a thin tissue of God-fearing devotion had held her back. She would have disgraced herself, for what?

There was something about him that made her want to jump out of her clothes and dive atop him. The thought of lying naked in bed with him caused her to sob in heartfelt anguish. Duane Braddock had forced her to comprehend that her marriage was a sham, she really didn't love her husband, and she desperately needed a real man before she died of shrunken unfulfilled longing.

"Give me strength, Lord," she whispered. "I am a weak vessel beset with temptation." She thought of Duane Braddock's broad shoulders, well-formed lips, and aquiline nose. He had eyes that she could gaze at until the end of time. Lethal, beautiful, and in need of a woman's love, he'd stood only inches away. She imagined the taut muscles of his body pressing against her. Her head swam as she took a deep breath and tried to regain her equilibrium.

"Are you all right, Patricia?"

Her heart nearly stopped with fright and dismay. Her husband, Reverend Herbert Berclair, stood at the end of the pew. She became aware of her tear-streaked cheeks. "I'm fine," she said.

"Doesn't appear that way to me, my

dear. Who knows you better than I myself? I think we'd better talk about it."

He led her to the parlor and prepared tea. Small windows admitted narrow shafts of bright sunlight, but the room was mostly dark and lugubrious. "Don't believe I've ever seen you so distraught," he said, as he carried the teapot toward her. "Are you sick?"

She tried to smile. "I'm perfectly fine. Don't worry about me."

"Of course I worry about you! Where would I be without your help, encouragement, and inspiration? My dear, you are the foundation of my very life itself. How can I soothe your unhappiness? Have I said anything wrong?"

She looked him over. He was a good man, but unfortunately excited no great passion in her. "It's not you, Herbert. I haven't been feeling well lately. Perhaps it's the weather."

"You're accustomed to the finer things, but this is where God needs us. Did Duane Braddock say something improper when you were alone in the shed?"

"What makes you think that?"

"It was as if I'd caught you in the act of adultery with him. What happened?"

"Perhaps I'm coming down with the catarrh."

He touched the back of his hand to her forehead. "You don't have a fever. I've been living with you four years, and know you as I know myself. I wish you'd tell me what's bothering you."

She wanted to unburden herself, but feared unexpected consequences. "There's nothing to tell."

"Sometimes I think I don't know you at all. Next thing you'll be having a squalid romance with poor, lost Duane Braddock."

"How can you say such a thing, or even *think* it?"

"Well," he said, scratching his nose, "I suppose a woman might find the lad possessed of a certain roughshod appeal. You don't view him that way, do you?"

"He's just a boy, Herbert. You're being absurd."

"He's not *that* much younger than you." Reverend Berclair narrowed his eyes and furrowed his brow. "I'm not the fool that you think, Patricia. Just because I spend my time in the Lord's ministry, it doesn't mean I'm an idiot. I think you have a girlish crush on Duane Braddock, but you're not honest enough to admit it to the man who loves you most!"

At that tense matrimonial moment, a dam cracked within Patricia Berclair's soul, and all the crippled passion of a thwarted life came ripping out of her throat. "Who needs this kind of love!"

Her scream reverberated off the fireplace, the candlestick, and the bare cottonwood cross nailed to the wall. He stared at her in consternation, as the truth sank through him. *I'm not really her husband,* he said to himself, as his face drained of color.

She regretted the words the moment they rolled off her tongue, but a stronger person dwelling within her had rendered the verdict. Reverend Herbert Berclair realized that a new woman stood before him, with unfamiliar fire in her eyes. At that moment, the parson believed that he'd lost her.

His throat clogged, his eyes widened with panic, and he threw a punch at the wall. The building shook, his hand shrieked in pain, then he realized that clergymen weren't supposed to be violent. Summoning his willpower, he modulated his voice and said: "Forgive me for my display of bad manners, dear Patricia. I guess I expected too much of you."

She realized that she'd gone too far, and now the time had come to smooth everything over. "I'm sorry too, but I have a normal woman's feelings, I'm afraid."

"Are you going to him?"

"I could never throw myself at a man," she said adamantly. "Moreover, I'd never disgrace you or myself. Besides, if I ever confessed my feelings to the poor lad, he'd ride out of town the next instant. He's not sophisticated in the least, and in many ways, is probably more religious than the both of us put together."

Reverend Berclair smiled knowingly. "Love is blind, but let's attempt to keep our feet on the ground, shall we? He's killed seven men since arriving in Escondido, and some say he's the most dangerous gunfighter in this part of Texas."

"But he's so frightened, Herbert. You can see it in his eyes, and he's not imagining things. Somebody truly is trying to kill him."

"Sometimes I wish he'd succeed," the pastor said gloomily.

He didn't realize it, but his jealousy was pleasing her. They stood facing each other in the parlor, as if seeing each other for the first time. Then he cleared his throat. "I have a late Bible class, and hope you'll excuse me."

She waited until he was gone, then reclined on the sofa and stared at the ceiling. Is my marriage over? she wondered. The new Patricia Berclair terrified her, and appeared capable of anything.

"I've been getting complaints about you," Maggie said.

She was seated behind her desk, puffing a panatella, her flaming red hair tied with a maroon ribbon. Duane sprawled on the chair in front of her, his hat slanted low over his eyes. "Is it the undertaker?"

"Him and a few others. They say yer a-bangin' in their houses without a warrant, a-makin' insultin' remarks, a-gittin' narsty."

"I'm trying to find out who set fire to my barn. Am I supposed to forget about it?"

"The main thing is keep the people happy, Duane. That's what yer job's all about, remember?"

"But somebody's trying to kill me!"

"That's no cause to snoop around everybody's house and act like yer a-gonna shoot 'em. Leave the people alone, especially the undertaker. A town like this needs an undertaker."

"What do you know about him?"

"Not a hell of a lot. To tell you the truth, he scares the shit out of me."

"Did you ever hear him talk about the Pecos?"

She shook her head.

"Does he sleep with any of the girls here at the Last Chance Saloon?"

"They won't go near 'im."

"Who's his best friend?"

"Don't think he's got one. He's like Death a-walkin' around on two legs."

"What about the preacher? There's something strange about him."

"A woman in my line don't talk to preachers, but his wife's said hello in the street a few times. You don't think the preacher's a-tryin' to kill you!"

"Maybe."

Maggie didn't bat an eyelash. "I don't blame you, because I don't trust anybody in this town. I've told you afore and I'll tell you agin: If somebody wanted to kill me, I'd hop on old Paint and ride away. I'm not proud — hell no. If yer a-worrying 'bout Alice Markham, I'll give her a job here as my clerk. I've been a-thinkin' lately that I shouldn't be a-doin' all this dumb paperwork anyways. I should be a-buyin' and a-sellin' real estate, and maybe it's time Escondido had a real honest-to-goodness bank."

"If I hop on old Paint, who'll be the sheriff?"

"I'll hire somebody, and a few deputies

too. They won't be as good as you, but if you keep botherin' the townspeople, they'll fire you anyways."

Patricia Berclair was kneading dough in the kitchen when her husband appeared in the doorway. "I've got to speak with you," he said.

He was returning from Bible class, and this was their first encounter since the great revelation. She wondered if he'd pull a gun and shoot her, or drop to his knees and beg forgiveness for his emotional outburst. She'd never seen him so agitated. "Are you all right?" she asked, as she reached for the rolling pin.

He paced nervously back and forth behind the stove, hands clasped behind his back. "You and I have trained ourselves to search for deeper meanings in life, Patricia. The way I see it, we're the only ministers in town, and the devil is trying to drive a wedge between us. Have you ever stopped to think that Duane Braddock might be an agent of Satan?"

She smiled faintly. "Are you trying to make a joke, Herbert?"

"We know that the devil is constantly trying to beguile us, and isn't it strange how Duane Braddock dresses in *black* most of the time. There's something cunning in his eyes — haven't you noticed? Perhaps he's hiding a pair of horns beneath his cowboy hat."

Patricia stopped kneading the dough. She wiped her hands on a towel, looked out the window, and realized, for the first time, that her husband might be insane. "Are you speaking symbolically, Herbert, or do you really think he has two horns?"

"Not in actuality, because the devil is much more subtle than that. Isn't it interesting how he's working on your mind? I'd imagine that a holy woman like you would pose quite a challenge to him."

"Pretty soon you'll be seeing little red devils underneath your bed, my dear. How do you know *I'm* not Satan's daughter?"

"I've seen your many good works, but the Evil One has come to you today, and you must resist him with all your heart. Otherwise you'll burn forever in the fires of hell."

"You're becoming quite insulting. If you don't mind, I'd like to be alone."

He retreated on his pegleg to his office and sat at his desk, drumming his fingers on the blotter, looking out the window. Five gaily tasseled hobgoblins danced merrily hand in hand amid the outbuildings, wearing funny hats. Ever since Vicksburg, Herbert Berclair had been seeing visions and hearing strange tunes in his head. Am I just another religious crackpot? he wondered.

The sight of Patricia in the shed with Duane Braddock had disorganized him deeply, for he considered her the fountain of his inspiration. Sometimes he thought himself cruel to have married her, but everything had been fine before Duane Braddock came along. The parson wanted to hate his rival, but Braddock was too young, naive, and polite to be despicable. Wouldn't the devil use such a guise, the better to cloud our minds? Reverend Berclair was afraid that Patricia would run off with Duane Braddock, despite her protestations. The parson loved his wife in a strange, antiseptic way, and believed that she cared for him similarly.

But she hadn't been wounded at Vicksburg like he. God had rendered him incapable of carnal love, while she was whole, brimming with life, and primed for adultery. A terrible thought surfaced in a deep cranny of his mind. I couldn't be a real husband, but married her anyway, taking advantage of her religiosity, forcing her to sin through my own craven selfishness. Perhaps *I'm* the agent of the devil, not Duane Braddock.

He opened the drawer of his desk, pulled out his old Colt Army revolver, drew back the hammer, and aimed the barrel at his ear. His finger tightened around the trigger, the Colt quivered in the air for several seconds, and then his finger relaxed. He eased back the hammer, returned the Colt to its position of meditation next to the pens, and covered his face with his hands.

I am the Evil One.

"What do you want?" asked Alice Markham through the crack in her door.

"I've got something to tell you," said Duane. "Open up."

"I'm busy studying."

"It'll only take a minute."

She opened the door. The desk was covered with books, and the small room reminded Duane of a monk's cell.

"I've got good news," he announced. "You're going to be Maggie's new clerk."

He expected a smile, a word of gratitude, and possibly a kiss on the cheek, but instead she set her stubborn jaw.

"Aren't you glad?" he asked.

She placed her hands on her hips.

"You're the one who's glad. So you're finally getting rid of me. I know how much you hate me — don't think I don't."

Duane was hurt by her remarks. "I don't hate you at all, and in fact, I've always liked you."

She squinched her face like a hurt little child. "You think I'm trash because you caught me with a certain somebody, isn't that right, Mister Pecos Kid? I know what's in yer mind. Since that happened, you barely talked to me."

He shook his head in despair. "Somebody's trying to kill me, but everybody thinks it's nothing for me to worry about. You're the only person in town that I can trust, because you were with me when the stable was set afire. But you don't want to be my friend because once I mentioned somebody's name by mistake."

"You made me feel cheap."

"I didn't do it on purpose."

"You're just making excuses. The truth is you don't think I'm good enough for you."

I could argue with her till the end of time, and still not change her mind, he said to himself. He threw up his hands and headed for the door. Women are nothing but trouble, he told himself, as he made his way down the corridor.

Carpenters hammered a new corral on the site of his former stable, and retrieved horses were hobbled and waiting patiently for their new home. Unfortunately, no one had seen hide nor hair of Steve. I guess we weren't that close, Duane lamented. I'll have to try harder with my next horse.

He no longer had obligations in Escondido, and the time had come to hit the trail. But first he had to refit for the ride to the Pecos, and he had to buy the new horse. Maggie doesn't really need a clerk, he suspected, but she hired Alice because that's what I wanted. Maggie O'Day is the best friend I've got in this town.

Duane returned to his office and made a list of things to do. His remaining wealth totaled approximately three hundred dollars, and the town owed him a month's wages. That ought to get me to the Pecos with plenty of room to maneuver.

There was a knock on the door, then Reverend Herbert Berclair walked numbly into the office. "I've got to talk with you," he said in a disembodied voice.

"Have a seat, Reverend. What's on your mind?"

The pastor placed his fists on Duane's

desk, leaned forward, and peered into Duane's eyes. "Have you been making improper advances to my wife?"

Duane nearly fell off the chair. No man had ever said such a thing to him before. "What makes you think that, Reverend?"

"Because she's madly and hopelessly in love with you, you fool." The parson sighed and went slack on the chair.

Duane vaguely remembered the odd behavior of Mrs. Berclair when he was alone with her in the shed. What is it about me that makes people think I'm a low-down skunk? "Surely you know that your wife would never do such a thing, Reverend Berclair."

"Animal lust has ruined many a good man and woman," the reverend replied. "The devil comes in infinite disguises, as I'm sure you know. I thought of killing you, Mister Sheriff, but you're not guilty either. I thought of killing myself, but the scriptures tell us that suicide is evil. So are false promises and ill-gotten gains. Do you know what I'm saying, Sheriff Braddock?"

"Not in the least," Duane replied.

"I have committed a terrible crime against God and my beloved wife, and you must punish me. Beneath my coat, I have my old Army Colt. I'm going to draw it and shoot you for the estrangement of my wife's affections. You will be obliged to defend yourself, and all my worries will be over."

The pastor drew the Colt, and Duane couldn't jump over the desk in time. All he could do was haul iron, but he couldn't shoot the only man in Escondido who'd gone to divinity school. Both men aimed the creations of Colonel Colt at each other and waited for something to happen.

"Go ahead," goaded Reverend Berclair, an uncertain smile on his face. "Shoot me."

"I can't kill an innocent man."

"Try."

"Impossible, and you're not a murderer either. Put away the gun and try to be reasonable. You're not setting a good example for your flock."

"I can't kill you, and can't kill myself either," the preacher moaned. His Colt hung down his side as he shuffled unhappily out of the sheriff's office. Citizens and bystanders gazed at their parson curiously as he moved jerkily along the planked sidewalk, a sorrowful expression in his half-closed eyes.

CHAPTER 9

The horse shortage continued, with prices for available mounts doubling and tripling. Then word was received that fresh horses would be offered for sale by local ranches at the end of the month. Duane waited for the animals to arrive, made plans, and gathered equipment.

He visited the gunsmith and negotiated a slightly used no-frills .44 caliber Winchester Model 1866 with brass receiver and 24-inch barrel for accuracy at long distances. Then he crossed to the general store and purchased sturdy black leather saddlebags, an extra shirt, a blanket, and a poncho. He carried his belongings to the desert and stashed them in a cave.

He sat cross-legged in gullies for hours, shaded by cottonwood trees, and contemplated the long, harsh, hazardous journey before him. His body had become soft due to excessive food and drink during his aimless nights in Escondido, so he placed himself on a regimen of running up and down mountains for long periods each day, as when he'd lived among the Apaches.

Escondido wasn't a total loss, because now at last he knew who his mother was. *Kathleen O'Shea.* He'd wanted to question Dolores Goines further, but didn't dare endanger her life. I'll find out everything I need to know in the Pecos country, he promised himself.

He didn't know what form his vengeance would take, and possibly Sam Archer wasn't even alive anymore. No matter what I do, it won't bring my father and mother back. The former acolyte had killed previously only in self-defense, and couldn't imagine holding a gun calmly to a man's head, then pulling the trigger. It was opposite everything he'd been taught by learned priests and brothers. I'll worry about it when I've got Sam Archer cornered, he thought.

He suspected that the killer had left Escondido after the fire, since no further attempts had been made on his life. Meanwhile, freighters arrived from the north with loads of lumber, and the reconstruction of the stable began. Duane sat on a bench across the street and smoked one cigarette after another as he watched the building materialize before his very eyes. Outlaws and wastrels worked as carpenters, and Duane learned that they weren't completely worthless after all. Occasionally Maggie would step out of the Last Chance Saloon, issue a stream of curse-laden directives, and return to her smoky gloomy tavern.

Duane spent most of his time on the desert traveling from spot to spot so no one could anticipate his position. Sometimes he had the uncomfortable sensation that someone was stalking him, but he moved in a zigzag fashion, maintaining a low silhouette.

The only thing standing between him and old man Archer was a horse. Occasionally he thought of stealing one but didn't want to add horse thievery to his other low crimes and misdemeanors. At night he sat in the hills and gazed at the twinkling lights of Escondido in the distance, occasionally hearing the flat notes of the off-key pianist in the Last Chance Saloon. The only person he missed was Maggie, and he resolved to have a long talk with her before leaving for the Pecos country.

He slept in a cave like a coyote. The

shrouded ghosts of Amos Twilby, the blacksmith, Hazel Sanders, and Marty Schlack paraded through his dreams, their mournful dirges disturbing his rest, as their poor lost souls cried for vengeance.

CHAPTER 10

At the end of the month, horses arrived for sale in Escondido, accompanied by wild-eyed cowboys, cigar-chomping ranchers, and sharp-eyed traders. Customers gathered from miles around to attend the auspicious sale, colored ribbons hung between buildings, and the piano player from the Last Chance Saloon pounded his keys on a platform constructed in the street before that great emporium of sin.

The horse fair was a gala event in the humdrum life of Escondido, and the leading performers were the horses themselves, from proud sleek prancing stallions to worn-out old nags a few strides ahead of the glue factory.

The merchandise was herded into the corral, as hawkers extolled the virtues of their animals, while ignoring their faults, such as no teeth, spavined limbs, and the desire to stomp a man to death.

Duane was spotted in the crowd at mid-morning, and folks gawked at him respectfully as he made his way toward the corral. Self-conscious, he tried to ignore unwanted attention as he appraised horses. He immediately spotted good prospects, but there'd be more of a selection later in the day, for horses still were arriving even as he leaned languidly on the top corral rail. He decided to have a talk with Maggie O'Day, then return later and make his choice.

He passed a lanky, clean-shaven deputy who scrutinized him anxiously, but Duane continued moving along. When they write the history of Escondido, Duane thought, maybe they'll remember I was first sheriff. He entered the Last Chance Saloon, nodded to Smiley the bartender, saluted Bradley Metzger, winked at the girls, and knocked on the door of Maggie's office. She bade him enter, and he sat on the chair in front of her.

She reached forward and touched his bearded chin. "You look like a mountain goat. Where've you been?"

"Nowhere, and after I buy a horse today, I'm gone. I'll miss you, Maggie. If it hadn't been for you, I'd probably be dead right now."

"You'll probably be dead anyway, if you go to the Pecos country. Why look fer lead, Duane? I was you, I'd lay back and find a rich old gal to take care of me."

Her eyes twinkled mischievously, but he pretended not to notice. "How's Alice doing?"

"She'll be awful hurt if you don't say goodbye to her. I think the gal's in love with you."

"It's a funny thing about love," Duane replied. "People say they love you, and a few days later they love somebody else."

"I cain't argue with that, but it ain't healthy to live alone."

"I can't see where it's hurt you."

"Just because you cain't see, don't mean it ain't thar."

"You've been good to me, Maggie. I'll never forget you."

"Oh yes you will," she replied in her throaty worldly voice.

He kissed her cheek, backed out of her office, and found Alice Markham in a smaller room down the hall, sitting at a desk covered with paper, adding up numbers. She looked at Duane, dropped her pen, recovered it, and fingered it nervously.

"I'll be leaving sometime today, Alice. I've come to say goodbye."

A teardrop appeared in her left eye which she wiped away hastily. "Good riddance," she replied.

"There's something I've got to do, but I'll come back someday."

"Horseshit," she replied.

"A lady shouldn't cuss." He pecked her cheek, then smiled warmly, but she looked like a disappointed petulant child. He backed out the door and headed for the stable. It pained him to be desired by someone he couldn't love back. Despite the passage of time, for reasons he couldn't fully articulate, his heart still belonged to Miss Vanessa Fontaine, worst bitch of them all. One part of him hoped he'd never see her again, and the other prayed she'd arrive on the next stagecoach.

The new stable had been constructed similarly to the previous one, with horses lined in stalls along unpainted walls. The office was located in the same spot, and Duane found Sam Goines behind the desk.

"Thought I'd say goodbye," Duane told him, holding out his hand. He looked around, to make sure no one was within earshot. "Thank your mother for me."

Sam Goines shook his hand. "Good luck, boss. Thanks for bein' a gentleman about that little thang that happened in the loft."

"Don't know what you're talking about," Duane replied. He noticed the box of old books in the corner. "Mind if I take something to read along with me?"

"The books belong to you, boss."

Duane found the volume he was seeking atop the pile: *The Prince* by Niccolo Machiavelli.

He opened it, and his studious eyes fell on these words:

> *The Prince should read history and reflect upon the deeds of great men, studying how they conducted themselves in war, examining the causes of their victories and defeats, and learning to emulate the former, while avoiding the latter.*

Again it seemed as if the old courtier were talking directly to him. Duane tucked the book into his belt and strolled out of the stable. More horses had been brought to the corral while he'd been making the rounds, and a larger selection was now offered, as he'd anticipated. He rambled closer, rested his elbows on the top corral rail, and evaluated the horseflesh for sale.

His brief cowboy experience had taught

him that the most important quality in a horse was long-range endurance. Good lines didn't necessarily indicate quality, and a healthy-appearing horse might die suddenly of a strange illness, while a well-behaved mount often was the worst choice of all. Buying a horse was mysterious business, and Duane tended to follow his gut instincts. He liked a certain wildness in the horse's eyes, because wildness was where endurance came from.

After several minutes of careful observation, he decided that the best-looking horse in the corral was a big russet stallion with a shiny black mane, solid lines, and skittish dancing. Duane climbed over the animal, pointed at the stallion's nose, and said: "Who belongs to this horse!"

"I do!"

A white-whiskered old man headed toward Duane, his hand extended, with a confirmed swindler's gap-toothed grin. "My name's Hodge, and this here's Nestor. You got good taste in horses — I can see that. Why don't you take 'im fer a ride?"

"What do you want for him?"

"A hundred dollars."

"No horse is worth a hundred dollars."

"He's not for everybody, that's fer sure. But if you've got the money, you can't buy a better horse in Texas."

"If he's so good, how come you're selling him?"

"It's my bizness to sell horses, but I ain't innerested in nags. I caters to the connoisseur, if you gits what I mean." The old man winked.

Duane examined Nestor's strong white teeth, and noticed his clear bright eyes.

"Only three years old," the horse trader said. "This animal will give years of good solid service if you take care of him."

"Where'd he come from?"

The old horse trader of the plains wrinkled his nose. "It ain't polite to ask a man where his horse came from, but 'twixt you and me, he was confiscated by the cavalry from Apaches." The horse trader lowered his voice. "I bought him on a special consignment from a friend of mines in the Army."

Nestor didn't wear the Fourth Cavalry brand, and evidently had been sold with no official papers, while the thieving soldiers pocketed the proceeds. The trader marketed his wares in outlying border towns to well-heeled outlaws who wouldn't ask questions.

The trader bridled and saddled Nestor, while Nestor glanced at Duane warily out the corner of his eye. Nestor had been born on a ranch, raised by cowboys, stolen by Apaches, recovered by bluecoats after a series of running gun battles, and now was being sold again. All the faithful animal could do was try to make a good impression. Hodge led Nestor to the gate, and a cowboy opened it. Then Hodge handed the reins to Duane. "He's all your'n, but if you cripple 'im, you pay for 'im."

The ex-sheriff adjusted the stirrups, then climbed into the saddle. Nestor danced to the side as Duane gripped the reins. He aimed Nestor toward the open desert, touched his spurs to the animal's flanks, and said: "Show me what you've got."

Nestor walked out of town, glad to be free from the corral, but not especially pleased by the weight on his back. He cleared the outbuildings and broke into a lope, to loosen his limbs and get the old lungs pumping.

Duane thought the horse felt like steel springs beneath the saddle. Then Nestor gathered speed, working himself to a full gallop, as Duane accelerated past cactus and juniper, wind whistling around his silver concho hatband. Nestor stretched his long legs forward and put on a burst of speed, overjoyed to be on open land. He turned his head to the side to let a long stream of saliva escape his lips, then found an old wagon trail, turned onto it, and raced for the mountains in the distance.

Duane crouched low in the saddle, as wind whipped his black shirt and jeans. It felt as if Nestor could keep galloping eternally. What a horse! Duane thought exultantly. If a posse were following me right now, what's a hundred dollars against the hangman's noose?

Duane paid the dealer, put Nestor in the stable, and spent the rest of the afternoon gathering final supplies. He intended to depart after sundown, travel at night, and sleep during the day. Within a month, he'd be at the banks of the Pecos.

When his chores were completed, he strolled into the Apocalypse Church, found an empty pew, dropped to his knees, and clasped his hands together. He intended to pray for safe passage, but his mind went blank, unlike in his monastic days when he fell into religious ecstasies almost at will. I've become a worldly man, and I carry Machiavelli instead of the Bible. He pulled out the black leather-bound book, cracked it open, and read: "*Whoever organizes a state and makes its laws must assume that all men are wicked, and will behave wickedly at every opportunity.*"

This hombre really makes sense, Duane thought. First chance I get, I'm going to read this all the way through. "*The mob is always impressed by appearances, and the world is composed of the mob.*"

"I hope you're not planning to leave without saying goodbye, Mister Braddock."

Duane saw the preacher's wife, Patricia Berclair, standing with a smile at the end of the pew. "How inspiring to see you reading your Bible when everybody else is getting drunk and boisterous."

Duane raised himself from the pew and stood only inches away, hiding the title of the book. Her bosom heaved. She balled her fists and closed her eyes.

"Are you all right?" he asked.

"Of course I'm all right." She smiled, and opened her lids. "Sometimes the desert air makes me dizzy."

He wondered how desert air could make her swoon in a church with small windows, but grinned politely. "It's been nice knowing you," he said. He became aware of a shadow in the doorway leading back to the sacristy. "Is the reverend about?"

"He's with his Bible class."

"Please say goodbye to him for me. God bless you, Mrs. Berclair." He took her hands in his, kissed her fingertips, then turned abruptly and walked out of the church.

She watched him go, her fingertips tingling with pleasure. She closed her eyes, took a deep breath, and whispered, "Thank you, Jesus." Then she turned toward the doorway, noticing for the first time the shadow lingering there. Frightened, she turned to run, when the voice of her husband came to her ears.

"Thank you," he said, emerging from the darkness, his wide pastoral hat covering his eyes.

He wore a cloak and carried something underneath it, like a pistol or knife. "For what?" she asked cautiously.

"I thought you would leave with him," he replied.

She looked at the bulge beneath his garments. "Are you planning to kill me, Herbert?"

He opened the folds and revealed his Bible. "I couldn't possibly harm you more than I have already," he said earnestly, holding the scriptures in the air. "I was the most selfish man in the world when I asked you to be my wife, since . . . I couldn't be your husband in reality. If you went with Braddock, you'd be perfectly justified, but I don't think I could've held up knowing that you were making love with him every night."

"You're being silly," she replied with a little laugh. "Why would he want an old lady like me when he can have any woman in town?"

"I've always thought you were the most beautiful woman in the world, Patricia. I know that he was taken by your charm."

"Really, Herbert. What would I do with the Pecos Kid? Lawmen all over Texas are looking for him, and did you expect *me*, of all people, to go on the dodge? By the way, why aren't you in your Bible class?"

"I sent the students home so that I could spy on you. I honestly thought you'd throw yourself at his feet. How little I know you."

"You should call your students back, because we don't want them to miss the Lord's holy instruction, or do we?"

His eyes filled with tears and he shook with a sob. He dropped to his knees before her, bowed his head, and said, "Forgive me, for I have doubted you. Forgive me, for I thought I was superior to you. Forgive me for thinking that God loved me more than he loved you. And forgive me most of all for being the most ridiculous, disgusting, and hideous fool in Escondido."

She looked at him for a long time, her chin perched in her fingertips, and then replied thoughtfully, "I think I like you better this way."

Duane sauntered toward the saloon district, unaware that he'd just helped improve a marriage. A chasm yawned in his stomach, and he thought he'd have one last good meal at the Last Chance Saloon before hitting the trail.

A little voice told him to pass the Last Chance by, but prudence offended his fundamentally rebellious nature. He pushed open the swinging doors of the drinking establishment, where outlaws from two nations were spread wall to wall, flaring sombreros beside wide-brimmed cowboy hats, with a derby or stovepipe hat tossed in for good measure. Bradley Metzger welcomed Duane like a lost cousin, slapped him on the shoulder, led him to a table in back, and forced its occupants to leave. "You can have this one, Sheriff," he said. "I'll send a waitress right over."

Duane gazed at Bradley Metzger's receding back. Once, long ago, they'd punched each other in their faces, and now were almost friends. It's enough to make you believe in God, Duane said to himself.

A Mexican waitress with flashing eyes brought him a glass of whisky. "On the house," she said. "My name is Conchita. Can I get you something to eat, Señor Pecos Kid?"

"Steak with all the trimmings, and an extra helping of collard greens, if you've got 'em."

She launched herself toward the chop counter, as Duane sipped whisky, his tension disintegrating in alcoholic fumes. He felt that part of his life was ending, with the next installment about to begin. I'll go to Edgewood first and visit my mother's grave. Maybe I'll find an old gal friend of my mother's who can tell me more about her, and who knows, a daguerreotype of Miss Kathleen O'Shea might be lying around.

Former deputy Derek Wright appeared in the aisle, his old Confederate cavalry hat tilted at a rakish angle. "Heard you're leaving town. Mind if I sit down?" Without waiting for an answer, he dropped to the chair opposite Duane. "Headed for the Pecos?"

Duane nodded slowly. "That's right."

Wright sighed. "Let me tell you something, sonny jim. You don't have a chance against the Archers. They've got their own private army."

"What's it to you?"

Wright appeared uncomfortable. "Just a li'l worried about you, damn fool kid."

"Last time somebody was worried about me, I found out afterwards that he'd been a friend of my father's. How about you, Derek? Were you a friend of my father's?"

Wright drew his head back as if someone tweaked his nose. "What a crazy damned thing to say. I wasn't even in Texas back in those days. Hey kid, I never rode with the Polka Dots or any other outlaw gang."

Duane smiled sagely. "Are you afraid of the Archers too?"

Wright looked at Duane intently for a few moments. "The damnedest things come out of your mouth, but if I'm ever in the Pecos country, I'll put some posies on your grave." Wright leaned forward, placed his hand on Duane's shoulder, and squeezed. "Don't be a horse's ass, kid. Go to Mexico."

"Too hot in Mexico," Duane replied. "I'm off to the Pecos soon as I finish supper."

"I tried," uttered the ex-cavalry officer. "Good luck, Pecos."

Wright lurched toward the bar, and Duane wondered if the ex-officer had actually ridden with the Polka Dots in the old days. I know what kind of man Derek Wright is, and he'd go to the Pecos country too if he was me.

The saloon churned with horse traders and customers, while waitresses ran frantically about with trays of beer, whisky, and steak platters. Absentmindedly, to pass the time, Duane drew his Colt and checked the loads. A gun can be used for both good and evil, he realized. Vengeance is mine, sayeth the Lord God.

He holstered the gun as Conchita arrived with the steak platter. She placed it in front of him, winked flirtatiously, and asked, "Anything else?"

"Not at the moment," he replied.

"I'm new in town."

"I'm on my way out."

"You don't like it here?"

"I don't like it anywhere."

"That is because you do not like yourself, Señor Pecos Kid."

She walked away, tray balanced on fingertips. Duane picked up his knife and tested it against his thumb. It was razor sharp. Then he cut himself a thick chunk of meat. His mouth watered as he raised it to his mouth, when something moved in the corner of his eye. Duane's hand stopped in midair. A big shaggy dog with one blind eye was looking at him hopefully. "Okay feller," Duane said. "You get the bone first, and all the rest'll be for me, all right?"

Duane sawed the massive bone away and threw it into the air. The dog leapt high, snatched it in his yellow fangs, dropped to the floor at Duane's feet, and commenced to gnaw. "Now it's my turn," said the former sheriff.

A voluptuous figure approached down the aisle, as Duane was lifting the chunk of beef to his lips. "Do you always talk to animals?" asked Maggie, a wry grin on her face.

Duane set the fork down again. "I've had some of my best conversations with dogs and horses. They understand more than you think."

She peered at his steak. "It looks a little raw. I'll get you another."

"I like it that way. This is my last supper in Escondido, Maggie. When I finish here, I'm on my way north."

"You've put on quite a show, Duane," she said, "and I'll miss you. Say, why don't you take little Alice with you? I passed her office a while ago and heard her crying."

"Maybe she was crying for somebody you don't know about."

"She talks about you all the time. I guess she wasn't happy in the business, but it's better than starvin' to death. You might look down on old Maggie O'Day, but I give my gals three square meals, and what they make of the job is up to them."

"I don't look down on you, Maggie. You're the nicest lady I ever met."

She blushed, searched for a change of subject, and her eyes fell on the floor. "What's wrong with the dog?"

"He's eating the bone that I just throwed him."

"Looks like he's daid!"

The dog lay still with the bone in his mouth, his tongue hanging out, eyes glazed over. "Hey, are you all right?" Duane prodded the dog with his boot, but the animal didn't respond. A faint white foam smeared the animal's lips. Duane beheld the animal in astonishment. "I do believe you're right. Maybe he had a stroke."

"Pore ugly son of a bitch," said Maggie tenderly. "He's been livin' off other people's plates fer five years. I'll find somebody to carry 'im away."

She set off in search of Bradley Metzger, as Duane lifted the dead dog tenderly and laid him on the table. The ex-sheriff examined the animal carefully, and the only thing unusual was the white stuff on the dog's mouth. Duane lowered his nose to the steak and sniffed a faint medicinal odor. His brow wrinkled with disbelief. Did somebody just try to poison me?

He arose from the chair, checked the position of his Colt, then scanned the crowd for Conchita. He saw her at the far end of the saloon, taking a drink order from a group of blackjack players. Duane threaded among tables and touched his hand to her shoulder.

"Anything wrong, Señor Braddock?"

"Somebody just tried to poison me, I'm afraid."

She let out a coy laugh. "The food here is not *that* bad."

He took her hand and led her to the dog lying on the table with his white tongue hanging out. "I tossed him the bone, and he died straightaway. You didn't put any special sauce on, did you?"

"I carried the steak directly from the chop counter, Señor. There was no sauce on it that I could see."

"Come with me."

They headed for the chop counter, where a Negro cook in a bloodstained white apron was flipping steaks and frying potatoes laced with onions. The fragrance permeated the saloon, but Duane's appetite had vanished with the dog's expiration. He tucked his head underneath the counter, came up beside the cook, and examined the work area at close range.

"What's up, boss?" asked the Negro, beads of perspiration on his ebony forehead.

"What's your name?"

"George Goines."

"You didn't try to poison me just now, did you George?"

The cook appeared surprised. "Why'd I do that?"

"You tell me."

"This steak was butchered this morning. I only used a little salt and pepper."

Duane looked at him closely. His reaction appeared genuine, and he was a Goines, which predisposed Duane to trust him, but there was no way to be sure. Duane returned to the far side of the chop counter, where Conchita was waiting. "Did you carry the steak directly to my table?"

"I had to stop at the bar."

Duane glanced in that direction. A crowd was gathered in front of the brass rail, but Smiley wasn't visible. Duane drew his gun, approached the area from the side, and looked behind the counter. The bartender who never smiled was gone.

"Where's the bartender?" asked Duane.

"Ran out back fer a minute," replied the nearest drunkard.

Duane headed toward the rear corridor, as Maggie and Bradley Metzger appeared at its entrance. "What's your hurry?" asked Maggie.

"Have you seen the bartender?"

"Ain't he behind the bar where he belongs?"

"No."

Maggie was confused and looked to Bradley for help. Duane ran down the corridor to the rear of the building, pushed open the rear door, and aimed his gun into the backyard. Then he cautiously stepped toward the privy. So it's been the bartender all along, he deliberated. He was in front of me all these weeks, watching me coming and going, stalking me, pouring me whisky, and trying to kill me. Anticipating the showdown, Duane knocked on the door of the privy. "Come out with your hands up, or I'll shoot you through the door."

"What the hell's goin' on hyar!" replied a baritone voice. The door flew open, and a beer-bellied horse trader stepped out, buttoning his fly. "Who the hell're you?"

"Sorry," Duane said. "Made a mistake."

"Goddamn," said the drunkard, wobbling toward the saloon. "A man can't take a piss in this town without somebody a-threatenin' his life!"

The ex-sheriff searched the backyard for traces of the bartender. Where would I go if I were he? His brow wrinkled in thought, and a possible solution came to mind. He ran down the middle of the street, gun in hand, as loungers wondered what was wrong with the Pecos Kid. Duane charged into the stable, paused in the darkness, and said: "Sam?"

He was answered by hoofbeats exploding toward him down the center aisle. It was Smiley, the bartender, still wearing his white apron and putting spurs to his horse, his gun aimed at Duane. Duane saw the evil bartender's grin of shame and leapt out of the way. The gun fired and floorboards splintered near Duane's feet. Duane dived out of the way, landed on a pile of hay, rolled, and took a wild shot at the bartender riding toward the door.

Smiley was on the street before Duane could fire again.

Duane rushed toward Nestor, scooped a bridle off a peg, and positioned the bit in Nestor's mouth. "I don't have time for a saddle," Duane said, "so I'll have to ride you Apache-style."

Duane jumped onto Nestor's back, wheeled him around, and nudged him toward the door. Nestor burst across the floorboards, then charged outside and galloped at top speed down the middle of the street. Townspeople were gathered on both sides, entertained by the spectacle of the ex-sheriff chasing the bartender of the Last Chance Saloon.

Nestor's hooves pounded the ground steadily, carrying Duane onto the desert. Duane saw a dot of white in the night ahead, the bartender's shirt and apron. Nestor loved to run free, with the bit loose in his mouth and not too much weight on his back. Duane hung on with his knees as the horse plummeted through the night, gaining steadily on the bartender, who glanced back fearfully and fired a haphazard shot.

Duane crouched low against Nestor's undulating black mane, as the russet stallion leapt over a cholla cactus, saw his quarry turn right, and angled to cut him off. Sharp needles scratched Duane's pants and Nestor's legs, but the spirited animal loved a good race. Smiley aimed another inaccurate shot as he rode for the hills or anywhere else where he could make his last stand.

But Nestor was gaining rapidly on the bartender, and Duane readied his Colt for a shot. "Stop, or I'll plug you!" he hollered.

"Never!" replied Smiley, punctuating his reply with another bullet whizzing harmlessly through the air.

They sped down an arroyo, their hoofbeats echoing off rows of cottonwood trees. The bartender tried to aim at Duane, but his horse was in motion and the bullet went astray. Duane could see stark terror on the bartender's face.

"You don't have a chance!" Duane hollered. "Stop!"

"Damn you to hell!" bellowed the bartender.

They were ten feet apart, and Smiley rode with his reins in his teeth as he feverishly reloaded his gun. Then he turned around and tried another shot. The yellow flash illuminated the night instantaneously, but Duane kept coming. He was six feet behind Smiley, and could shoot him in the back, but a dead bartender spoke no tales.

Duane pulled Nestor's reins toward Smiley's horse, but Nestor was as close as he wanted to go. Duane raised one boot onto Nestor's bobbing back and dived through the air. He landed on the bartender, tore him out of the saddle, and together they fell toward blurred cactus beneath them.

They landed, jostled, and rolled over, and when the dust had cleared, Duane was on top, pressing the barrel of his Colt against Smiley's sweat-stained forehead. "Why'd you try to kill me?" Duane asked between clenched teeth. "And you'd better tell the truth, because I ain't playing."

Smiley gasped for air, thinking his hour had come. His eyes were bloodshot and his tongue lashed the air. "I did it fer the money!" he screamed. "Don't shoot!"

"Who paid you?"

"If I tell you, he'll kill me!"

"If you don't tell me, *I'll* kill you!"

The bartender seemed at war with himself. "The man who gave me the poison," he hissed.

"Tell me his name, or you're a dead man."

"I'm a dead man anyways!" shrieked the bartender.

He gave a mighty pitch, managing to upset Duane's balance. Duane fell to the side, as Smiley dived for the gun he'd dropped. He scooped it up, pointed to his own temple, and closed his eyes.

"Don't shoot!" Duane shouted.

Smiley snarled, then pulled the trigger. Blood, brains, and bone flew in all directions. Smiley grinned victoriously as he sagged toward the ground. Duane didn't have to feel his pulse to know he was dead. Disappointed and disgusted with himself, Duane searched the bartender's pockets, finding keys, a tobacco pouch, wooden matches, and a hundred dollars in coins. I'll search his room, Duane thought, but where does he live?

Duane realized that he knew nothing about Smiley the bartender, yet Smiley had known everything about him. Who had paid him to do the job? Nestor returned, a solemn expression on his face. Duane decided to leave the bartender for the buzzards, so he climbed onto his new mount and headed toward the bright lights of Escondido.

If that poor dog had chewed on somebody else's steak bone, he'd be alive right now, Duane acknowledged, and I'd be lying on the floor of the Last Chance Saloon with white stuff on my lips. What kind of poison was it? How did it come to Escondido? Do they sell it in the general store, or does somebody in town make it? Duane flashed on rows of chemical bottles in the undertaker's office.

He'd been suspicious of the undertaker from the moment they'd first met. There was something diabolical about Snodgras, but Duane had ascribed it to his macabre profession. The undertaker definitely has poison in his house, and I think it's time I had a little talk with him.

But I shouldn't persecute a man who may be innocent, Duane cautioned himself. Just because he deals in dead bodies, that doesn't mean he's killing them too. And just because he has chemicals, he requires them in his profession. But I haven't seen chemicals anywhere else. If he's allied with Smiley, he probably left town by now, or maybe he's hiding, waiting to spring another bushwhack.

Duane drifted into Escondido behind sheds and privies, avoided the saloon district, and approached the undertaker's house from the rear. A lamp burned in the parlor, and all was silent as Duane climbed down from Nestor's bare back. Then he tied the animal to a tree, drew his Colt, and snuck silently toward an open window.

He saw the undertaker pacing back and forth in the parlor, hands clasped behind his back, wearing black pants, white shirt, and black suspenders. Duane raised his face above the sill, aimed his gun at the undertaker, and said, "Howdy."

The undertaker blanched, and appeared as though his worst nightmare had come true. Then he pulled his shoulders up and tried to compose himself. "What are you doing lurking beneath my window, young man?"

"I've come to pay you a visit, Mister Undertaker Man."

Duane raised his leg over the sill and climbed into the parlor, his gun aimed at the undertaker's chest. "Guess what? Smiley told me that you paid him to poison me."

It was humbug, but seemed to be working. The undertaker's lips quivered with barely concealed emotions. "I never paid him to poison you or anybody else, and I don't care what he said!"

"I saw bottles of chemicals in your laboratory. You know how people die, and I wouldn't be surprised if you help them sometimes. How much is Old Man Archer paying you?"

"I don't know what you're talking about," Snodgras replied, his eyes darting about excitedly.

"Raise your hands high."

Snodgras followed orders. Duane patted him down, searching for a hidden derringer, but found nothing except a small pocketknife. Duane aimed his gun at the undertaker's nose. "I wonder if you're the low-down skunk who took a potshot at me when I was riding on the desert a few weeks ago."

"Not me," replied the undertaker, gazing at the barrel of Duane's gun. "I knew you were loco, but not *this* loco."

"Are there poisonous chemicals in your office?"

"Of course. I'm an undertaker and my work requires them."

"Have you noticed any missing?"

"As a matter of fact . . . I have," Snodgras said shakily.

"You'd better start telling the truth." Duane pressed the barrel of the Colt against the undertaker's nose, squashing it down.

"Don't shoot!" the undertaker screamed. "It wasn't me!"

"Liar," Duane replied, as he tightened his finger around the trigger.

Sweat poured down Snodgras's face. He gasped for air, and his eyes crossed as he stared fearfully at Duane's Colt. But Duane couldn't shoot him in cold blood, and his latest bluff appeared a failure. Maybe he was innocent after all, Duane speculated, his conviction wavering. He loosened his finger on the trigger, and the undertaker realized that he'd been given a reprieve. "This is an outrage," he said in a quavering voice. "I'm an innocent man."

"There's an old Apache trick that I learned a while back," Duane replied. "You take a man onto the desert, wrap green rawhide around his head, and stake him in the sun. The rawhide contracts and crushes his skull in a slow agonizing process, and maybe, while it's going on, you'll tell me who you're working for, what he paid you, and where I can find him."

"You have no proof!" asserted the undertaker. "You're loco, do you hear me!"

Am I pushing too hard? Duane wondered. But on the other hand, he's got an office full of poison. The truth remained elusive as usual, and Duane pondered whether to ride out of town, head for the Pecos country, and forget the mess in

Escondido. Then Snodgras's eyebrows raised, as Duane became aware of a sound in the doorway behind him. "Drop the gun, Señor, or I'll shoot you where you stand."

Duane let his Colt go, and it clunked to the floor. Sanchez bent to pick it up, his Remington aimed at Duane's stomach. Sanchez took a step backward, gazed at Duane with amusement in his eyes, and laughed. "So we have you at last, eh?"

"I should've known it was you," replied Duane, as he gazed at the long barrel of the Remington. "I always figured you cried crocodile tears." Duane clenched his teeth and prepared to die. "Well, go ahead, shoot straight, and let's get it over with."

"What is your hurry, Señor?" asked Sanchez. "We have been after you a long time, no? You snoop and sniff like a dog, and look where it has got you, eh?"

"Are you working for Sam Archer?"

"Who's Sam Archer?" Sanchez asked with mock innocence. Then he threw back his head and laughed. "I have never met a bigger *idiota* in my life than you, my friend."

Snodgras narrowed his eyes. "This is no time for palaver, Sanchez. He's dangerous. Shoot him and get it over with."

"I will, do not worry about that. But first I want to have some fun. So this is the famous Pecos Kid, eh? He does not seem so *peligroso* to me. No, he looks like a frightened boy who is about to join his *diablito* father in hell. The father had no brains, and the son is no different. If you want to know more about the Polka Dots, you can ask them yourself." Sanchez aimed his gun at Duane's nose. "You will be seeing them soon, Señor."

Duane steadied himself for the inevitable bullet. This is what happens when you don't think beyond the obvious, he acknowledged bitterly. He saw Sanchez's knuckle tighten around the trigger, as a choir of angels sang Gregorian Chant through the open window.

"What are you waiting for?" asked a new voice.

Just when Duane thought he couldn't be surprised anew, Derek Wright trailed into the parlor, old Confederate cavalry hat low over his eyes. "Let's get it over with."

Duane stared malevolently at his former deputy, as the ramifications of the evil plot deepened. "I was right about you all along, Derek. I figured you asked too many questions, and I should've shot you while I had the chance."

"But you didn't, fortunately for me. You've bit off more than you can chew, kid. I told you to forget about your thieving father, but you were stubborn as a jackass. We did everything to persuade you to go to Mexico, so don't blame us. It is your ignorance and immaturity that has brought us to this sorry pass. Say your prayers, my lad. The party is over."

Duane couldn't believe that his life was coming to an end, but any other conclusion would be irrational. He glowered at Derek Wright and said in a deadly tone: "I can understand how men like Snodgras and Sanchez can go wrong, because they were the scum of the earth to begin with, but you fought in the Stonewall Brigade. Or did you?"

Wright removed his old Confederate cavalry hat, examined it critically, and shrugged. "You can buy one of these quite cheaply these days. I never fought for either side during the war. What for?" Wright smiled ingratiatingly. "I fooled you with my charming line of horseshit."

"Not really, because I always figured there was something false about you, and you made one big mistake that I recall. If you're so smart, why didn't you let that cowboy shoot me in the back at the Longhorn Saloon. It would've saved you a lot of trouble."

"When we first heard about you, we weren't sure who you were. Regardless of what you might think, we only kill when we have to."

"And for some strange reason," Duane replied sarcastically, "you have to kill all the time."

Sanchez took a step closer to Duane and grinned like a dog, showing tobacco-stained teeth. "I like to see how a man faces death. Sometimes they cry, other times they beg, but this young fool appears lost in the sound of his own voice. Are you afraid to die, Señor Pecos?"

"Just tell me one thing, you flea-bitten varmint. Who killed Twilby?"

Derek replied. "I did. And Sanchez killed the women, of course. Snodgras tried to bushwhack you a few times, and he took care of Marty Schlack, while I had to silence that damned fool blacksmith. Then somebody else tried to bushwhack you in front of your office, and we don't even know to this day who the hell he was. We tried to keep you from finding out the truth about the Polka Dots, but it soon became clear that too many people knew. Then we hoped to scare you away, but you wouldn't take the hint." Derek smiled cruelly. "You even thought I was a Polka Dot myself. In point of fact, I hated the damned Polka Dots. They were nothing but a bunch of dirty outlaws, and *I* rode with the posse that tracked them down, you fool. A lot of lead flew that day in the Sierra Madre, and maybe I'm the one who killed the son of a bitch horse thief known as Joe Braddock."

Duane thought his head would explode, but Derek and Sanchez both leveled guns at him, and the Pecos Kid realized that his only hope was to play for time. "How'd you know the blacksmith told me about my father?"

The undertaker replied, "You were talking about Mister Archer an awful lot after you saw the blacksmith, so it wasn't hard to figure out.

"We knew, of course, that Rafferty had lived in the Pecos country, and the Polka Dots stopped at his shop while they were making their last run. So Mister Wright paid Mister Rafferty a visit, and one thing led to another, you might say." The undertaker snickered at his little joke.

It had never occurred to Duane that his nemesis might be three bungling blood-soaked fools, but his worst rancor was reserved for his former deputy. “You’re a polecat, Derek Wright. You act friendly with people, but you’re just looking for a soft spot to stick your knife.”

“Derek Wright isn’t my name, you horse’s ass. Your ignorance and gullibility astonished me on numerous occasions, but we have no more time to waste with you.” Wright turned toward Sanchez. “Are you going to shoot him, or shall I have the pleasure?”

“I will do it, Señor. I have never liked this young son-of-a-whore.”

Sanchez aimed his gun at Duane’s chest, and Duane knew that he was going to die. All he could do was close his eyes, and whisper, “Hail Mary, full of grace, the Lord is with thee.”

A shot resounded in the small parlor, and Duane felt sharp pain in his heart. Smoke filled the air. He was certain he was dead, but had somehow remained standing. Sanchez’s expression of triumph became blank despair, as the whoremaster dropped to the side like deadweight, his shirt blanketed with blood. Duane spotted the double barrels of a shotgun poking through the window.

An expression of panic came over the man Duane knew as Derek Wright as the second barrel fired. Buckshot caught him in the face and sent him slamming against the wall. He slid down, wearing a ghastly red mask, dead as a mackerel.

"Looks like I arrived in the nick of time," said Maggie O'Day, smiling in the window.

Duane gaped at her in amazement, as Snodgras dashed toward the kitchen in the momentary confusion. Duane came to his senses, pursued the undertaker down the corridor, tackled him, and brought him down. As Snodgras lost his balance, he grabbed a frying pan off a hook and slammed Duane upside his head. Duane lost consciousness, and Snodgras fled down the corridor to his office. Duane cleared the cobwebs out of his head, followed the undertaker's trail, and turned the knob, but the door to the office was latched from the inside. Duane took two steps backwards, then slammed his shoulder against the door and it burst open.

Snodgras stood beside his desk, an empty goblet in his hand. There was a strange glazed expression in his eyes and a faint smile on his pale craggy features. "So you finally know," he said dreamily.

"I haven't figured out everything," replied Duane. "How do you communicate with Sam Archer?"

The undertaker laughed weakly. "You can't arrest a corpse." He swayed, stumbled, burped, and went crashing to the floor. Duane ogled him in wonderment, when he heard footsteps in the hall. It was Maggie O'Day smiling cheerily, a double-barreled shotgun in her hand. "So this is where you went." Then she noticed the undertaker lying on the floor. "What happened to him?"

"He poisoned himself, just as he tried to poison me at your saloon. How'd you know I was here?"

"I've been keeping an eye on you in more ways than one. After you left my saloon in such a hurry, I figured out who might've poisoned you. Then, when you came back to town, somebody told me that you was headed here."

Duane picked up his Colt, checked the loads, and holstered the weapon. Then he returned to the parlor and regarded Sanchez, killer of women, and felt a certain perverse satisfaction at his passing. Duane turned to Derek Wright, who'd pretended to be a friend and nearly won Duane over. "I was thinking about going to Mexico with him," Duane said.

"He would've shot you in the back when

you wasn't looking, and brought your head back to Old Man Archer."

Duane thought of Twilby, the blacksmith, the dead prostitutes, Marty Schlack, and his father. And in back of them all, hovering maliciously in the distance, was Old Man Archer. Duane gazed for a long time at Derek Wright bleeding on the parlor floor. You fooled me and everybody else in this town, but you didn't fool Maggie O'Day.

His head whirling, Duane opened the front door for Maggie. A crowd had congregated outside, and Duane saw the gunsmith, the bartender from the Silver Spur, merchants, prostitutes, and others he'd known and sometimes suspected during his brief stay in Escondido.

"I just killed two sons of bitches!" Maggie declared proudly. "And the other one killed himself."

The townspeople cautiously entered the undertaker's house, and one of them hollered, "Holy Jesus, lookit this!"

Duane and Maggie headed toward the center of town. Lamplight twinkled behind windows, and a big cowboy moon hung high over the rooftops. "What're you gonna do now?" Maggie asked.

"I'm headed for the Pecos, I guess."

"If you ever need help, just get in touch with Maggie O'Day."

They came to the Last Chance Saloon, where half-empty glasses could be seen through the window, and horses lined the hitching rails. Desert bats flew eccentric patterns in the sky, as crickets sang loudly in the vast sea of grama grass.

"Care for a last drink on the house?" she asked.

Duane opened his mouth to respond in the affirmative, when his Apache ears perceived strange rumbles from the north. "Something's coming," he said, wrinkling his forehead.

"I can't hear nothin'."

Duane dropped to the street and pressed his ear against the ground. Massed hoofbeats were on the desert, and he heard the distant bleat of a man hollering at the top of his lungs. Duane narrowed his Apache eyes and picked out a black bouncing dot in the dark night. "The Fourth Cavalry's on the way!" yelled the faraway voice. "Run fer yer lives!"

Duane's body tensed, because the Fourth Cavalry had chased him in the past, and for all he knew they were coming specifically for him now. The dark outline in the desert became an old cowboy with a long gray beard riding his pinto nag down the main street of Escondido. "The Fourth Cavalry'll be hyar in 'bout an hour, boys! Hit the trail!"

Pandemonium broke out all over town, as outlaws stopped what they were doing and prepared for the sudden imminent journey across the Rio Grande. Coins were dug from beneath floorboards, supplies stuffed into gunnysacks, and horses saddled rapidly. Maggie's eyes misted as she looked at Duane standing before her like a big gangly boy, anxious to move on. "I wish you'd forget about the Pecos," she said.

"Old Man Archer isn't getting away with killing my parents," Duane replied. Then he raised his right hand to the sky and said solemnly, "So help me God."

She gazed at him, her eyes filled with tears, and then she clasped him to her. They hugged tightly. Then he kissed her forehead and said, "Please take care of Alice for me. Give her a chance, all right? She's a good girl, smart as a whip, and can be a big help to you."

"As long as there's a roof over my head, there'll be a roof over Alice's head. It might not be much of a roof, but . . ."

They separated reluctantly. "I never knew my mother," Duane said, "but you're the closest thing I ever had to a mother, and I promise I'll see you again someday."

Horses trotted down the middle of the street, as outlaws and banditos headed for Mexico. Men bellowed, laughed, and yawped at each other, because the chess game with the Fourth Cavalry had begun again. The stable was a hubbub of madness and curses when Duane arrived, men frantically saddling horses in the lamplight.

"To hell with the Fourth Cavalry!" somebody yelled, as he rode his prancing charger to the door. "They'll never catch me!"

Duane saddled Nestor in the darkness at the end of the row. "We're going for a long ride," Duane said to the horse. "You won't be getting oats or apples for a while, but sooner or later things'll settle down, you'll see."

Nestor didn't appear convinced as Duane led him out of the stable with other horses and riders. Duane's plan was to head for Mexico and hide out for a few weeks, then turn around and cross the Rio Grande upriver, his trip to the Pecos temporarily rerouted thanks to the Fourth Cavalry. The notes of a brass bugle sounded in the distance, and a great tumult could be heard coming through the stillness. The Fighting Fourth advanced on Escondido, while the town's outlaw citizens fled south.

Duane climbed onto Nestor's back, wheeled the horse around, and nudged him with his spurs. Nestor heard the bluecoats coming as he joined the mass of other horses and riders departing in earnest. Nestor turned into the nearest alley, leapt over a sleeping drunkard, loped through the backyard, vaulted over a pile of firewood, and broke onto the open desert, heading for Duane's stash in the hills. Fragrant night wind streamed through Duane's beard as Escondido twinkled and faded into the black pitch darkness behind him.

The Pecos Kid was on the dodge yet again, headed for the ancient home of the Aztecs. Rattlesnakes or scorpions could get him, not to mention the Mexican Army, and Comancheros might string him up by his heels. Nestor kicked clods of desert behind him, as his youthful rider gazed back at outlaw hell falling behind in the distance. At least I know who my mother is, Duane thought gratefully, and thank you, dear father, for being a man that others admired and trusted to lead them. I knew you weren't an outlaw, and I'll clear your name even if it kills me.

The clatter of cavalry reverberated off mountains, as bugles blew and officers shouted orders on the horizon. The detachment of the Fighting Fourth charged helpless little Escondido, but the hard-riding Pecos Kid was long gone.

The mighty Rio Grande gleamed like an iridescent silver snake in the Texas night, but Nestor kept barreling onward. When the horse dived off the riverbank, a massive splash of cold water baptized horse and rider. The Pecos Kid yelled with strange inexplicable joy as his hundred-dollar stolen stallion stroked powerfully toward the distant shore.

The employees of Thorndike Press hope you have enjoyed this Large Print book. All our Thorndike and Wheeler Large Print titles are designed for easy reading, and all our books are made to last. Other Thorndike Press Large Print books are available at your library, through selected bookstores, or directly from us.

For information about titles, please call:

(800) 223-1244

or visit our Web site at:

www.gale.com/thorndike
www.gale.com/wheeler

To share your comments, please write:

Publisher
Thorndike Press
295 Kennedy Memorial Drive
Waterville, ME 04901